THE ENDLESS SKY

ADAM P. KNAVE

The Endless Sky
Adam P. Knave

ISBN: 978-1926946-061

Trade edition.
This book is also available in ebook formats.

Published in Canada by Creative Guy Publishing
Victoria, BC, Canada

THE ENDLESS SKY

ADAM P. KNAVE

Thanks to:

Lauren for her edits, as always.

The flight attendant who had a pen when the moment was desperate.

And to J, D, D, L & P.

CHAPTER 1

GRAVITY PULLED THE SHIP toward the planet, hungrily, a toddler with a new favorite toy. Stress fractures erupted along the hull, the squat emergency cruiser barely built for slow planetary incursions. The engineers, in their wisdom, assumed no one would be dumb enough to throw themselves into a planet's gravity well with no attempt to slow themselves down.

"Bee, so help me, if you crash another ship..." Mud said, slapping at his safety harness's release. He grabbed the side of his chair tightly, using all the strength he had to pull himself to standing.

"I'm not going to crash," Bee insisted. It hurt to talk, the forces pushing her into her chair making it hard to breathe, to see, to work the controls of the cruiser.

"You're going to crash," Mud said. "Again."

"You keep talking shit like this and I'll crash on purpose, I swear."

Mud threw himself toward the side of the ship, grabbing at the wall and using it to inch his way back toward the engine compartment. If Bee was wrong, when she cut the engines in to slow them, everything would blow at once. Mud wasn't sure what he could do to stop that. Honestly, he felt pretty sure nothing could stop it, but trying remained high on his list.

"Sure, blame me. Just flatten out the arc so when you cut the engines..."

"I know what I'm doing," Bee said. She knew

she could pull the landing off, assuming the ship held. Proud of the work she'd done to the engine overhauling it, she could list the new specs off the top of her head. She'd just never had to field test them. "If your work on the superstructure holds, that is."

"It won't," Mud said, looking over the indicators for the engine. "That's what I've been saying. Even if the engines don't blow, we won't have a hull to sit in once you fire them up. Not the way you plan to."

Bee cursed under her breath. There wasn't time to redo the plan. Hell, she reminded herself, there hadn't been time to make a plan, not really. Once again, the Insertion Team worked too fast, something Bee pointed out every debrief. No one disagreed with her, but they also provided no good solution. When your job description consists solely of "Go fix things when they get really ugly," no one ever finds an abundance of planning time just sitting at the edges.

"So, Captain," Bee said, accenting the title harshly, "I have a status update."

"We're gonna crash?"

"Oh, you already got the update? My bad. Now strap down and brace for it—I can aim at the beach and bounce us safely."

Mud gave the engine readouts one last look and started clawing his way back to his seat. "Official report will blame me?"

"Mud. Sir," Bee said, wishing she could roll her eyes without them feeling like they would escape her head, "that might be because it's your fault."

"Just leave us something to get back out of atmo with, will you?" Mud fell heavily into his chair, struggling to get his harness back on. He wished he could see and briefly considered flipping the windshield screens to open, knowing that all he would see were flames as the air around them burnt. Instead he ran the scenario in his head with what new data he could muster. A beach crash put them a solid three miles from target. The beach itself sat ringed by a small glade of trees, but they'd be painfully obvious coming in, what with currently imitating a fireball and soon a small bomb going off as they hit, so the utter lack of cover to the tree line became a giant hurdle.

"Can you bounce us off the water on our way in?" he asked. His head hurt from the gravity pressing in on them. Technically their ship had internal gravity dampers, much like his GravPack. Which, he thought, they could've used, if the packs hadn't been sitting at their target site instead. The ship's internal gravity dampers were weak to begin with, the cruiser not built for this sort of work—plus Bee'd rerouted about half their power to use as a forward shield, hoping it would help keep the ship intact.

It left them both in a painful place, pinned by gravity. Their organs squished and shifted, joints cracking under the stress. Mud's eyes felt ready to pop any second. The Hurkz, Mud's race, hated this sort of pressure. Their skin kept extra moisture, and their eyes were almost three times the size of a human's. A landing like this left him feeling like a wrung-out sponge. Not that Bee felt much better. Humans, after all, weren't exactly designed with high-gravity maneuvers in mind either.

The ship rumbled less, and Mud could feel them

leveling out, if still sliding around out of control. They'd hit low enough atmosphere, he knew from the feel, that Bee should be getting some control back. Still too fast to risk the engines, given the hull's stress limits, but they weren't a giant fireball anymore.

No, now they were only a large hunk of metal making planetfall at explosive speeds. Possibly literally explosive speeds.

"Bee, water bounce?" Mud asked again, worried she'd passed out.

"Trying for it, but if I miss, we're dead."

"If you hit the sand clean we'll be dead a different way," Mud said, wishing the conversation would stop so his gravity-sore jaw might rest.

"No, I can..."

"Bee, they'll be waiting for us. Hit the water first, then bounce into the sand. Trust me."

Bee didn't respond, concentrating instead on hitting the water at the right angle. A few degrees off and the ship would simply burst. Sand she could glide in on, counting on the silicate to wear down the ship, and slow it as well. Water, on the other hand, would—Bee smiled, or tried to, her face fighting the gesture. Muscles strained against gravity, but the smile eked out at the edges. Water would hit harder, but if she could hit the angle right, the resulting steam would work for them.

Arcing down, falling out of control, the cruiser approached the ground far too fast. It turned, nosing up degree by degree, until it seemed to be gliding with possible purpose. Sentry towers on the ground continued to follow the descent, mobilizing a recovery team, then quickly adding a Force Squad

4

to the mix when their view of the ship resolved to not be a bundle of debris. Yet. They watched the ship fall. A small emergency cruiser, no weapons, minimal crew capacity—the shape it looked to be in as it fell assured them there would be no takeoff later.

"Impact in five...four..." Bee said, knowing Mud didn't need the count down. He could see the instruments as easily as she could. Saying it, though, intoning the countdown, put it at a distance for her. She could shift her anxiety about hitting the mark to a simulation, a dry run where you made sure to say the right things and always knew you could feel good about protocol, even if you "died."

This wasn't a simulation.

The cruiser hit the water.

Steam vomited upward, billowing thickly toward the beach, followed by the ship. The hull cracked and curled back as it cooled too quickly. The bounce itself took out a large section of metal, and the sand they skidded on after tore the rest of the bottom out of the ship.

Sand, thrown high into the air, mixed with steam. Force Squad C watched, holding the recovery team back. Waiting.

CHAPTER 2

MUD AND BEE CROUCHED near the scorched, torn hull of the cruiser. The steam-and-sand mix caught the wind and dissipated—too quickly, Mud knew. His half-a-plan started to blow away with it. Knowing there would be a reception for them, but unsure of who or how many, left both Mud and Bee nervous. Their instruments couldn't parse the data with precision, the ship too busy falling apart on entry. Mud had hoped to blind them and skirt whatever laid in wait, heading right for the trees. But that breeze rose faster than hoped, and so they crouched, considering their options.

"We could just go right at them," Mud said, whispering so softly Bee wouldn't have heard him, even though she stood right next to him, if not for their comm units.

"Outside of my sonic gun, and your Acadian blaster, what do we have to pull that off?" Bee asked, checking the charge on her gun. It'd last a while but not long enough, she knew.

"Nothing, outside of general suit countermeasures."

"So let's not die, then."

"Good call," Mud said, and he pulled his Acadian blaster free of its holster. A gift from his father, an illegal blaster that could stun if dialed wide enough, and burn through most ship hulls when focused. He considered it and smiled, nudging Bee with an elbow. "I got this. Follow me exactly."

They moved into position, Mud in front, Bee

directly behind him, one hand grabbing the back of his belt. The team practiced this sort of thing regularly enough for them to feel confident in it. At a dead run, eyes down, you didn't want to lose the person you followed, not for a step, in case of mines. So you made a human chain, able to react to their lateral movements with something faking grace.

Mud started to run, blaster held out in front of him, right toward the vanishing steam. Bee kept her eyes down, trusting that this new plan wasn't the one they'd just discarded. It wasn't. Quite.

They still ran directly at Force Group C, who, of course, started to see the shapes resolve in the quickly dispersing steam. They raised weapons, ready to fire. Mud fired first, though, setting his Acadian blaster for wide dispersal, a flat beam about four feet across. He aimed it at the beach, striking sand.

The blast hit the sand at an angle to throw up heaping clouds. Mud played the blaster back and forth, crating a wall of sand that moved forward as they ran. He pulled to the left, Bee's grip on his belt letting her know even as he started to move. She followed and together they broke left, Mud keeping the aim of the gun to appear as if they still ran directly at the oncoming horde.

Sonic fire made whirling holes in the sand barrier that spiraled in the air before vanishing, allowing maddeningly tiny glimpses that only showed stretches of beach and water. Strike Force C hesitated. Outside of suppressing fire, which seemed to do nothing, they were unable to run into the abrasive wall of angry sand standing in front of

7

them. No way of knowing what lay behind stumped any plans they had. So they kept firing, trying to keep a pattern up to pierce the wall long enough to map the enemy.

"Jump in five steps," Mud said as he ran at the tree line. The blaster range would still throw sand but already the angle had shifted, and Force Group C noticed, starting to head for the trees. Bee let go of Mud's belt and they jumped into the trees together.

"You know, if we had our GravPacks this would be so much easier," Mud said, dodging behind another tree.

"If we had our GravPacks we'd be with the rest of the team, and the *Arrow*. Which is why we need to get to them." Bee dove from one tree to another, wishing for some more tech herself.

"And hope they got the bomb locked down," Mud added. The team had separated to finish a mission and that's when everything went south, he knew. He felt the blame settle into his chest and wiped his goggles to distract himself. His extra-large Hurkz eyes needed to be moist, and so on most human-inhabited planets he needed the goggles to not dry out and go blind. He hated them, always getting scuffed and seeming to magically attract debris and damp leaves.

Both of them stood, backs to trees a few feet apart, and thought. They wore their uniforms: solid black thinsuits, with blue piping running from the outer line of the boots along the leg and turning to travel along the back before winding over the shoulders and across the chest in a loose curve. Over the left breast of each suit an inverted V made of five arrows sat, with their names under it in small block

8

letters. Camouflage they weren't.

Except.

Hurkz naturally possessed limited biological stealth capabilities. Glands running in stripes along their bodies allowed them to match their skin tones to their environment. Scarred and tattooed over against his will, Mud couldn't shift naturally, not quite. An abandoned foundling, he was given no standing and rejected by his own people. Found, and raised, instead by Jonah and Shae Madison, he had gained much more. Including a work-around to access his natural abilities.

Hundreds of small, painful needles lined the inside of his thinsuit. They buried themselves along his tattooed clan markings, accessing the special properties that still lay in wait. Enhancing and completing certain chemical and bioelectrical processes, the special thinsuit let him blend as well as any Hurkz could. He hated it, the stabbing of the needles flooding him with memories of the pain and shame of the tattoo needles. It never faded.

Slightly reluctantly, Mud again chose survival over pain and triggered the needles. "I'll fade, make a break for the compound. You start to loop around the long way," he told Bee, even as the black fabric and blue stripes of his thinsuit became browns and greens.

"I'd rather not be bait," she said, bracing for it regardless. She figured her sonic gun could shatter some trees, the shrapnel slowing down anyone after her.

"No need, I'll send random pot shots toward them—they've only seen my blaster in use so far so they can't be sure that's not the only weapon we have. They'll be forced to follow me. You keep clear and we'll meet up at the compound doors."

"Sounds good, boss," Bee said, relieved. Not that everyone would follow Mud's shots, but enough to instill some confidence of survival in her.

"While we're moving, figure out how we're gonna get in the compound, huh?" Mud said, and she heard him move away from her.

Great, she thought, nothing like multitasking while being chased. Invigorating, she told herself, a real character builder. She counted to ten and then started to move, just as Mud's blaster sent a focused, deadly bolt between two trees. Grinning now, Bee picked up speed, knowing she'd have to move faster than him to meet up in time. Force Group C, she saw glancing over her shoulder, followed Mud's random shots but were pointing all over the place, not able to spot him with any certainty. Still, while she was in range she felt she ought to make life a bit more exciting for them all.

Aiming at the ground, she pulled the trigger on her gun, the sonic weapon set to its maximum field of disruption. Dirt, leaves, twigs, and a few small creatures went flying into the air, along with a thrum of noise loud enough to stop her pursuers. They'd dealt with sonics before, but when you aren't expecting them—well, disruption is about right.

The small creatures displaced, none bigger than a fat earthworm, all landed safely, accepting their new location and short flight as just one of those things that happens. They adapted far better than anyone else in the vicinity, and if their consciousnesses had allowed for that fact to filter through, they would have been smug as hell.

A few members of the Force Group broke off to follow this new insurgent. The leader of the smaller segment felt proud. He'd insisted there were multiple invaders and had been told initially to shut up, his commander maintaining that if there were then they would obviously all fire a weapon. Arrogant as the earthworms could have felt but didn't, he ran after Bee with four members of his group. They'd catch up while the main force took care of the clear leader of the intruders, and back at base they could celebrate and possibly he could even get a promotion.

He brushed aside an internal pang telling him that no one got promoted for being smarter than their boss, and concentrated instead on the chase. A tree exploded in front of him, becoming a cloud of shrapnel. It pinged off his chest armor and helmet, but ripped along his face and hands, flaying his exposed flesh like a badly rushed and drunken chef.

Bee heard the screams behind her and changed direction as she ran. They'd really be after her now, she knew. Those who could still give chase, at least, and no way she'd taken them all out first try. They'd be faster, smarter, and, frankly, meaner now.

Mud, for his part, ducked behind a tree early, letting his eight pursuers go right by him. He waited for them to get a good distance ahead and then took off after them. He reached down, while running, and scooped a few stones up, running his fingers over them. Dropping the few that didn't pass muster, he threw the others in a high arc, knowing they'd be fairly invisible until they hit their target.

Clonking off a tree, a good solid heavy clonk

11

about ten feet up, the stones fell back to the ground, rustling leaves as they went. The Force Group members ahead of him turned toward the noise. Mud took the chance to leap. Literally.

He sprang hard at the two armored folk in the rear, those closest to him, arms and legs spread like a flying squirrel on a mission. They caught his shadow as he reached them, his hands each grabbing a helmet and yanking them toward each other. The three of them went down in a tumble of bodies, but only Mud expected it, his legs clamping around the two other bodies, forcing them down as awkwardly as possible with himself on top. Grabbing their guns from holsters, Mud landed and rolled, coming back up and diving behind another tree.

Now Force Company C started to fall apart. They were sure of one invader, then two, but this meant, to their reasoning, three. The six still standing halted, bunching up into a protective ring.

Mud worked quickly, and silently. Considering his options, he fell back on an old habit: running through what his parents would do. Dad would run right at the guys, blasting hard, and try to take them on. He'd probably walk away from it, but chances of a random injury in a six-on-one fight were extremely high. Mom would lob a grenade and be done with it.

He had no grenades. Except. He thanked his mom silently as he dismantled the blaster packs in the two low-yield energy pistols he'd stolen. Each pack held enough charge to fire a hundred or so blasts, each powerful enough to kill a person with no armor. So, cross wired together, with the leads in the wrong places to short them, Mud guessed a good building charge should do the trick.

Patting the slender pockets on his thinsuit, Mud found a spool of tape and stuck the two guns together, barrels pointed at each other, saving some tape for a final loop to hold the triggers down on both guns. He tugged the tape tight and the guns started trying to build enough charge to fire, the packs unable to work as spec demanded. Instead they whined, the noise growing into a troubling buzz.

Mud threw the mess right into the center of the scrum and turned his head away, hunkering down to shield himself. The explosion rattled his joints and made the ground under him bounce a little.

Glancing over his shoulder, Mud saw four more of the people chasing him on the ground. He peered further out and saw the last two heading further into the trees ahead, down the same route Mud wanted, right to the compound. They'd decided, it seemed to Mud, that getting to base and standing nearby a fortress would be smarter. They weren't wrong, but Mud also knew that if they got there before him, Bee wouldn't be expecting them. She could handle herself, but Mud didn't intend to give her a mean surprise of the shooting variety.

Standing, stretching joints and muscles sore from sitting too close to an explosion, Mud started after them. Bruises from proximity detonations rated high on his list of annoying occupational hazards.

Bee heard the explosion and hoped Mud had caused it instead of being on the receiving end. Only one way to find out, and that entailed getting the last two goons on her trail off it directly. She'd been through training, basic and advanced, and could hold her own in a fight, but self-doubt held her back. Worse yet, she knew it. She felt graceless, clumsy compared to her trainers and most of her teammates.

Regardless, she thought, when needs must you show up. She skidded to a halt in the leaves, letting her knees buckle, and dropped suddenly to the ground. Two blasts burned the air above her, right through where she'd been standing.

She lay, waiting for them to investigate. They did, as a matter of procedure, assuming they'd hit her. While they stood above her, checking for a wound, she kicked out, each foot going in a different direction, each one making contact with a knee and shoving the joint out of true. Her two pursuers screamed and fell, and Bee rolled so that they were in reach. Covering their mouths so they wouldn't keep drawing attention, she hit them each with a low-level sonic blast to the temple, knocking them out.

Standing, she took up a run toward the compound to meet Mud.

Mud lined up his shot as carefully as he could while moving, and tagged both the Force Group C folk in front him with a wide-angle beam from his blaster. Kicking their helmeted heads hard to ensure they stayed down a while as he ran past, Mud got to the compound doors only a few seconds before Bee.

"That blaster fire just now you, or we still have someone on us?" she asked.

"We're clean," Mud said, "so now the hard part."

"We get in the front door and they'll cut us down

hard."

Mud ran a hand along the thick, imposing doors. They ran up roughly ten feet and stood eight feet wide. "We couldn't get through anyway. Maybe you could get through the scanner, but—"

"I couldn't, dual biometrics, it'd take way more time than we could possibly have," Bee said.

"Right, so. How do we get in?"

"Not how," Bee said. "Where."

"Sure, if I had a GravPack I'd hit the roof, come in from above hard and fast, no problem. But this place..." Mud looked at the compound. A large, gray, featureless mound rising a good sixty feet into the sky. No telling from here how far down the structure went. Round, it seemed to his eye to sit at least seven thousand feet in diameter. No easy entry leapt out to him—windowless and apparently seamless, the walls looked designed to be exactly the impenetrable fortress he'd worried it might be. Sure, they'd need air, he knew, but putting the vents on the roof along with a few gun turrets made life far simpler.

Bee nudged the ground with the edge of her boot. "Walls will be too thick, up here..."

"You're thinking a dig?" Mud asked.

"We don't have long before they come looking for us, minutes most. Still, they'd expect us to come in from the front, so where do you keep things?" She knelt and stuck the business end of her sonic into the ground, gently pulling the trigger a few times.

"Prisoners down a level, everything else up. So we have to backtrack and cut ourselves off. So if we go in low—"

"And no one fortifies underground walls the

15

same," Bee said, standing. "Sonic bounces funny, so the walls go down straight. Dig?" They moved to the relative back of the compound to avoid anyone using the doors.

Mud took out his blaster and fiddled with it a bit. "Stand back, this'll be fast and messy." Bee came around to stand behind him. An arc of energy shot free of the gun and blasted dirt up and elsewhere. Whipping the beam back and forth, Mud dug a hole deeper and deeper. Bee glanced around nervously as he did. Not noisy work, but certainly visible— and taking far too long, she felt.

The digging ceased. "I think I have enough charge left," Mud said, starting to cut into the wall while standing in the large, boxy hole he'd dug. The ground level sat above his head, and Bee crouched at the edge, still keeping a lookout as the Acadian blaster sliced through the much thinner walls with a tight, focused beam.

Bee dropped down into the hole and nodded at Mud. Leaning back, he braced and kicked the cut section of wall in, the two of them diving into the hole after the slice of metal, not giving anyone inside time to react.

CHAPTER 3

Blaster fire cut across the air. Between reports of intruders, silence from Force Group C, and then watching a cutting arc slice through their wall, the people in the fortress were far from surprised as Mud and Bee jumped through. They were, instead, frankly pissed. Mud and Bee shot back, going for wide blasts, trying to clear a path forward.

A searing bolt sliced along Mud's leg, cutting his thinsuit and charring some of the skin under it. Stumbling, Mud bit back a scream and shot wildly twice. Bee helped him up, pinging sonic blasts off the walls to send people sprawling.

"Bee, find the cells, I'll cover."

"That blaster won't hold out!" Bee insisted.

"I'll borrow one. Go. Order." Mud grinned at her and ran a hand over his smooth head, knowing as he did it that his father's example rose high in his own muscle memory.

Bee took off with a frown, and Mud unleashed wide-angle blasts to either side of her, clearing a path. Running for one of the downed soldiers, he grabbed a blaster free and then sought another, and one after that. Five blasters in his belt and one in each hand later, he still fired, ducking behind any random object he could. More and more people came down a wide staircase along one wall, creating a choke point that Mud kept firing at to discourage them. The level they were on was mostly wide space, with a few hallways spun off. Bee'd run down one of those, and Mud made sure no one tried to follow her. Damn but his leg hurt. The burn ached, stabbily, making Mud want to hit someone. So he did. Grabbing the nearest mook by the shoulders, Mud smacked him hard with a headbutt, feeling the guy's nose flatten.

Kicking him away, Mud looked around the room. They were cringing at the top of the stairs, unsure of the full situation, knowing only that blaster fire greeted anyone who tried to go downstairs. Three guards still stood in the space, looking for backup. Mud wanted to sneer, to say something big and heroic and badass, but his damned leg hurt. It distracted him, preoccupied his brain just long enough for the mass of people along the stairs to let someone through. And she had grenades.

Mud cursed, taking a few shots at her. One of them hit her arm, but not soon enough. Three grenades lazily flew through the open space toward him. He watched their arcs and tried to work out which way to go to get clear. Except the spread widened as they arced, cutting him off completely.

Taking the only option he could think of, Mud shot at one of the grenades. Missing twice, he nailed it on the third try, blowing it before it reached him. The explosion still hurt, ringing his ears and vision, but it did the same to the people who were coming down the stairs freely now.

Having a safe-ish space to run, Mud took it, limping in a wobbly line as his inner ear caught up to a post-explosion world once more. Unfortunately his path intersected with the mass of people coming down the stairway. Nothing for it, he thought— they needed to eventually get upstairs regardless. Someone had to clear the way. Somehow.

Mud had started shooting, trying to hold them back, when he felt a hand on his shoulder. Before he could fully react, a voice said, "These guns for us?" and took one of the pistols from the back of Mud's belt.

Looking back over his shoulder quickly, Mud saw Steelbox, the Insertion Team's navigator, grinning. "Pass them around, we have to get upstairs and then find the *Arrow*." Steelbox, still using the gang name he grew up with, hailed from the same settlement planet as Bee and looked up to her.

"The *Arrow*'s on the upper level, it's a top hangar," said Chellox, the lizard-looking Tsyfarian pilot. Mud didn't reply, trying to work out how to get to his team's ship. He kept firing, Steelbox joining his side.

"Look, Cap—" Steelbox started.

"Mud. Just...Mud."

"Sure, Cap. Look, we're in good shape. They didn't know what to do with us when we didn't have the—"

"You don't have it?!" Mud said. His head hurt, now. All this trouble, all this bullshit, and they didn't have even the cargo. Now they'd have to start again.

"Before you work on a stress headache, Cap, we stashed it. They just don't know where. So they had to keep us here, hoping to bargain with you. Same with the *Arrow*. Now. Olivet has an idea."

Olivet, their human science officer from the settlement world of Bercuser—the strangest planet in the system in that it changed what sun it orbited, changed the very solar system it inhabited, and no one why or how. One of the only people from his world to leave, Olivet's work sometimes involved inhaling from jars of vapors brought from his home

19

world, mists that allowed him to see limited and strange visions of the future.

"Olivet? Ideas welcome," Mud said. They weren't gaining ground and wouldn't be able to even hold firm for long.

"I made these from scraps as we got here," Olivet said, pressing two shapes into Mud's free hand. They felt, and looked, mostly like grenades. Enough to fool these guys? Mud decided to try it.

"Fire in the hole," he said, loud enough for the enemy to hear him, and lobbed both spheres toward the stairs. People scattered, backing up and making a path. Mud waved his team forward, gaining the ground quickly. "Good call. Now sound off, everyone in good shape back there?"

Everyone, including Bee, sounded off, and the crew, now all armed, took the stairs, fanning out onto the upper landing. They fought hard, Mud's limp slowing them down more than anything, and focused only on getting to the top hangar.

They gained ground inch by inch and foot by foot, using everything possible as cover and watching each other's backs. Mud watched his team, proud of them all. They'd come together haphazardly, helping his father. With time and effort, though, they'd grown into a team. A team that seemed to be figuring out how to work together. Mostly, Mud mentally amended, as he watched Steelbox and Olivet narrowly avoid catching each other in their own crossfire. They were exchanging words that didn't seem friendly, but Mud couldn't make out specifics.

He also couldn't get to them to break it up and set them back on mission. Sighing, he shot the foot of another guard, working out a path to his crew. Bee got there first and shoved them apart. The three of them turned back toward fighting the actual enemy, and this time actually remembered how to stagger defense so each of them could hopscotch forward behind various boxes and pillars, making their winding way up to the hangar.

Mud took the rear position as they gained the final level, inching up the stairs backward, keeping suppressing fire going. His Acadian blaster sat in the holster, out of energy. He relied instead on a standard-issue blaster, annoyed at its limited use. His heel hit air instead of another step and Mud turned, seeing the *Arrow* sitting there, shining with a slight shimmer around it.

"They put a shield around it?" he asked Chellox.

"We did," the Tsyfarian replied. "Bee set a safety before you left us."

"Bee," Mud said loudly, raising his voice so she could hear him further toward the ship, "you *can* turn that thing off, right?"

"You can," she replied, waving him over. "Got your blaster?"

Mud handed her his blaster and waited. She sighed at him and dropped the gun to the floor dismissively. "No, the Acadian."

"Sure, but it's out of juice. Couldn't cut through a shield anyway, though."

"Of course not," Bee said. She popped the energy cartridge out of the gun and reached into the cavity with a finger, wiggling it around, searching for something.

"Please don't break—"

"Mud," Bee said. Her tone filled in the rest of the

sentence.

He looked behind them, then back at her. "Fine, but quickly? They're right behind us."

"Sorry, your mom mentioned this old trick," Bee said. She pulled a small cylinder out of the gun and pressed it against the shield, squeezing the cylinder hard. The shimmer vanished with a pop and Bee smiled, shoving the gun back together quickly and handing it over to Mud. "Acadians have unique energy translators. I keyed the ship's shield to it. Simple."

"Unless I didn't make it," Mud said. He wasn't sure he liked this plan. Too easy to strand everyone else.

"I would've made sure the gun, at least, made it."

"And if we both died?"

Steelbox up-nodded at Mud as the *Arrow*'s hatch opened. "Bicker on board? Let's get moving, right?"

Mud shook his head and started onto the ship. "Bee, we have to—"

"If we both died, the mission would've been so off map it wouldn't matter."

"Nope. Have to make sure everyone has an out, no matter what. Don't do it again." Mud strapped in, his seat against a side bank of computers. Chellox and Steelbox took their front positions as pilot and navigator, respectively, Chellox putting on a large, hard-sided bird helmet, the fighting gear of his culture, and Steelbox grinned at it. "One day I gotta get me one of those," he said, with the feeling of an old well-worn conversation starting up.

"One day you shall earn one," Chellox replied, checking out the ship and prepping it for takeoff.

Bee strapped in near Mud, in front of her engineering consoles, and glanced back to make sure Olivet had settled into his science station. "I had to secure the ship," Bee said to Mud, quietly.

"Ship second. Crew first. You know that," Mud said. They were still new, no matter how well they could fight out of a base camp together. Edges like that were what got people killed. It kept Mud up at night, even if, when his father asked whether that specific issue ever wore him down, he would certainly lie.

"Shooting through hangar," Chellox said, making sure everyone could hear him, "and going for hard burn in three...two..."

Mud braced and didn't catch the end of the countdown. An explosion rattled him as Steelbox fired the ship's guns, and before that bone rattle could die the *Arrow*'s strange Tsyfarian engines came to life, pressing Mud deeply into his seat.

Once more into the black.

They hit orbit and slowed, drifting lightly while Chellox teased them to a full stop.

The *Arrow* sat just outside the tug of the gravity well, pointed down at the planet. The crew waited, knowing. "Crew of the *Arrow*," the transmission began, they always started this way, "stand down. We have you locked on. We can blow you from the sky."

Mud clapped his hands once, getting ready. Flipping switches in front of him, he set his seat's mic to live. "Hey down there. We're fully armed and a mile or so above you. This quickly looks like mutual destruction, right? Only problem is we can dodge. Buildings can't. But I'll be honest with you. We don't have the canister, either. Neither side has it, right now. So let's go our separate ways and no one has to die today. Deal? *Arrow* out."

The crew waited. No one on board wanted to kill anyone. They tried to avoid it, outside of raw self-preservation. At first some among them had fought against that aim, thinking Mud to be soft. He swore though, with examples to back him up, that on a long time frame, enemies you left alive with dignity could become allies at the strangest times. Mercy had saved members of Mud's family more times than he could list.

Chellox, one of those who could have been an enemy at one point, as well as Steelbox, backed Mud's theory up. So the crew waited, and hoped.

"Crew of the *Arrow*, we will launch missiles in five minutes. Stand down," came their reply.

Mud smiled, leaving his mic off. "You heard them, guys. We're fine."

"Cap?" Steelbox asked. "They said they'd fire."

"Five minutes is a long time," Chellox said, before Mud could respond. "They save face, we go grab the canister—"

"Which we totally don't have right now, but will soon," Mud put in.

"—and everyone is happy," Chellox finished. "Well, for now."

"By the time they find out and get angry, they'll be grateful to be alive," Mud said. He flipped his mic to live again. "Five minutes. We copy. *Arrow* out," he said, flipping the mic off quickly. "Chellox, take us to where you stashed this dumb thing." Pleased with himself—and his crew, for the most part—Mud sat back and closed his eyes, trying to ignore the pain in his leg.

CHAPTER 4

SOMEONE, WHICHEVER ONE of you is free, tell me where you hid the cargo?" Mud said once they got underway.

"We left the cargo attached to that comet we passed coming in," Olivet said. "Steelbox has a mapping of its trajectory."

The *Arrow* slid through the void easily, an elongated teardrop body sprouting multiple rotating Tsyfarian engines, the fastest known. Chellox threw them around open space, keeping any directional vector changes just under the limit of the ship's gravity compensation.

"Great," Mud said, "I'm going to bandage this leg. Get me when it's on board." He limped aft, climbing into his small crew quarters. Just big enough for a bed, and enough space to hold clothes and change in—the accommodations weren't great, but they were better than sleeping in your chair.

Mud cleaned and bandaged his wound, taking his time and trying to not gaze longingly at his pillow. Bone tired, he found he could fight it easier with other people around—alone it felt all too easy to just tip sideways and let sleep take him. He fought back and stood, opening the door into the small hallway.

"Cap, we're good to go," Steelbox's voice came through the speaker set into the wall.

Making his way to the hatch's airlock, he stood with Olivet and Bee as they wrangled the canister on board. "Was this really the safest place to stick the cargo?"

"It's still here, right?" Bee asked. Mud nodded—he griped out of a need to gripe, rather than any particular complaint.

Sitting in his chair, he keyed his mic, dialing in a homing frequency. "*Ratzinger*, this is the *Arrow*. Cargo acquired and secured. Headed back to base."

No reply. Mud rekeyed the mic and tried again. The same silence remained. "Bee, did the comm unit get bungled recently?"

Bee returned to her seat and studied a few screens. "Everything's working on this end. *Ratzinger* not getting back?"

"Dead air," Mud confirmed. "Could be a problem at base, or—"

"Or nothing," Bee finished for him.

Mud closed his eyes, took off his goggles, and cleaned them without looking. "How often is it nothing?" he asked as he reseated them, blinking quickly a few times.

"Full burn to base, Mud?" Chellox craned his head to look back at his captain.

"Damn it, I guess so. And Bee, keep trying them. Olivet, make sure the cargo is secure. And everyone else, brace for, you know, Chellox's flying."

"I resent—"

"Oh shush, Chel," Steelbox said, slapping the pilot on the shoulder, "he's just jealous he can't fly like you."

The crew settled in, straps secure, and braced for the engines to go full out. Chellox didn't disappoint them, burning fuel hard and fast, taking turns that their internal gravity adjusters couldn't always handle. Little lurches and spasms in local gravity made them all, with the exception of their Tsyfarian pilot, uneasy—but they trusted him. He could throw a ship through space with a grace normally reserved for angels and the theoretical.

The five day trip remained otherwise uneventful. The crew passed the time as such teams have since the dawn of time: sleeping, eating, playing small games, and cheerily bickering with each other.

No reply from the *Ratzinger*. The small-city sized ship housed some of the best the Gov had to offer, and served as the current home base to the Insertion Team. Recently floating out near Jupiter, in humanity's home system, the *Ratzinger* had been restocked for a long-haul tour. They'd be underway not long after the *Arrow* returned, Mud knew, if everything stayed on schedule.

Then they'd all be off for a five-year tour around some of the outer settlement planets, relieving the *Dozier*, while a sister ship, the *Farnsworth*, relieved the *Swann*, which would make the same loop counterclockwise.

Lieutenant Commander Mills would be waiting for them by now. In fact, there should've been a message waiting, Mills bugging Mud about timetables on the current mission. Nothing, though. Silence, same as their attempts to reach back.

"Hey Bee, patch me in to anyone?" Mud asked on day two of the trip. The absence of communication ate at him, even as he played it off with the others. He knew they didn't buy it, regardless.

"That's a bit vague."

"Seriously, any ship in the fleet. Can we hear anything or talk to anyone at all? We need to know how localized this is."

Bee tried, and using long-range comms, nothing seemed to go in or out. She insisted the equipment worked. When Mud questioned her for the eighth time, she did a total tear down and rebuild on the unit, showing him the problem wasn't on their end.

On day three of the five-day trip they got a ping back. Going off in the middle of their designated night shift, Olivet caught the ping alone in the forward compartment of the *Arrow*. He considered waking Mud, or Bee, but held off long enough to answer, making sure the console knew to record.

"This is the *Arrow*. Go ahead," he said, hoping for the best.

"*Arrow*, this is *Ratzinger*. Where are you?"

"Identify, please," he requested, still wary.

"Olivet, is that you? It's Brockston."

"Brockston. Good to hear you," Olivet said. Brockston still owed him money, never having learned to refuse offers to gamble with someone who could occasionally see the future. A friendly voice settled Olivet down. "We're two days out. Thought there was a problem, couldn't get a message through."

"We know. Get here fastest."

"Chellox has us at a hard burn already," Olivet said, starting to reach for the internal ship mic, to wake Mud.

"Good, *Ratzinger* out," Brockston said crisply, sounding stressed.

"Wait," Olivet said, "can you wait for me to wake the Captain and—"

"Just get here. We're not in danger, but get here. Soonest." The unit clicked off, and Olivet double-checked the recording to make sure everything had

28

worked before keying internal communications and waking Mud, and, on second thought, Bee.

The three of them debated any meaning behind the message, at length. Brockston wasn't surprised by the communication issues, so something widespread must have been going on, but a reassurance of no danger meant this could be possibly nothing more than a known glitch. If he hadn't also asked for a return soonest. That spelled trouble.

Trouble that the rest of his message denied. Which left them in a strange place. They needed to plan their approach. On the one hand, soonest meant soonest: you came in hard and fast, took no detours, and docked with engines still cooling off. On the other hand, the message could be taken to construe a need for stealth and erring on the side of caution.

The contradiction stood out to the whole team, each coming in at different points in the debate as they woke up for their shifts. Mud knew at the end of the day his call would be the final one. But he'd learned long ago to listen, and to take advice from capable people seriously. If his own team members didn't get a voice, why trust them enough to add them to the team in the first place?

They'd started the team together, and it was with them that Mud had started finding his footing as a leader. He couldn't just discount them now. Still, the group leaned toward stealth and caution, and something in Mud's mind, a feeling he couldn't pin down, told him to just go in as if the message caused no confusion at all. Just land as normal, as requested, and go from there.

He also refused to call the *Ratzinger* back and talk to Mills. Either way—problem or not—nothing could be gained from that. And that gave Mud his reasoning. If there was a problem, Mills or one of his assistants would have reached out to the *Arrow* by now, back channel and subtle, to give them a heads up. If things were so odd and wrong that they couldn't even do that, then any effort to act warned could put them in jeopardy.

Reassured by his own logic, he laid out the thoughts to the crew and they agreed. Set on course, they headed into the unknown with a sense of resolve and at least half the start of a quarter of a plan. So, Mud thought, everything remained normal.

CHAPTER 5

THE *RATZINGER* HUNG LARGE in front of them, growing larger as they sped toward it. Docking Bay Seven slid open, surrounding lights flashing clear, and Chellox came in fast enough to worry even Steelbox, reversing thrust hard at the last possible moment.

"Bee, take the cargo to our normal operations room," Mud said, already standing at the hatch before it opened. "I'll go meet Mills and come back around with him. Let's see what's wrong." He moved off the ship quickly, refusing to actually give in and run. A fast walk would be fine. No problem, Brockston said, they weren't in trouble. So let them prove it.

Mud burst into the General Ops room, scanning for Mills. Over in a corner, discussing something quietly with another officer, stood Mud's boss, or liaison, or whatever he really was. The Insertion Team's status in the Gov remained unclear on purpose, just as it always had back in the days Mud's parents ran it. Mills, all five-foot-six of him, stood straight backed and sure of himself. He saw Mud coming toward him and moved away from his previous conversation.

"Captain Madison—"

"I'm not my dad. Mud, it's Mud."

"And he's Jonah and no one in your family seems to accept the use of rank or titles," Mills said, touching Mud's shoulder lightly. Mud tensed slightly—Mills never touched him, that wasn't Mills at all. Which meant...something.

Mills steered Mud out of the room and spoke quietly, leaning his head closer to Mud as they went. "Look," Mills said, "let's go brief your guys, but this isn't common information yet. It will be soon, but not just now, all right?"

"Sure thing, Mills," Mud said, wondering if he even knew Mills' first name. He'd never heard it, thinking back. He'd never asked. They were friendly and Mud considered Mills an actual friend, the sort you drink and hang out with late between missions, but despite stories told and card hands played, he couldn't think of any time he'd heard the man's first name. He'd have to ask him. Later.

For now they had to debrief on their mission, as well as find out what needed them back so hot and fast. They entered Insertion Teams Ops, really just a ready room that no one else had claimed, Mills nodding as the rest of the team stood as he entered.

"We don't stand for Mills, guys. It's Mills. You don't even have official ranks," Mud said, shaking his head.

"You stand for me," Mills said, waving his hands for them to sit back down, "because I'm your boss."

"Or something."

"Can we," Steelbox asked, rolling his eyes, "get on with it?"

"Of course," Mills said, sitting down in a chair himself. "I'll cut the preamble. Over the last few months we've had occasional issues with long-range communications. Blackouts lasting from a few minutes to a few hours, along various degrees of space at a time."

"Someone is managing to block Gov

communications an entire degree worth of space at once?" Bee asked, leaning forward, elbows on knees.

"Seems like it," Mills said, nodding. "Which, of course, makes no sense. That is, plainly put, not a thing that can be done. There have been no traces left, no markers, no one claiming credit, nothing to show anything other than utter failure along a cone of space each time."

"All right," Mud said, leaning back in his chair and stretching his legs out, "so how're they doing it?"

"No, we really have no idea. Not a single solitary clue. Except one. During this blackout, the one that hit you guys, we might have gotten our first break. We had a small fighter array on maneuvers in the same open degree. Like you—us, everyone affected—they lost all long-range communications. But they tried something no one else seems to have tried yet."

"Got out and pushed?" Steelbox asked.

"Pushed...the transmission beam itself?" Chellox replied.

"No one else would try it, right?"

"They didn't push," Mills said, refusing to rise to the attempt to lighten the mood, "they supermagnetized their hull in an effort to focus all communications through one unit, using their engine as a starter and the magnetics as—"

"Fighters aren't ferrous hulled, you can't magnetize one," Olivet said, shaking his head.

"Bee?" Mills asked, waiting.

"You could if you played with the gravity shield and—" Bee cut herself off, a look of worry playing across her face quickly. "How is she?" she asked quickly.

"Bushfield's fine. Probably wishing she never listened to your ranting about strange fixes for problems that don't exist, but she's fine."

"So what happened?" Mud asked. He, too, was concerned about Bushfield, but they needed to work out the problem, and if Mills said she was fine, he had no reason to lie.

"Her ship tore itself apart. She was prepped for hard vacuum so she's fine, but it tore itself apart right under her. Like someone just grabbed it and pulled."

Mud sat up straight and felt his mouth open and close involuntarily a few times. "Say that again?" Mud stood, hands on the back of his chair, leaning hard on it. His team watched him, concerned.

"Her ship tore itself apart. Just pulled apart like taffy," Mills said.

"Do you still have my old ship docked somewhere on this huge whale?" Mud asked.

"The T194? It's in a storage dock, but it should be untouched, sure. Why?"

"I'll be back. Guys, tell Mills about what just happened with our incoming cargo, and I'll be back. If I'm right...I'm right, I know it." Mud left the room without waiting to hear any complaints.

Mills watched him go and shrugged, turning back to the rest of the group. "So, what happened and how many people are pissed?"

"Well, we owe someone a small cruiser," Bee said, still watching the door Mud had left by. "Had to steal it, then Mud made us crash. But we got the cargo."

"Splitting the team, getting us captured, stealing civilian vessels, and basically bungling through it,"

Steelbox said, with a shake of the head. "But hey, we got the cargo."

"Details go in the full report," Mills said. He shook off his annoyance at the team. They were still learning, and even so they'd pulled off a few missions no one else would have considered sane. He felt sure he could paper over any issues with this last excursion. "But the cargo is fine, you're sure?"

"What is it?" Chellox pointed at the table where the canister lay, safe and shiny.

"A viable sample of an engineered disease the likes of which none of us want to think about."

"And you let us just carry it home?" Steelbox asked, angrily.

"You knew to not open it," Mills said.

"What if the canister got damaged in transport, or during retrieval?" Bee felt her own anger rise to match Steelbox's for a change.

"Then the three sub-canisters would have contained it. And if the fourth had been so much as dented, it would have immolated everything inside. Which we hoped wouldn't happen, and didn't, it seems. So thanks."

"So now you will save this to wage your wars?" Chellox asked.

"No, they will study it long enough to find a way to kill it, and then do so," Olivet said softly.

"Is that a premonition?" Mills asked him.

"No, just a hope."

"Well, it's still dead on," Mills said, leaning back in his chair. Silence fell over the group. Mills told himself that his actions were one hundred percent correct, but a nagging doubt crept in. Mistrust, not giving full information to your teams, had proved to be a mistake in the past. He'd counted himself as better than that—right until he dived into the same issue. Why hadn't he just told them? He ran the chain back through his mind. Fears that they would be overly cautious and not get the job done, that they were too new.

Which was, he felt, also ridiculous; he used the team to do all sorts of things no new team should cope with. He couldn't have it both ways, but there he sat, trying to anyway. Deciding to not apologize but to do better in the future, Mills watched the team, trying to not stare but still get a read of the room. To see if this would cause problems down the road when they explained it all to Mud.

Shaking his head, remaining silent, Mills swallowed his concerns as best he could and tried to focus on the new problem at hand. This new Insertion Team still faced pressure from above Mills' pay grade. Higher-ups wanted them but didn't like the relative autonomy they worked under—only one member technically even holding rank—and they certainly hated the cost.

They got the job done, but that couldn't be enough. Not for the high brass. Results alone, without low cost and easily explainable risks, worried the top end of the chain of command. Mills fought for them because he believed in them, never mind that his own career now lay tied into theirs.

He looked around the room, sparse and simple, just a bunch of chairs in a large room, empty except for a table against one wall and a whiteboard stuck up next to a series of monitors opposite the entrance. They didn't rate a better operations center, and honestly had never even asked for one.

The team, for their part, sat waiting. Until Mud came back, none of them felt they could do anything useful. They couldn't push back against Mills—not as hard as any of them wanted, not without their leader. They all knew it, without having to check with one another. They also couldn't start briefing on the new matter, no more than had been said, until they knew why Mud had run off. So they sat at ease, as they did on long trips, only resisting the urge to find a mindless game to play. That didn't feel appropriate given the tense air in the room, with Mills still there.

So everyone in the room felt easier when Mud came back in, carrying a sealed bag. He walked over to the table across the room and tore the bag open. "Guys, Mills, come see this," he said.

They gathered around him and looked at the table. Two pieces of metal sat on the table, heavy and thick enough, Bee judged, to be pieces of a small ship's hull. "Where'd you cut those from?" she asked.

"No, look at the edges," Mills said, pointing. Sure enough, the two pieces had ragged edges, looking torn, or pulled, apart from the whole.

"I found these ages ago, right before I, uhhh," Mud shrugged, glancing at Mills, "snuck onto the *Dozier* that time." Mills certainly remembered that. The others had heard the story, both from Mud and from his dad. "At the time I didn't know what it was, I guess I still don't, but I found a ship broken apart at points, and the hull—well, here, see for yourselves. Mills, is this what you meant about Bushfield's ship?"

Mills studied the pieces of hull. "This is the same

stress and tear patterning, yeah. So what does *that* mean?"

"It means someone else thought of Bee's idea to go around a communication breakdown before, with the same result," Olivet said.

"So this happened before? The same thing?" Steelbox asked.

"Seems like it," Mills said, not liking that one bit. "All right, this is definitely yours. With backup for a change."

"Backup?" Mud asked. Backup meant a close eye on them, something he wasn't too fond of, mostly because it meant they had to play by the rules more than they liked.

"There's some other data. We'll have a full brief in a few hours once your backup arrives," Mills said, walking away from the table. "For now—good job."

Mills grabbed the cargo, tucking it under one arm, and started out of the room. He closed the door behind him and the team turned to Mud. "Yeah, about that good job, wait till we tell you what we were lugging," Steelbox said. "Just wait to yell until we finish."

CHAPTER 6

THE INSERTION TEAM WANDERED away from the room, needing a break of even a few scant hours before they found themselves facing the next problem. Mud, still fuming from what Steelbox had explained, stalked off to his quarters on the *Ratzinger*, Bee trailing behind him, unfortunately going the same way.

The others went to the Mess to grab food, leaving their Captain and his Second to fume. Bee let Mud rant softly under his breath, issuing the occasional mutter of agreement, for most of a hallway. At a junction, people crisscrossing this way and that, to and from various duties, Bee noticed a familiar shape and slid off without a word.

Mud kept talking to her for about thirty feet before he noticed her absence. Shaking his head, annoyed more with himself than anyone else, he turned to see where she'd escaped to. Not that he blamed her. She didn't need him venting any more than he'd need to hear it from himself. Still, bad form.

He caught Bee, fairly skipping back toward him, hand in hand with someone decidedly not skipping but no less pleased to be there.

"Bushfield," Mud said, watching the couple come down the hallway. Bee stopped her half-skip to walk normally, trying to feign looking embarrassed. She wasn't, Mud knew.

"Hey Mud," Bee said, smiling, "look, it's Sarah!"

"Yah, just said hi to her. You were there. It was

three seconds ago."

"I'm allowed to be excited," Bee said.

"She is," Bushfield said, shaking Mud's hand. "Mud. Heard you had some trouble of your own?"

"Ditto," Mud said, shrugging, "and isn't that just odd. Think they'll send us out together this time?"

"Backup, reporting for duty," Bushfield said. She leaned down to quickly kiss Bee, then stood military straight again, grinning.

"You could just join the team," Mud said.

"Mud, you know I think of you—hell, your family—as my own, but I never want to work for you," Bushfield said, the words coming out like an incantation. A conversation they'd repeated many times, that neither of them grew tired of.

"But we'd get to travel together and see each other more," Bee said.

"And you'd get sick of me, and I wouldn't be your pilot, and...and...and," Bushfield said. "When all that changes, then maybe. But for now? Backup. As requested."

"No offense, but not requested. We were told."

"I didn't ask to ride shotgun myself, Madison," Bushfield said, needling him, "but orders are orders."

"Mostly."

"Mostly," she agreed, with a smile. "Briefing in two hours, right?"

"Something like that," Bee said, checking the time readout on the cuff of her thinsuit.

"Mud, we'll see you in Ops in about two hours then. Go get a nap, or a drink." And with that, Bushfield and Bee wandered off to catch up as best they could in the small time they had.

Stepping around strangers in the hallway, Mud wandered aimlessly, unsure what he needed. Food and sleep both sounded good, but neither sat right in his gut. He stopped, having wandered down to navigation, and activated his team's communicator. "Olivet, meet me, your quarters, in ten," he said. Without waiting for a reply, Mud started back in the direction of the crew's suite of rooms, spread along a hallway near the hangars. Not the best location, but good for a quick rollout and launch, which was what they'd asked for.

"Copy," came Olivet's delayed response a few minutes later. Mud kept walking, stopping by Medical for some painkillers for his leg. He refused to let them get a look, needing to keep moving. The pressure bandage job would hold a bit longer.

The crew around him subtly changed as he moved down levels and aft on the large ship. Management types vanished and more and more flight deck crew could be spotted. Mud felt no difference between the two types, mentally, but he admitted the former were far worse at getting out of your way in a tight corridor. Mud felt like a snob even noticing the issue. He shook it off, finding the corridor where his crew lived when not on missions.

He knocked on Olivet's door and waited. Then he knocked again. "Mud, relax," Olivet said behind him. "You beat me here. I decided to grab us both some pie. Whatever it is, pie will help."

"Is that one of your big future feelings?" Mud asked lightly, following Olivet into the room.

"If you'd like."

They sat in the small, sparse room. Olivet leaned back in his desk chair and Mud perched on the edge of his dresser. Olivet hadn't decorated to any serious degree. A small clutch of empty jars sat in one corner. Mud eyed them, thinking. Olivet noticed and raised an eyebrow. "You need the mists?"

"How's your stock?"

"I am waiting for another shipment from Bercuser," Olivet said. They both knew what that meant. Shipments from the planet could take months, because, inexplicably, the planet changed which of the two possible stars it orbited on a random-seeming basis. No one knew why, but you couldn't count on Bercuser being in the same star system you'd thought it was in when you headed there. Considered off-limits to everyone until recently, there were still, obviously, major problems with trade.

"So you're out?" Mud asked. The idea kept tickling the back of his brain, and he didn't want to let go just yet.

"Not quite," Olivet said, thinking out loud, "but my stock is low and I would not be able to incur many visions. They would be sporadic, and weak at best, I fear."

"No, that's fine. Something is better than nothing. Make sure you bring what you can on the *Arrow*, all right?" Mud sat still, letting his mind work on the problem.

"Of course, but can I ask?"

"Why I'm suddenly all about your prophecy, if I generally want you to just deal in hard science instead?" Mud asked in return, smiling at his science officer.

"Yes, pretty much," Olivet agreed.

"I have a feeling," Mud said.

"You? Listening to your gut, to some strange sense of—"

"Oh, all right, I listen to my gut all the time. I just don't huff paint to do it," Mud said, smiling. Olivet felt his visions were true, and that his success rate was extremely high. Which remained something that Mud fought back on, pointing out that they were often vague enough to be able to claim success or failure depending on how you looked at it. They disagreed on which way to look at it, and yet had turned it into a friendly distrust and not a team-breaking one.

"I'll make sure I have what stores I can gather loaded on the ship, Captain," Olivet said, not rising to Mud's dig.

Mud stood, nodding at Olivet. "Thanks. I'll see you in Ops in a while."

"If I may," Olivet said quickly before Mud could leave, "beyond your gut, what's setting you off?"

"That's the thing," Mud said, stepping out of the small room, "I'm not even sure. Anyway, briefing in a bit."

"You didn't even have any pie."

"Thanks, I'm good." Mud closed the door behind him and started back down the hallway. He headed to Medical, to see to his leg, figuring he might as well get it dealt with by professionals while he had some time to do so.

While Mud wandered, Olivet ate pie, and Bee and Bushfield spent quality time together, Steelbox studied charts. When Mud had officially formed a new Insertion Team he'd asked Steelbox to be a part of it, knowing what the man had done for his father. A fighter, Steelbox didn't let anything stop him if at all possible. He could push harder than any of them, just about, to keep going.

The thing of it was, he had no practical skills the team needed. They didn't need a bruiser, and so after a lot of thought, and beers, he'd decided to become a navigator. It was a job he'd done before, rawly and untrained, and he enjoyed it enough—he set his mind to the task.

He studied. He spent downtime—nights off-shift on the *Arrow*, whatever time he could spare and still end up alert and ready for missions—working on his new calling. So he sat, in a small corner of the primary mess hall, and pored over star charts. Bercuser remained his favorite side project. He'd map out both systems that the planet lived in, overlap them, anything to try to make sense out of the behavior of the strangest world known.

Not that he got anywhere. People studied those systems, wrote dissertations, built entire careers on them, and had for decades. The point, to Steelbox, wasn't to discover and solve the problem, necessarily, but to rediscover on his own everything that humanity knew. To reverse-engineer the data, and reprove it. To become good enough to have earned those degrees himself.

This time, he thought he saw something. He looked at the maps, them laid them over each other. Scrounging for a pencil, he marked both maps up and started doing calculations, roughly, in the margins. Even as he worked, he decided someone else must have either noticed what he saw or already dismissed it. Regardless, he did the work and noted the data carefully. Olivet might know about this, he considered—but then, most Bercusans didn't study

44

their planet, instead choosing to accept its behavior and the fogs along its surface: simply a thing that was and always would be.

He'd started to sum up his thoughts, writing longhand on the back of one of the maps, when his suit's clock alarm went off, reminding him of the briefing. If he left now, he thought, he could just manage to arrive only a minute or two late. Sighing at himself, he quickly folded up his maps, being one of those strange people who could actually refold a map properly on the first try, and hurried out of the room.

CHAPTER 7

THE INSERTION TEAM'S OPS room felt fairly full by the time Steelbox got there. Besides his team, Mills, and Bushfield, one of Bushfield's squad took up a seat and a bunch of secure boxes hemmed in the chairs, seeming to sprout uncontrollably from somewhere else. They intruded on the small space, making people draw their chairs closer together, huddling into a semi-circle aimed directly at the video wall and whiteboard where Mills stood.

Bee turned to look at Steelbox as he entered, the last one in the room, and just shook her head at him. Not in anger; more along a sisterly annoyance. He shrugged in reply and found a seat.

"...So once you're on mission, you can deploy the scanning equipment," Mills was saying, "which will hopefully let us track what's going on. Hopefully it will be a waste of time." Everyone chuckled politely, mostly because growling was rude.

"Can't you deploy this stuff," Mud waved at one row of boxes, "some easier way? By easier, just to be clear, I mean 'using anything but us.'" No one dared chuckle at that, because they would have meant it, and Mills could tell the difference.

"It'll need to go along your flight path, regardless, so you get to do it. Look," Mills said, trying to not sigh. "We need this stuff. You don't have the only payload, trust me, but we need to be able to at least make a stab at tracking an origin point for these comm blackouts."

"But you're sending us to deal with the primary

suspect," Mud said. He leaned back in his chair but kept his legs curled back, under the chair, to avoid disturbing anyone else or taking up extra space. He could've gotten away with it, and he knew it, and that only added to his reluctance to actually do it.

"Yes," Mills agreed, "but the primary suspect in this case is fairly thin. Now, I admit, we want these guys brought in anyway, so lucky us. But we can't put more than a best guess on them for this in particular. So we double down. You saying I shouldn't?"

"No, sir," Bushfield said, "he's saying he's lazy."

"That's the one," Mud said. The laughter came from everyone, including Mills, this time. "So fine," he continued, "we set up your equipment. What's the actual mission?"

"You need to take out the Brand Syndicate. Family run, we'd like Sybil and Tiago Brand back here, optimally. They're in the city of Kenzo, planet is McDallison." Mills called images up on the screen next to him. Pictures of an Earth-like planet, followed by slowly zoomed-in shots all the way down to the city level. Tiny facts, added by helpful people who didn't realize the data would be too small to read when run on a screen like that, sat in small boxes along the edges of each image.

"McDallison," Bushfield said. "Isn't that pretty farspun, sir?"

"I couldn't make them live closer, Bushfield. You'll carry extra fuel and leave some along the flight path back, with two of the sensor packages. The *Arrow* should be fine for it, both ways."

Bee nodded, "If I remember where McDallison is, we should have fuel to spare."

47

"We will," said Steelbox. "McDallison is farspun all right, but only a few days out from where we just were. Timewise. Directionally, whole other ballpark."

"So we know where, but why them? And what," Mud asked, "will we be facing that you want us to have backup for? No offense, Bushfield."

"None taken. Not a single one of us wants an unnecessary field trip."

"The Brands have been on our radar for years. They run their local city and have fingers in most of the crime spread throughout at least one continent on McDallison. But they export, which is where we get involved. They focus on aerial and orbital defense, illegal gun mods, and communications jamming. They minor in Beta-wave disruption and recreational drugs. They've made some advances in comm jammers that are damned strange, so we think there's a good chance they're our goal. Also, three of the jamming waves have been from their degree of the sky, more than anywhere else. It points right down their throat, frankly."

"Wait," Steelbox said, "they minor in drugs? And they still have a big reach? We might not have to move on them—they're apparently bad at business."

"Sorry, that list was for off-world. Around home they balance it all about how you'd think they would. No, they're good at what they do—very good. And dangerous."

"Let me guess," Bushfield said, "that whole aerial and orbital bit there, that's why you're calling me and Beef up."

"Your callsign is Beef?" Bee asked Bushfield's

48

squad member.

"Yours is Bee?" he asked in return.

"No, my name is Bee," she said.

"Oh, my name is Ted. But yeah, Beef. I think I was passed out when they handed out call signs, or something."

"It's because you wouldn't stop talking about types of cows that one day," Bushfield said, punching him in the shoulder. "Hours of ancient types of cows on Earth."

"Oh, yeah, that'd do it," Beef said, happily agreeing.

"Guys, up here," Mills said, trying to recover the room. "To your point, yes, Bushfield, that's exactly why you and Oblick were called in for backup. The Brands will have something, at least one something, and we have no way to know what it is—only that it'll be ugly and deadly. You hold the door open for the *Arrow*, retreat, then reenter the field to open the door on exit."

"No planetary run?"

"Not unless unavoidable," Mills said. "You leave tomorrow morning. Take the rest of today, get ships and gear in order, do your prep. I'll run Ops from here, assuming I can and they don't jam us. If they jam us, Mud, you're in charge on ground, Bushfield in orbital combat."

"Thank you," Olivet said, "for getting that straight now."

"Are you trying to say something?" Mud and Bushfield asked him, almost simultaneously.

"I think you just explained it for us," Olivet said.

"All right, get out of here," Mills said, "before this turns into what it usually does."

"That was kind of quick," Mud said, even as he

stood.

"It's a simple mission. Go get these folk. Don't die," Mills said. "Fix the problem."

CHAPTER 8

THE NEXT MORNING THEY prepared for launch. Mud and Bee went over the GravPacks that the Insertion Team both loved and hated. They were too useful not to wear, and use, during missions. But they'd also gone out of fashion decades ago. Mud's parents, and the original Insertion Team, were the last people to use them on a regular basis. Trained on them as a normal part of growing up, Mud remained the most comfortable with them, and even he preferred to not use them when he could.

Though ultimately faster and far more maneuverable than any ship in the sky, GravPacks left the wearer with only a gravity envelope around them instead of a hull, which would also allow them to carry more food, atmosphere, and waste removal along for the ride.

They took a long time to learn to control well, their specialized, contact-based HUD disorienting at first. Plus there was math involved in the use, and angles to consider, and generally no one felt they were worth the trouble.

Mud's parents proved the exception to that rule, however, and imparted the overall use of them to their adopted son. Being able to hold your own in space came in handy, and flying in a planet's gravity well certainly expanded mission possibilities.

They also gave physicists small nightmares. Doctor Terrance Williams, Mud's grandfather, had invented the GravPack, and even he wasn't sure how they worked. Not fully. Basic gravity shields for internal ship use and limited propulsion in smaller vessels made some sense, but the GravPack could throw itself faster than light and didn't seem to be bothered or to incur time dilation, which fell into the "simply impossible" range of the universe.

The packs didn't care and went on working, and Mud's team kept using them.

Checking out each pack carefully, Mud and Bee stored them, sorting out everything else going with them on the trip. The boxes of scanning equipment and extra fuel for Bushfield (mission callsign Deep Water) and Beef's fighters couldn't all fit in the *Arrow*, forcing them to use a trailer sled. Chellox secured it, strapping the boxes into a larger container that could be towed by the *Arrow*. The tow would limit his maneuverability and speed, adding to their time to target, but deployment of the scanners would eat time regardless.

All three ships checked out. Their cargo sat secured and verified. The crews loaded into their positions and refueling finished. They backed out slowly, dropping out of the docking ports into the vastness of space casually, like lost luggage. Only Mud's call of "*Arrow* clear, mission clock started," plus Deep Water and Beef's confirmations, signaled the start of something. Mills' reply, a simple "Copy," and they were off and on the job.

Due to the cargo trailer, they took a good half day to their first sensor drop-off. Steelbox and Olivet took the job, going, as Steelbox put it, "for a walk." They wore their thinsuits, invisible gravity bubbles working as shields around their heads once the suits detected a slim enough oxygen level.

They also wore their GravPacks, setting them to a very slender protective field. Only centimeters from their body, the field would help redirect any stray matter winging through space at speeds best described as catastrophic. No one wanted a micro-meteor to punch a hole in their suit, or their organs.

Deployment went smooth, including base communication, so the teams moved on, continuing their route. Over the next two-and-a-half days, the pattern continued: they would reach a deployment location, deploy and adjust the sensors, and move on. Twice they also left fuel depots behind, but outside of that, nothing changed.

They grew bored, but never lost mission awareness. Each of the seven of them knew that something could not only crop up at any moment, but, worse, something incredibly stupid could happen and endanger all of them. None of them wanted to be the cause of that potential mishap. For one thing, the mocking would never die down, but for another much more important reason, too: none of them wanted to cause anyone's death.

They were professionals, even though not all of the Insertion Team felt that way. Like many proficient people, each of them remained gut sure they were the only one involved who felt like a fraud, so they worked harder and hid their insecurities from everyone else.

They moved on, running low on sensors to deploy. Finally, at the start of day four, ship time, they deployed the last sensor array, flipped it on, and confirmed it worked.

"Deep Water, Beef, this is the *Arrow*," Chellox said, relaxing now that the cargo trailer drifted, slaved to the last of the arrays. "Are we good for slaved hard burn?"

Slaved burns were a simple idea. The trailing ships linked their flight controls to the lead, so they could fly as a pack without having to work at it, or worry. Deep Water and Beef both hated it, as did Chellox when he sat on the receiving end of a flight slaving. The maneuver still remained their fastest route in, however, and so two short agreements came back over the comms.

Chellox flipped a few switches, confirmed vectors and status chains with Steelbox, and sent out a final warning, both to his crew and the linked ships. He'd have to fly a little slower than full out, so the ship linkages wouldn't lag, but not by much. Everyone strapped in and braced for him to start tossing them through the black.

The three ships moved through space as if they were angry at it, no longer on speaking terms and sure it knew what it had done. Speeding that way for another full day, the ships drew closer and closer to McDallison. Forward sensors scanned steadily, with Steelbox running the readings through his own homebrew systems to double-check some of the data. The pattern remained clear, nothing but the expected orbital bodies ahead, above, below, or around them.

They drew within visual sight of McDallison, still feeling clear and free. For a few hours they continued, getting ready to cut the fighters loose and spread out, to start preparing for possible trouble. About an hour before their planned decoupling, alarms went off in all three ships. Instantly, all three pilots silenced the alarms and cut into a communications channel.

"*Arrow*, this is Deep Water, drop us! We got incoming!"

"This is Beef, I got no visuals, no scans, only alarms? Repeat, I have nothing showing. False alarm?"

"Don't care—Deep Water, Beef, you're free to fly," Chellox said, flipping switches on his console quickly. Inside the *Arrow* they all braced for the unknown, aware that often meant nearby explosions.

"Copy, *Arrow*. Beef, go wide, could be false sensor readings. Could be an attack. Until we know, we assume worst."

"Copy, Deep Water, still seeing nothing."

"This is *Arrow*, we have nothing either. Are they just messing with our sensors to panic us?" Steelbox checked every instrument in reach, twice.

"That's current theory, *Arrow*," came Bushfield's reply. "This is Deep Water, assuming command," she said crisply.

Mud nodded to himself from his seat. Until further notice, this was a full-out combat situation. "You heard her," he said to his crew, "combat assumed." He switched his mic to a wider channel. "Deep Water, this is Mud. Want me out there?"

"Not yet. Stand-by position only."

Mud stood and made his way to the ship's airlock, strapping on his GravPack. Along the wall were a few small fold-out jump seats, one of which Mud flipped down and perched on. If Bushfield gave the order, he could be out of the ship and in combat in less than a full minute. Until then he sat, listened, and waited.

The three ships still sped toward McDallison. Further apart, they each scanned electronically and visually, wary of anything coming at them. Slowly, though, over the course of an hour, they started to feel safe. Nothing showed up anywhere. Bushfield wasn't quite ready to stand them down, however.

She weighted a stand-down versus constant vigilance through the very human problem of constant caution breeding a drift in attention. Diminishing returns would start kicking in soon, but she wanted to push the envelope as far as she could, for safety. She had reached for her communications switch when the blackness of space erupted in a series of white-hot explosions all around her.

"Status!" she yelled into her mic. "Report, everyone report!" Grabbing her controls tight, she juked her ship hard, throwing it through a series of turns and loops designed to shake off target locks. Her systems showed her Beef and the *Arrow* doing similar.

"We got explosions out here, Deep Water," Beef said over comms, "too many to count."

"Wide field," Chellox said, sounding almost calm. Bushfield knew he could pilot through a firestorm without breathing hard. "Nano-drones blowing small charges. Sensors show...what, Steelbox? Ahhh, sorry, yes. We're showing they could pierce hulls. Stay wide."

"Wide from what, we can't see them!" Beef said.

"Steady, Beef. *Arrow*, how're they avoiding sensors?"

"Working on it," came the reply. Inside the ship, Bee and Olivet traded notes and chewed at the problem as fast as they could, knowing their own lives, and more, very possibly hung on their work.

"Mud, stay off fie—No, damn it, Mud, get out here!" Bushfield's head hit the back of her chair hard as more explosions rocked her ship. One of them would get lucky and blow a hole in her ship, or worse, an engine, any time now.

Mud didn't wait for further orders—he leapt from his seat, slapping the quick release in his harness. He hit the airlock cycle pad before he fully stepped into the chamber, warming up his GravPack to full operation as quick as it would cycle. Blinking twice to call up the HUD controls for space flight, he stepped out into nothing, and hung there.

"I'm out for a walk, Deep Water. Talk to me."

"That bullet on your back throws fields hard. Time to push back."

"You want a wall?

"Copy, Mud."

GravPacks worked by throwing up a HUD in special contact lenses. Users could then blink-select gravity wells for attract and repel. In space that often meant whole planets. The overall effect ended up being somewhere between giant invisible rope swinging and a strange bit of tightrope walking, theoretically at super-light speeds. But the silver, bullet-shaped device that ran the length of Mud's back also put out a protective field. Close in it would deflect stray rocks and debris. Normal field size during free flight stood at around five feet. But the field could be widened and shaped when needed.

Mud lashed himself to the bow of the *Arrow*, swinging in front of the ship smoothly. "Form in," he said, glancing behind him to watch Bushfield and Beef tuck in close. Blinking quickly to select through menus, he turned his protective field into a wall in front of him and widened it as far as he could. Then he expanded it outward, with the field set to maximum density.

Smaller ships had deflector shields based on gravity tech as well, but the shaping and manipulation of them was crude, useless for this sort of work. The nano-drones started to explode as the shield hit them. They could blow tiny holes in it, to be sure—the charges were focused and ugly—but Mud's GravPack could put out far more energy to keep repairing the shield than they could manage to eat away at.

Setting a repel strand to the nose of the *Arrow*, Mud started moving, his shield in front of him, setting off charges. The *Arrow* gained speed, which meant Mud gained speed, and as they did, Mud, as tip of the spear, ran the numbers on how long this could work.

"*Arrow*, ETA on a better way to blow these things? I have no rear or side shields and will deplete pack before we reach planetfall. Please advise."

"Working on it, Mud," Chellox said. "Hold tight."

"Mud," Bushfield asked, "what are the chances one of these drones sneaks around the edge of your field?"

"This is why I want an ETA, Deep Water."

"Copy," she said, "*Arrow*?"

"On it. Over," came a reply from Steelbox.

"You guys seeing this?" Mud asked suddenly. Ahead of him, as they grew ever closer to McDallison, twinkling shapes started to grow in the

58

distance. Mud knew that twinkle: engine burn. He sighted, and sure enough the tiny twinkling ships could easily be traced straight-lined right back to the planet.

"Copy," Beef said. "Incoming. Reading twenty. No, ten. Forty...guys, they're jamming us and sending misreads."

"I count fifteen," Mud said. "With my eyeballs. That they haven't jammed."

"Mud, get back in the *Arrow* and—"

"Deep Water, they need to shut down the drones to fly into the field," Mud said, cutting her off.

"Not if they can ID friendlies they don't," she said.

"Damn it."

"Exactly. We'll take the drone hits. Don't stand there like a big dumb target. Over."

"Copy, Deep Water. No big dumb target." Mud pulled his shield in and reeled himself back to the *Arrow*, cycling the airlock.

"Bee? Olivet? Any progress on the drones?" he asked as soon as he got back on board.

"Not enough," Olivet said, not bothering to look up from his console. "They're shielded enough that we can't find a frequency to remote blow them, hijack their controls, or disarm them. The go off on firm matter contact, like our hull, or a strong enough energy signature, like a ship shield or the GravPack. But we can't fake a signature that strong or wave a big stick through the air to knock them about and set them off early."

"But they have to be able to avoid their own ships, right?" Mud asked, trying to sit comfortably with the GravPack still strapped to his back. Not an easy feat, and one he'd never gotten good at. He shifted constantly, forcing Bee to look somewhere else so the constant fidgeting didn't annoy her.

"Sure, so if we can work out what they broadcast—"

"They're too far and if they're as shielded as the drones—" Olivet started.

"Then we crack their shielding," Bee cut in. "Not sure we have another option."

Mud nodded at her and turned his chair to face the cockpit. "You two doing all right?" he asked as lightly as possible.

"Sure thing, Cap," Steelbox said, "we're just back to taking hits from the drones. Can't we just set off some explosions of our own and wipe them out?"

"We don't have ammo to waste," Chellox said, "but we need to clear the pattern before those fighters reach us."

"So we have about twenty minutes," Steelbox said, "give or take."

"An eternity," Mud said, rotating his chair to his own console. He keyed for Mills back on base and got static. "They're jamming long-range comms," he said over the larger group channel.

"Confirmed," Bushfield said, "but static?"

"Dead silence last time," Mud agreed.

"If this is the same thing," she pointed out.

"Damn it," Mud said, watching his screens, setting them to show him navigation data, "we know nothing and it's going to get us killed."

"Deep Water to all ships, new action plan."

"Go ahead, Deep Water," Chellox said.

"Hit me, boss," Beef replied.

"While *Arrow* continues work on drone disabling, we're going hard burn at McDallison."

"Front door?" Steelbox asked, looking over his shoulder at Mud.

"Confirmed, *Arrow*. Look," Bushfield said, inhaling slowly, enough to be heard over her mic, "we're taking the hits either way. But if we move fast enough they might not keep up, and better, if they can, they may not turn as well and we can throw them at upcoming targets."

"Deep Water," Mud said, "that's just mean."

"I love it," Beef said. "Starting hard burn in three."

"We love it, too," Steelbox said. "*Arrow* on hard burn in two..."

The three ships all lurched forward, engines pushing hard, and aimed themselves directly at the oncoming swarm. They got knocked around by drones, but kept going. At their speeds, the drones were starting to go off harder and harder, due to impact. Beef felt his bones rattle.

"This is Beef, we need to close fast, not sure how much more of this my ship can take."

"Copy, take tight evasives. Let's try to shake at least a few of them," Bushfield said, her voice shaking as a drone went off on her right side midmessage.

Rattling and taking damage as they went, the three ships closed with the fifteen enemy fighters as quickly as possible. As soon as they were in range, they tried to target the enemy, only to find the jamming being used wouldn't allow for a clean lock.

"Oh come on," Beef said. "Permission to go manual and start blowing them out of the sky."

"Affirmative. All weapons to manual," Bushfield said. "Mud, stay indoors until the drones are better dealt with."

"Copy, Deep Water. Will sit tight."

Steelbox readied the *Arrow*'s weapons array and launched two missiles quickly. One went off early, intersecting with a drone. The other exploded off one of the enemy's shields.

"They're using the drones to blow our shots," he said.

"Copy," Deep Water said. "*Arrow*, throw out some widespread terror, open the door for us so we can open it for you with the fighters."

"Copy," Steelbox said, manually targeting all fifteen fighters, knowing most of the shots wouldn't get to target. He thumbed the button hard and watched the missiles fly free.

"Beef, track and follow. Let's take them out and remind them it's our sky."

"Copy."

The two streamlined fighters shot ahead of the *Arrow*, following the missiles close, losing themselves in the scattered glare of the missiles' thrusters. They broke in different directions, Deep Water going relative up, with Beef taking a turn relative left, around the missile array, and they turned hard enough that their engines whined at a pitch necessitating their comms being turned off for a second.

The missiles started to explode as the drones intersected them, but Deep Water and Beef ignored that, taking a few drone hits to their own shields. Instead they opened fire on the mass of enemy ships in front of them, surprising them.

Blasters and small manual-targeted missiles from both ships wound their way into the enemy field. The sudden, unexpected flurry of fire caused the enemy ships to attempt to scatter. Except they didn't know where they could scatter to. In front of them their own drones exploded, along with incoming enemy missiles. From at least two sides they were also taking fire, and as they tried to work out whether they were about to take fire from any more angles, not yet sure that the ships attacking them were two of the three they'd been heading toward, they bounced and rolled from explosions.

Two of the ships caught shots from Beef's blasters and collided, trying to dodge. The *Arrow* came in behind their missiles, Steelbox taking a few potshots between the missile field at the enemy ships, knowing he couldn't really do much damage even if he did hit one, but enjoying adding to their confusion and panic.

The thirteen enemy ships, having worked out what they were up against, scattered effectively, forcing Deep Water and Beef to give chase and fight them in small batches. They also tried to draw the *Arrow* into the fighting full-time.

"Deep Water, this is Mud. Permission to go for a walk?"

"Negative, Mud," Bushfield replied quickly. "Drones still in play."

"Damn it, Deep Water, we need to even the score."

"Negative, repeat negative. Your mission is planetside. Punch through quick and get on the ground. This is our sandbox. Copy?"

"Copy, Deep Water. *Arrow* to proceed into atmo, on mission," Chellox said before Mud could reply. Unable to look away from what he was doing, he added over his shoulder, "I'm taking us in, Mud."

Mud didn't reply, instead heading back to the airlock and gathering up GravPacks, handing them out to everyone but Chellox and Steelbox. They couldn't take the time just then, so Mud set their packs near their seats and strapped himself back in.

Chellox aimed them at a pocket of enemy fighters and then, just as they opened fire, dove toward the planet at speed, leaving the battleground.

The *Arrow* hurtled toward the planet, daring the enemy fighters to break off and pursue. One took them up on it. Deep Water and Beef caught the trajectory change and considered their options quickly.

"Beef, get that thing off their tail. I'll keep the rest on the hunt after me."

"Boss, that's not the—"

"Beef, stay on mission. Keep the door open for them. Clear their six."

"Copy, Deep Water." Beef broke away from pursing fighters to trail after the *Arrow*. The fighter behind them had managed to tag the ship once already, giving it a bit of a wobble as it got close to the planet. Beef could see the damage didn't cross into critical, but his sensors were still jammed so he couldn't be too sure on what might've been knocked out.

He opened fire with blasters only, not wanting to risk a missile getting off-track and becoming friendly fire. The enemy fighter tried to stay directly behind the *Arrow*, so an easy dodge would put the ship at risk from Beef's shots. He cursed loudly, hoping his comms weren't hot, and pushed his engines as hard as they'd go, trying to overtake the enemy ship from relative above.

Chellox saw Beef's speed increase and took a gamble on the maneuver. He slowed down, turning as if to abandon planet fall, counting on the ship still firing on the *Arrow* to follow him. They did, and Chellox let a soft whoop escape from his lips as he used the Tsyfarian engines to do their thing and turn far faster than any ship had a right to, throwing the crew around the cabin unexpectedly. "Sorry," he said, not meaning it, "just have to lose this guy, hold on."

"You tell us to hold on before you do that, Chellox," Bee muttered, gripping her harness tightly in her hands. "Not after."

"Well, hold on," Chellox said again. The *Arrow* came around, turning to loop the enemy ship horizontally, giving him no good way to turn and fire for a moment. Beef took his shot. He took several. Enough of them hit that the enemy ship's engine started to sputter.

"*Arrow*'s in the clear," Beef said. "Headed back to you, Deep Water."

"Copy," Bushfield said. She turned her ship hard enough she could hear the metal of her hull complain. The enemy took the moment to focus solely on her, surrounding her with fire. The only good side to it that she could see was that their fire knocked a bunch of the remaining drones out of the way.

She dodged as best she could, hoping her shields continued to hold, but knowing that the damage her ship accumulated would overwhelm her ability to keep up with the fight sooner than later. They'd underprepared, she thought; she should've taken at least two more ships along. They could only react to the data they possessed, though, and nothing Mills showed her had lead them to believe orbital defenses would be quite as robust as they seemed to be now.

Beef came in hard from her right, firing everything he had, chasing a few of the enemy off her. In return she looped around and caught out one of them as they started to shift into position to take shots at Beef.

All in all, eleven ships remained in the darkness around them, with only their two quickly depleting weapons stores to protect them. It'd be a thin line between survival and failure for them, but they both knew they had to hold tight, keep up the fight, and be ready for round two when the *Arrow* took off. So they retreated, drawing the fighters off with them, hoping they'd turn back.

They did, and Beef and Bushfield cut engines, floating free for a few. "Beef, while we catch our breath, we need to EVA to try and do patch jobs. You good?"

"Good here, Deep Water, but they'll toss more drones in our way if we try to make it back into the full field."

"Of course they will," Bushfield agreed, "so let's hope the *Arrow* can stop them at the root while doing everything else they're on mission for."

"They'll get it done."

"They will, if they remember. And we can't comm them anymore to make sure—the jammers are too strong close to the planet for us to punch through."

"So what do we do?" Beef asked, checking his systems carefully, making special notice of weapons levels.

"Go EVA and patch job, like I said. One at a time, the other keeps an eye out for stray enemies."

"And if they send a drone wave back out this far?"

"Then we probably die. So let's hope they don't do that," Bushfield said, popping her ship's hatch open and latching a tie down to make sure she didn't drift off.

"Copy, Deep Water," Beef said, watching her work while keeping an eye out for signs of engine flare in the distance. "It's a good plan, Boss. I'm thrilled to be a part of it."

CHAPTER 9

ATMOSPHERE STARTED TO FORM around the *Arrow*. Flames followed, and Chellox adjusted his entry angle to let the shields do their work. He planned to land far from their target city, then fly over it, once they were securely in atmo and no longer looked like an invading force.

A good plan, but one that didn't count on explosions starting to go off in the sky all around them.

"Report!" Mud yelled, trying to see what his screens could tell him.

"Aerial defenses, Mud—we've got more of those drones, and missiles coming in hot," Steelbox said.

"Options?" Mud asked, sure he wouldn't like any of them.

"We can go down hard or we can try to fight back," Chellox said. "We can't exactly flee anywhere. If we retreat into orbit we won't be able to try another run, data suggests. If we just go the way we are, the ship might end up...unwell."

"So we crash? You're saying we crash?" Mud took a deep breath. "Why does it feel like we're always crashing?"

"Probably something you did," Bee said, hoping for a tension break.

"Probably is," Mud agreed, shaking his head. "Chellox, can you at least crash land us somewhere in one piece, without too much damage?"

"That's my current objective, Mud," Chellox said, "so just let me work on that."

"Shutting up then."

Mud glanced toward Olivet, who nodded and opened one of his jars of mist, sniffing deeply. Mud hoped that the process he didn't even really believe in would work for them. He knew it would take some time, so best to start now, doubly so if they had to abandon ship.

Explosions rocked them hard, but Chellox did his best to keep them fairly steady. After a few minutes, the ground rushing at them, they could all feel the ship start to respond badly. A shake and drift combined with a strange rattle from the engine that shouldn't be there. Olivet stored the jar of mist and joined Bee as she went to see to the engine. Mud heard a fire extinguisher go off and had started to unhook his harness when they came back out of the engine compartment together. "It's fine," Bee told him, "but we'll need repairs when we land."

Mud settled back into his seat, as best he could wearing his GravPack. "Plus repairs to the hull, chances are."

"Olivet can handle the engine, Chellox can work on the hull."

"Shouldn't you work on the engine, Bee?" Mud asked, looking between her and Olivet.

"You need one of us on mission with you," she said, as if that solved it.

"So I take Olivet and leave you to fix things here," he said.

"Mud, if Bee feels—" Olivet started.

"No, I need the best hands on engine. Also, Bee, you're better in combat situations than Olivet and we all know it. I need you here in case they come for the ship. Those're orders." Mud looked around as they continued to fall from the sky, mostly uncontrollably. "Anyone else think we're way too calm about crash landings?"

"Comes with the job, Cap," Steelbox said over his shoulder. "Also I'm better with the hull work than Chellox, if we're dividing up teams already."

"Chellox, can Steelbox make sure those Tsyfarian engines are properly tuned, yet?" Mud asked.

"Not yet," Chellox said, "but please let me crash this ship safely, thank you."

"Sure thing, Chel, sorry. Steelbox, you come with me and Olivet. Bee and Chellox fix the *Arrow* so we have a way back off world. New side mission parameter, too. We need to knock out whatever controls those drones, otherwise when we launch, and while we retreat, we'll get blown out of the sky again. Also Deep Water and Beef would probably welcome the respite."

"Copy that, Cap," Steelbox said, returning to helping Chellox land the ship as smoothly as feasible.

"Well, let's crash this thing with dignity then," Mud said with only a small hint of a sigh.

Chellox kept them as level as he could manage, skimming through trees and bouncing them as gently as possible before they skidded to a bone-rattling, jarring stop.

They all hit harness releases and got out of their chairs quickly, Chellox and Steelbox stopping to don their GravPacks. They exited the *Arrow* and stood around outside of it, looking over the damage. "Olivet? Chellox?" Mud asked, looking between them both.

"Hull damage is minimal, Mud," Chellox said, "but

the engines will need realignment and that will take some time."

"Olivet?"

"Engine's fixable. Mostly. Take-off could be a big problem."

"Wait, why?" Mud asked.

Bee nodded at Olivet. "Because the engine will still generate thrust but the relatively long-term strain of leaving atmo might knock it back out."

"Wouldn't a hard burn home do the same?" Steelbox asked before Mud could say it.

"Oh, sure. But one thing at a time, right?" Bee shook her head and walked back toward the rear of the ship with Olivet, discussing a few ideas.

Olivet returned alone and stood near Mud. "Bee is going to get to work. I suggest we do the same."

"Agreed. Steelbox, you good to go?"

"All good, Cap."

"All right. We'll fly in low, grab the Brands, convince them to shut off the drones and tell us about the jammers, then blow the drone controls anyway. Simple," Mud said, knowing it would remain exactly that simple right up until the moment reality caught up with planning, as it always did.

Mud, Steelbox, and Olivet took off, leaving the *Arrow* behind. Bee watched them go, returning to the interior of the *Arrow* to work on the engine. She wanted to be part of the mission team, not left behind as support staff, but felt Mud was right; if there was trouble here, she had a better shot at dealing with it.

They weren't hard to track, landing the way they did, and given how anxious these people had proved so far about keeping them away, there remained a ton of reason to feel they would send a team to inspect, confiscate, or more likely destroy the *Arrow*.

She couldn't keep an eye out while working on the engine from inside, of course, but Chellox could while working on the hull. They talked it over briefly, and he went to work still wearing his Tsyfarian helmet, in case.

Chellox didn't mind being left behind to work on the ship; he preferred it. Fighting was fine, if you were in a ship, but hand-to-hand felt ungainly and strange to him. Also, even though it might logically follow that he would be the most natural with a GravPack, he found he hated the things. Flying a ship made sense to him. The crazy strand weaving of the GravPacks, selecting target after target for attract or repel, just never clicked in his brain well enough.

So they both worked on the *Arrow* tensely, waiting for attack.

CHAPTER 10

Mud, Olivet, and Steelbox flew over trees, the latter two a bit wobbly in their paths. Selecting planetary-surface mode allowed them to dial down to much smaller gravity sources than whole planets. The fine-tuning let them attract their GravPacks to some treetops and repel others, and if done at the proper speed, the flight path looked straight and clean.

"Let's slave your packs to mine for entry," Mud said. "It'll keep us lower." Neither of his teammates disagreed, and the linkage went live. Mud sped them over the trees, dropping as low as he dared. "Set shields to one foot," he said.

"That's a little thin," Steelbox said. He didn't like GravPacks, but put up with them when he had to.

"We'll be fine," Mud assured him. "Not my first tree topper."

"But it's mine," Steelbox pointed out.

"Same," Olivet added, "and a foot shield is close enough to dent us if you twitch wrong."

"Which I won't. Set for one foot, where's the trust?" Mud hated this. He needed his team to not take up time arguing about the finer points of perfectly solid plans. He felt torn—he didn't want to go full 'I'm the boss' right before they entered a probable firefight, but the reminder might help. He considered everything and ran it, eventually, through the filters of his parents. His father would absolutely enforce order. His mother remained a maybe, leaning toward a yes. He decided on something different. "I don't want to lay down law, pull rank, and piss us all off," he said, deciding to, instead, just be blunt with them. "But we need to do this solid, without missing. The rest of the team, our friends in the black right now, they need us to get this right the first time. So can we cut the democracy for a bit?"

He waited in what felt like an endless silence that only lasted a few seconds in reality.

"Copy, Cap," Steelbox said.

"Copy," echoed Olivet. They set their shields to only a foot of distance and both took a few deep, calming breaths. The three continued in silence for a while, Mud using his GravPack to pull and push them along the tree line like a gymnast. They hit speeds upwards of a hundred miles per hour, with Mud having to select new targets and disconnect from old ones a few steps of ahead of where they were. He did the sort of GravPack flying that he'd been raised to, the type he thought he'd never really need.

Soon enough, Kenzo came into view. Large, spire-shaped buildings rose up, straining for the sky. The rest of the city sprawled around them, edging out into the woods. From their vantage point, the team could see a distinct lack of careful city planning, meaning the place grew wild, expanding as needed—and quickly, from the gleam of most of the buildings. So it sprang up and edged out into the wildness out of necessity, claiming what land it needed without thought to checking growth.

Other cities on McDallison, they knew from their map checks, had been planned out before construction, almost sterile in their mapping. The tiny town of Kenzo had started that way, but the last decade had seen an influx of money and a decrease in care.

Mud knew that the Brands lived in one of the taller spires, but their power base laid distributed throughout a lot of the smaller buildings in town. Knowing an attack headed their way, what were the chances they'd stay home and not seek a reinforced hiding hole? The question then became where they hid, and where their attack controls were.

The controls were going to be easier—there was only one small spaceport in the city large enough to launch a small cruiser, or maybe fifteen small fighters. Why wouldn't, Mud reasoned, you want your drones to be controlled from the same place they'd probably launch their payload rockets from?

He turned them toward the spaceport and quickly laid out his reasoning. "So the problem left is where the Brands themselves are," he said, finishing his chain of thought. "We'll work it out while we get rid of the drone problem. Setting you both to free flight in five. Steelbox, take the control tower; Olivet, provide covering fire; I'll find the tech room and knock it out."

They came in over the spaceport quickly and dropped to the ground just as fast. Guards came out of the four terminals, yelling and brandishing guns. Steelbox used his GravPack to shoot off to the tower, crashing through one of its large windows.

Tucking and rolling as he went through the window, Steelbox came to his feet gun drawn, spinning to do a quick head count. Only four people sat in the tower at the moment, and all four of them were cowering. "So hey, hi, we're gonna be grounding anything for the rest of the day, that good for you all?" Steelbox waved the four toward one spot in the room, across from the door, so he could track them easier. Locking and bracing the door shut, he turned his blaster back toward his new hostages. "I promise, the last thing I want to do is hurt anyone here. But nothing takes off, nothing lands, and no one gets any data from you. Just a while, then we'll be on our way. You can thank the Brands for today's disruption of service."

Outside, on the ground, Olivet sought cover, taking random shots from behind various structures and vehicles at the guards going after Mud. He kept them distracted, giving Mud openings, which Mud took advantage of happily. He leapt at one guard, lassoed him with an attractor field from his GravPack, then spun and set it to repel, throwing the guard hard into one of his friends.

Setting his Acadian blaster down to a thin beam, Mud burned through the door of one of the smaller structures at the edge of the spaceport. The small building built around the door seemed uselessly tiny, enough so that Mud felt sure the door only opened on an entrance down to some lower-level structure. Proven right, he took the stairs two at a time, blaster aimed in front of him. The bottom of the stairway dead-ended at another door. This one stood unlocked. Mud threw it open, moving to the side as best he could, and waited for a four count before looking into the new doorway. A long, empty hallway stood in front of him. "You guys good?" he asked softly into his thinsuit's comm.

"All good here, Cap."

"Still laying down cover but they'll be onto me soon. Mud, they're starting to gather at the door you just went through, they'll be on you soon, too,"

Olivet said.

"Thanks, don't worry about it, continue to secure site." Knowing his time grew short, Mud started to kick in doors along the hallways as he walked them, clearing each as fast as possible. The rooms all sat empty, full of terminals and tech still running various routines he couldn't identify at a glance. Nearing the last rooms and the end of the hallway, he could hear boots coming down the stairs he'd used to gain entrance. One small room, near the end of the hallway, sat empty in a different way than the others. It had the power controls for the area, breakers and circuits running to a few different power junctions.

"The hell with it," he muttered and started to open fire, blasting the power couplings into dust. Sparks flew, and the room, and hallway, went pitch black. Red emergency lights came to life, along with a siren. Mud reentered the hallway to see a gaggle of guards running toward him, only momentarily frozen by the loss of power and lighting change.

Before they could react, Mud set his GravPack to repel the wall behind him, and set his shield to a good two feet in front of him. He rammed through the guards like a bullet, landing himself at the foot of the stairs. Slamming the door behind him, he set his blaster to a fine beam and welded the door mostly shut. He ran up the stairs, wanting to see what havoc he had caused.

Back above ground, in the middle of the spaceport, Mud looked around. Nothing seemed changed. Nothing obvious, at least. He caught up with Olivet. "Any word?"

"On what? Steelbox has the tower locked down,

nothing is landing or taking off. But we have no idea where the drones are controlled from. The guards seem to have—"

"Locked them downstairs behind me. Unconscious."

"There'll be more, you know."

"I know. So let's work fast." He headed toward one of the other low buildings, while Olivet took a different one. Mud sighed, seeing the building was only a small, serviceable machine shop. Might come in handy if the needed a few parts for the *Arrow* and were desperate, but that was all.

He closed the door behind him, stopping to glance down at his hand on the doorknob, wondering why he bothered. Habit. Didn't matter. Time for the next—

Mud's next thought blew right out of his head as an explosion knocked the wind out of him, sending him to the ground. White heat washed over him, and a steamy breeze followed. He stood, as fast as he could manage, in the after effects.

"What was *that*?" Steelbox asked over comms, sounding concerned.

"No clue," Mud said. He looked in the direction of the explosion.

Olivet crouched nearby the wreckage of a building, flames still shooting up from where a roof had been. Mud ran to him.

"You all right?" he asked, helping Olivet up and drawing his own blaster.

"No, no—" Olivet stated.

Mud began to pat the Bercusan down, looking for injuries.

"No—I mean yes, I am fine, but no there is no

need for your gun, Mud. That explosion was my doing."

"You warn people before you blow something up like that," Mud said, shaking his head.

"I did not know it would go up like that, but I suppose the fuel cells for the drones were stored too close to the control units, and when I shot the controls to take them offline a few sparks flew further than I planned for, and—"

"And boom," Mud finished.

"Boom indeed," Olivet agreed.

"You get all that, Steelbox?" Mud asked over comms.

"Olivet made the world go boom?"

"Yeah. Let's just go find the Brands."

"I'll be right down, might have a lead on them."

Mud and Olivet took to the sky, setting their packs to hover while Steelbox joined them, leaping out of the same broken window he'd entered the control tower from. They took off, and Steelbox explained what he'd learned.

Meanwhile, Bee and Olivet continued to work on the *Arrow*. Bee felt pretty sure they could manage an orbital launch. The mix of human and Tsyfarian engines still messed with her a head a bit. She could almost understand how the Tsyfarian ones worked, but the *Arrow* didn't normally use those for launch, so Chellox took the lead there. If they could use both, launch would be doable.

That meant a slight reworking of some of the controls and wiring. She thought what they really needed was to tear down the ship and start over. Not because of this mishap, but in general. The ship was a mix of technologies and ideas, and they'd never found the time to redo their initial plans and fuse the thoughts based on experience.

Bee stood in front of the engine compartment, doors flung wide, and thought about how to rewire things for now. Chellox sat at the controls, ready to test her ideas. He found them sound, and remained excited about the prospect. One of his reasons for joining the team originally was to help find ways to merge and enhance both human and Tsyfarian technology.

While he sat there, looking over early readings, hearing Bee curse and bang about in the engine room, starting to adjust some connections, the main communication unit lit up. "*Arrow*, this is Deep Water, do you copy?"

"Deep Water, this is *Arrow*," Chellox said, cutting the mic as soon as he spoke and calling for Bee to join him. She hurried up.

"Chellox, that you?" Bushfield's voice came over the comm.

"Copy that, Deep Water. Bee is here with me."

"Rest of the team?" Beef's voice cut in.

"Not the point," Bee said. "How are you—"

"A few minutes ago, long-range comms came back on line," Bushfield said, "no more static. We got a quick status from them and thought maybe the jamming had died all around. Seems like."

"Mission team must have killed it," Chellox said, smiling at Bee.

She nodded. But if they'd known what they'd done, they would have reached out. "Not that they know that," she added.

"Either way. Need assistance, *Arrow*?" Deep Water asked.

"Negative," Chellox said.

Bee cut his mic. "We could use the launch assist, Chellox. And if all jamming has dropped, we could find the Brands far faster than whatever Mud is doing, I'd bet my pay. They don't know they've dropped it—they can't, or they would've told us."

"Are you sure, *Arrow*?" Bushfield asked again.

Bee kept a hand over the mic switch. "Then again, we don't know drone status, or if those fighters are still out there. We ask Deep Water and Beef to come calling and we might be dragging them into a death field again. We can't risk it."

"So let's ask Mud," Chellox said.

"What? But he's—"

"Reachable without jamming now," Chellox pointed out, "so secure comms should be online. They might not know it, but they'll realize it once we tell them."

Bee moved her hand from the switch.

"Deep Water, hold for final. Need to count eggs and baskets down here," Chellox said.

"Copy that, *Arrow*. Get back to us. Soonest."

Chellox flipped the communications array over to their team's secure channel. He sent two back-to-back pings. "Bee," he said while they waited, "how much more work do you think we have until we're launch capable?"

"On our own, another hour. With the fighters down here to help a bit, or maybe a GravPack-assisted launch? We'd be good to go."

"Good," Chellox said.

"*Arrow*, this is Mud, you got secure comms back?" Mud asked suddenly.

"Good of you to notice," Chellox said, shrugging

at Bee.

"How'd you manage that?" Steelbox asked. "We're on route to where we think the Brands might be, but it's only a good guess based on—"

"Guys," Bee said, cutting him off, "you took out all their jamming. We can do sensor sweeps now."

"Are you in the air?" Mud asked.

"Negative, still getting us fully launch capable, but Deep Water wants to know if you need help."

"Ha!" Mud laughed. "Tell them we also knocked out drone control. Doors open, if they can clear fighters. Any set of you guys want to come hunt, let me know. Your sensors will outstrip our thinsuits any day."

"Confirm, please," Chellox said. "Drone control is down?"

"Confirmed. Drone control, jammers, and the space port is closed, so those fighters up there are getting minimal ground support," Steelbox said.

"Guys, seek cover and wait for us to get everyone in the loop," Bee said. "We'll get you scanner support, maybe heavy air support, soonest."

"Copy. We're dropping low to wait now."

Bee looked at Chellox. "I'll go finish the hotwire— it'll hold for launch and then I can adjust it for a hard burn home. You get Bushfield down here if they think they can punch through the ships remaining and have a plan for opening the door on the way out. But only then. Agreed?"

"Agreed," Chellox said.

Chellox started to negotiate entry with Bushfield while Mud and crew settled down from their flight. They stood on the roof of a six-story building, feeling exposed. Mud forced open an access door and they entered the building, finding it to be a simple apartment structure. They considered making their way downstairs and hiding in whatever basement the building possessed, but Mud noticed cameras along the hallways, so instead they hit the roof and lit off again.

They landed quickly on a street, figuring three flying people would be readily noticed and probably already had been. With all eyes on the nearby spaceport explosions and commotion, they had worked out a small window where they could afford to be seen, but that window was closing in on them quickly.

Ducking into a random store along the street, Olivet bought three large ponchos and, donning one, took the other two to the alley where his teammates waited. With their thinsuits and GravPacks concealed, even if badly, they could walk the streets somewhat easier.

For their part, Bushfield and Beef finished repairs on their ships and fired up sensors to locate the other fighters in the area around McDallison. Nine of them remained, and they still hung about the planet, waiting.

Nine-on-two weren't impossible odds, but they made precise timing suspect. Bushfield ran through a few scenarios while waiting to hear back from the *Arrow*. She had a plan in mind by the time Bee came back over comms.

"*Arrow* to Deep Water, do you copy?"

"Go ahead, *Arrow*," she said.

"Mission team could use scanning help. But you need to open door."

"Nine remain upstairs with us. But if Beef swings

low for a scan pass, we can shoot the data to you, and the *Arrow* can take it from there," Bushfield said.

"Why not have us do the sensor run, too, then, Deep Water?" Chellox asked.

"Do that and these fighters will come for you. If we tangle them here and make them think you had to've gone down firm, it should buy you time to run the mission and get upstairs while we hold doors. Copy?"

"Copy that, Deep Water. We'll relay orders and start a clock soon. Status green?"

"We're itching to get back into it, *Arrow*—don't sleep on the dance floor on our account. Deep Water out." She switched to ship-to-ship communications and started to work out the exact plan with Beef.

Back planetside, Mud and Bee worked out the plan quickly as well. They looped Deep Water in and started the mission clock. Chellox fired up the *Arrow* and waited.

Deep Water and Beef nudged throttles high and aimed themselves at McDallison. The nine fighters around the planet fanned out to engage in response. They'd lost communication with their ground group and could no longer confirm drone deployment, so they acted as if they were alone, which they were.

Beef turned hard, unleashing a barrage of blaster fire from his ship, forcing a few of the enemy ship to turn and give chase. Deep Water came at the remaining fighters head on, flying tight evasive patterns to avoid a lock. She didn't fire a single shot, making the fighters she closed in on nervous.

"Beef, you getting that tinkling on your hull?" she

asked.

"Scattered, useless drones," he said, confirming her suspicions.

"Yup, complete the mission, Beef, go for dive."

Beef changed his ship's angle of attack quickly and dove toward McDallison, four enemy ships following him. Deep Water changed her approach as well, turning away from the confused group in front of her to follow Beef, coming behind the four on his tail. The five fighters now behind her took after her quickly.

A hard flip turned Beef's ship around so it started to fall into McDallison's gravity well backwards. Pointed back up at the sky, he started to fire at the ships chasing him. Deep Water took the sign to break off before she hit atmosphere, flipping her own ship and heading right into the clutch of five ships firing at her. She opened fire and zipped between them, leading them back away from the planet.

Beef flipped his ship again, the hull enjoying the strain, so he could use his engines to control his descent. This is where things got tricky for him. His group was excellent at deep space combat flights, but in atmosphere the fighters behind him had logged more time, gaining experience he didn't have. He lost all advantage, but also only had to do one simple sweep. So he led them on a chase over the planet until he could do a low flyby over Kenzo.

He set his sensors to a very specific search and let the ship's computer drink in data while trying to dodge blaster shots from the ships behind him. They winged him a few times, smoldering bits of hull glowing red beneath his shields. He tight beamed the data his sensors had scooped up over to the *Arrow* and hit thrusters hard in a wide arc of climb, heading back out of the sky and into the black. The climb felt as if it took days, the sky unending around him. He took on more fire, the fighters behind him climbing and starting to gain on him.

Beef tried to nudge his throttle faster but nothing happened. The engines strained against atmo, reaching for the silence of space, but the shots behind him were getting closer and closer. Suddenly a ship flew past him, headed down into the gravity well. It went by in a blur, blasters firing.

"Thanks, Deep Water," he said on comms, feeling his ship react to the thinning air around it. Another few seconds and he would be back in open space.

Bushfield's ship came up alongside him. "They're still on us, but we'll have time to climb," she said. "I left four up there to greet. Let's keep them busy and hold the door open. Clock's running."

"Copy that, Deep Water."

In the *Arrow*, Bee ran through the sensor data as Chellox took off. They headed directly for Kenzo, stopping just short of the sprawling city itself. She fed the results of the scans to the mission team's thinsuits and waited. She checked the mission clock and tried to tamp down the anxiousness that welled up in her chest.

Mud, Steelbox, and Olivet took off at the coordinates the scan results gave them. A small building, only three stories, marked off as their target. Fortified for battle, the building would be hard to crack if they wanted to be subtle. But the clock running down didn't get them the time.

Instead, they rammed the building with gravity shields repeatedly while Mud burned through the superstructure with his Acadian blaster. The fortifications were as good as most long-range ship hulls, and it took longer than they'd hoped. But by the time they'd gotten through, they'd caused so much damage to the structure that the internal defenses were offline and the guards inside were rattled, if even still conscious, from the falling debris.

It was, overall, the wrong way to get to their target in any condition other than the one they found themselves in. Keeping their fields at a set two feet, the three crewmembers of the *Arrow* walked through the building, letting still-falling bits of wall and ceiling bounce off their shields and shatter on the floor. They walked to the basement, easily laying down enough fire to fill the hallway among the three of them.

The guards, realizing this would never go their way, started to flee. They, quite honestly, were not paid enough for this level of brute force. With the leading crime family in town obviously going down, their hired hands left at speed, hoping to guess the correct next-in-line family and to secure jobs with them.

They came upon a reinforced door, the walls around it still intact, and looked at each other. "I got it," Mud said, checking the charge on his blaster. Seeing it was low, Mud considered a door-knocker move with his GravPack. He looked behind him and realized the space provided was too small for dodging a door flying at the speed of sound right at your face. He patted at his leg and confirmed a back-up charge for his blaster. Steelbox and Olivet took up positions on either side of the doorframe.

Setting the Acadian blaster for the highest possible burn—his spare clip in hand, ready to deploy—Mud took three shots, barrel against one edge of the door itself. Three shots and the hinges on the other side simply vanished into smoke. He pushed the door in, ejecting the empty blaster clip and slotting home the replacement in a smooth motion.

Four guards started to fire and Mud hit the floor. Steelbox and Olivet came around the frame of the door from either side, firing quick to disable the guards. They shot on stun settings only, seeing no reason to kill. Two people, similar in looks—both thin, with almost glowingly white skin and green hair—sat in matching suits, lounging in ornate recliners.

"Sybil and Tiago Brand," Mud said, "we need to go. This building won't last long."

"Mission team to *Arrow*," Steelbox said into his suit's comm, "we're a go, see you in three."

Sybil and Tiago didn't move. "We're fine here, thank you *very* much," Sybil said. She looked at her brother. "You can kill us if you wish, but I do not think we'll be coming with yo-" she was cut off by a shot from Olivet's blaster. A second shot stunned Tiago. Olivet moved to collect Tiago and nodded at Steelbox, who lugged Sybil onto his shoulder.

"We do not have time," Olivet said to no one in particular as they left the room, their cargo slumped in fireman's carries.

They walked out of the building in time to see the *Arrow* hovering overhead. GravPacks shot them up and into the ship, passing through the wide-open airlock quickly. Olivet and Steelbox walked the Brand siblings to what the crew of the *Arrow* called their holding cell. Really the room was just the smallest crew room, and unnecessary since it would be the sixth of the living quarters when they only had five crew members. Some reinforcements and a security door later and they had a nice comfy holding cell they almost never had cause to use.

Cargo stored and strapped in, everyone took their seats, keeping GravPacks on and adjusting harnesses to fit properly.

"Ship status?" Mud asked, looking at streams of data across his screens.

"We'll be able to break orbit," Bee said, "and get home, just not under full burn. It'll add a day to the trip. Also not sure if our backup have enough fuel to make the first depot. Assuming they're doing all right."

"Let's make sure," Chellox said over his shoulder, keying the mic. "*Arrow* to Deep Water. Is the door open?"

"Door open, *Arrow*, but make it quick," came Bushfield's reply.

"Copy that, Deep Water, see you soon." Chellox looked back at the crew, his bird helmet hiding his smile. "So you want me to say 'Hold on' now, instead of about three seconds from now, correct?"

"Just get us back into the black," Mud said, shaking his head.

Chellox nodded, turning back to his instruments. Steelbox fed him data in soft tones and the *Arrow* thrummed to life, arcing cleanly to escape the sky.

They started back toward base, as fast as they

could safely manage. They let the *Ratzinger* know they were under way, and that it would take an extra day, but left out any other details for the actual debriefing.

A while out from the first depot they ran into a snag: Deep Water and Beef didn't have the fuel to reach the depot, after all. So, with a shrug and map, Mud and Bee got out and pushed using their GravPacks. The smaller fighters were easy to hang onto, and from there it was a simple long-range use of the GravPacks that the team had prepared for.

They got to the first depot, refueled both fighters, and made the rest of the multi-day trip without incident. They docked at the *Ratzinger* easily, with Steelbox marching the Brands out and turning them over to the ship's guards. While he did, Bee and Chellox left instructions that they would need a complete teardown of the *Arrow* soon, so it could be loaded into a work bay.

They felt good about the mission, or at least good enough. Right up until Mills marched into the docking bay, his face showing anger.

"My office," he said. "All of you. Soonest." And with that he turned and left before they could ask him anything.

CHAPTER 11

UNADORNED, FULL OF CLEAN LINES and very little personalization, Mills' office took up just enough space to fit the seven people filing in to it. He himself sat behind a small desk, too small for the room, actually—it's size betraying, to Bushfield's eyes at least, that he had only recently moved into the office and didn't know what to do with it yet.

Two chairs sat in front of the small desk, and Mud and the crew of the *Arrow* stood behind them, leaving room along one side for Bushfield and Beef to stand as well.

"You wanted to see us?" Mud asked lightly.

"No," Mills said, "I really didn't. I need to, but let's not mistake it for desire."

"Sir," Bushfield said, "what—"

"Bushfield, you and Oblick—"

"Who?" Mud asked quickly.

"Me," Beef said, "Ted Oblick."

"Oh, sorry, I—"

"Mud." Mills said harshly, "do you mind? Thank you. Bushfield, you and Oblick were supposed to be backup. Only backup."

"Sir, we were, sir," Bushfield said, growing more and more uncertain as to what was even going on.

"As for you, Mud, *Arrow* crew," Mills said, looking away from Bushfield, "would it have been possible for you to have made more of a mess?"

"Mills," Mud said, "I'm not sure what's going on here, but we completed the mission objectives and then some."

"Really?" Mills asked. He shook his head and flipped open a folder. "Because I am already dealing with complaints about a spaceport that is unusable and a citizenry that seems terrified of, and I quote, 'flying invaders,' which feels like it may have been you."

"Sure, and those terrified people were probably all working for the two we have in storage now," Mud said. "I mean, this is all just ridiculous. But the thing that gets me...that really nags at me...why are you playing their game, Mills? You know we did our jobs and did them well."

"Right up until you had Gov ships do a fly-over of a city where we weren't supposed to have ships at all, much less on some mission. The *Arrow*? That I can disavow easily, I've done it a bunch of times, that's why we use you guys—why you don't even have ranks! But once Bushfield and Oblick entered atmo—"

"Sir, with respect," Bushfield cut in, "there was nothing in the mission brief about us not being seen at any cost."

"Backup. You stay out of atmo and hold open the door, that was it."

"And you think," Mud said, his own anger starting to seep in, "that none of the fighters we faced could have taken a picture of Gov ships up there? What's really going on here, Mills? Hell, even this dressing down doesn't need everyone present."

Mills stood and walked over to his office door. Locking it, he then walked around the assembled groups to the back wall of his office. He slid open a panel in the wall and took out a small, squat, brass-colored device.

"Is that a—" Bee started to ask.

"When I ask for your input," he said harshly, cutting her off. Twisting the brass device, he stared at it, holding a finger up to the group. Confident the device worked, he lowered his hand as he walked back to his desk. "Anyway, now that we're shielded, sorry about that. Needed a record of me yelling and you being clueless for the archives when this gets combed through by the higher ups."

"Mills, just spill it," Mud said.

"The Brands sell some of their tech to Gov holdings. Going after them was a huge mistake on my part. I need to dress it up a bit to get away with it. I thought I was covered when I sent you guys out, and I'm sorry about that, but now I need to clean this up so we all still have jobs."

Bushfield smiled, moving closer to the desk. "So what you'd need, then," she said slowly, "would be something that the Brands didn't want to sell, but keep for themselves—something the Gov didn't have and would utterly love and could now, realistically, have for free?"

"That would be a thing to have, for sure," Mills said, agreeably.

Beef took a metal cylinder out of his suit's cargo pocket and set it on Mills' desk.

"Oblick?" Mills asked, picking up the container and turning it over in his hands.

"Drones. Explosive warding drones. There's one in there—in a few pieces, admittedly, but both my ship and Deep Water's have a good number of them intact and disabled in our intake storage tanks."

"How'd you disarm them?" Chellox ask.

"They were disabled without control so we

figured that was off enough to work."

"That—" Mud stopped and chose his words carefully. "That was incredibly stupid. Both of you. Contact-explosive micro-drones just sitting in the intake holders?"

"They aren't contact unless they're active," Bushfield explained. "We noticed when they started just bouncing off our hulls with no effect. It was safe, Mud, don't insult my intelligence."

"Or mine," Oblick added.

"You can insult his," Bushfield said.

"Hey now."

"Folks," Mills broke in, "this will help, but still— do me a favor and act dressed down while we sort through this jamming problem."

"It wasn't the Brands," Bee said, "their jamming is utterly different."

"We know, we had a comm blackout while you were gone, just a different degree of space than you sat along. Regardless. Go along, all right. You're all grounded for the next few days."

"We need to overhaul the *Arrow* anyway," Mud said.

"Good. And look, let's solve this comms problem, and then we can look into why some of my bosses are buying from mobsters, OK?" Mills twisted the device again and looked at the assembled tams. "So don't get any more ideas that you're untouchable."

"Sir, yes sir," Bushfield said, leaving the room. The others followed suit. Given Mills' performance, they didn't feel they could talk freely in the hallways of the *Ratzinger*, at least not about the mission. So they made their way back to the *Arrow*, under the guise of starting work on the ship early.

Bee turned on the internal countermeasures and they relaxed, leaning against the bulkhead and slumping in various chairs.

"Really, this became our problem?" Steelbox said when no one else wanted to say anything first. "We get to now work out some sort of corruption going on?"

"Nope," Oblick said. "We do our jobs, which is this communications blackout. I mean," he turned to Bushfield, "sir, if that's still our mission."

"We help the *Arrow* as we can," she said. "But it isn't our mission, no. So we go where Mills tells us. I have a feeling it might just be something sneaky."

"Wait, but the Gov buying from some high-tech syndicate, is that really strange?" Mud asked the room. Everyone just looked at him.

"It was normal on Trasker Four," Bee said. "Steelbox and I knew about it, everyone knew about it."

"But Trasker Four also locked itself out from the Gov for the most part," Steelbox added. "Does the larger Gov do that sort of thing?"

"More than any one would like. I don't know why this one is such an issue. There's something else there, but it really isn't our problem right now."

Sitting in his normal seat, Olivet started to sway gently. No one noticed.

"But Mud—" Chellox started.

"Nope. We have a communications problem that could threaten the ability of the Gov to get anything done and we still don't have any leads except it also happened a few years ago. Now it's back, and worse. We need to stop it. I trust Mills. This sort of thing, it's not what we do. It's all sneak and lie, and depends on having access we just don't possess. We do our jobs, not his."

"And we'll keep an eye open," Bushfield added.

"Right. And thanks. And if you need us, let us know," Mud said.

"Ditto," Oblick told him. "Now, we're gonna go and get some downtime, and you guys might want to do the same."

Everyone stood and started saying goodbyes, which is when they noticed Olivet slumped over the arm of his chair. Awake, his eyes unfocused, the Bercusan just draped there over his seat, like a rag doll left in the sun.

"Olivet?" Bee rushed to his side.

"Is he all right?" Chellox asked, coming around to Olivet's other side. They started to right him in his seat, checking for vitals.

"He's fine, Mud told them, unconcerned. "Just give him a minute. He took in a bunch of mist, by request, a while ago. This must be a hell of a vision."

"He's Bercusan?" Bushfield asked. "I thought that was some sort of joke you guys had. You mean he has the visions? Really?"

"Not a street performer," Mud said gently, "but yes, he is and he does."

Olivet slowly righted himself, still staring ahead blankly, seeing things the others couldn't. "A rending," he said softly, "a tear and a folding. Gone through. The claws of the side mark the intent of the other."

Beef started to say something but found himself shushed by Mud before any noise could be made. They all stood and watched, Mud having his suit record the second Olivet started talking.

"One dies in darkness, another rises to take the place," Olivet continued. He blinked several times and looked around the room. "Stop staring," he said softly.

"Sorry," Steelbox said as they all tried to look elsewhere, realized that impossible and somehow more insulting, and just tried to relax.

"I recorded it, in case you don't re—" Mud started.

"I remember—it's interesting that some of the stronger visions look like trances and all, but we always recall the visions," Olivet told him quickly.

"Good to know for the future," Mud said, the most at home with this process. "So."

"So," Olivet repeated. "That was the vision, the entire thing. I don't have insights past what I've said. No bigger clue toward meaning. We don't...we don't see them so much as feel them. The words are the closest we get to understanding what flashes through our minds. Will it help, Mud?"

"As always, yes and no."

"Of course," Olivet said, nodding. He stood, not in the least shaky, and looked at his teammates and friends. "I'm sorry, I just realized none of you except Mud has ever seen that. Apologies."

"Don't apologize," Bushfield said, "I mean I've heard, I knew that was why you originally went on the ship with Jonah, but—"

"But seeing it is different, I agree," Olivet said, nodding at her. "Anyway, I believe we were going to discuss the *Arrow* and how to rebuild it?"

"Shouldn't we discuss what you said?" Bee asked.

"No point just yet. What was said will be. The how and why is a mystery, even to me. So let us go back to what we were doing."

"We can't just ignore it, Olivet," Mud said. "You're the one who keeps reminding me they come true."

"And you remind me we can't use them to chart our course, only guide at best. And I agree. So let the words guide us as they begin to make sense, but let's not do what my people sometimes try, and work them to death until we force an answer."

Bee shrugged. "Right then. Chellox, Olivet, let's go look at engine linkages and try to get human and Tsyfarian tech to work together better. Steelbox, you and Mud reconsider the interior layout. Bushfield, Beef...sorry, Oblick—"

"Whichever."

"You guys go and get some rest, I suppose. Bushfield, dinner?" Bee smiled at Bushfield, who smiled back.

"You got it."

They left and the crew of the *Arrow* got to work—all them, including Olivet, regardless of what he had said—working over his words of prophecy.

CHAPTER 12

OVER THE NEXT SEVERAL DAYS, the crew of the *Arrow* tried to resume a normal life. As normal as one got living on a large, space-faring battle cruiser, at least. They took care of important things, such as sleeping and eating, as well as finding time for hobbies and friends.

Mud started his time by catching up on paperwork. Missions meant documentation, both on and off the record.

For the Gov and ship records he wrote up events as transpired, careful in what he said and how he said it. He wrote the report as he'd been taught to. Everything that went wrong ended up phrased in a way to make it his fault over anyone else's. Everything right found the proper crew member assigned credit. He wrote both missions up, attached various supporting documents—logs, scans, and such—and filed them with the central office.

That done, he started over from scratch and wrote up the missions again, an eye on deeper thoughts regarding the crew, linkages to older missions he found interesting even if coincidental, and any other strange sidebars he thought of along the way. This version of his reports also included tactical thoughts detailing his choices as well as the rest of the crew's, mostly written in terms of what worked and didn't, and why he thought each case did what it did.

Wrapping up that version, he sealed it under

special encryption and uploaded it to a different server, one off base entirely. The family mission drop, for historical archives. His father insisted, and catalogued them with the original Insertion Team's mission logs that he had kept. These second mission reports were an easy way of keeping the family up to date and seeing linkages that no one else could. Theoretically. Privately, he just thought it was a way for his parents to ensure he, in some way, constantly phoned home to keep them updated on the gossip out in space, now that they'd retired for good. Either way, the act of putting it down helped sort his thoughts.

Outside of that, Mud trained and helped out with the retrofit of the *Arrow*. Mud had other friends on the ship, and he would grab a meal and catch up with a few of them, but he had a problem nagging at him and it kept him focused down. He remained perfectly all right with that turn of events.

Olivet spent his time doing research. The communications problem bothered him. It bothered all of them, but as the science officer on the *Arrow*, he considered it rather more his problem. Right or wrong, he started to dig back, working to find out what could possibly block communications the way it was being done, and that meant being deeply and obsessively familiar with how the communications worked.

He discovered something on the second day that he chased for the next few, not telling anyone else about because, though he believed it, he couldn't actually believe it could be right. It was.

Steelbox spent most of his time working on his star charts and, remembering what he had noticed before they left on their last mission, diving back into his study of the Bercuser charts, and how the systems the planet inhabited overlayed. Someone else needed to have noticed what he'd seen, and if not, then they could reason why he was wrong. So he dug into stacks of data and studied.

When his eyes started to feel blurry and his brain felt soft, he went down to the *Arrow* and assisted with the retrofit, helping Chellox design and install new sensor arrays and navigation equipment. He also demanded he be allowed to redesign the crew quarters, sick of the tiny little impersonal spaces they all put up with because they were what were there.

Chellox talked to his people, when he could, helping teach them about humanity. He wanted the races to get along. They weren't fighting, but the truce still felt uneasy, and Chellox found that he liked humanity, over all. It was, in essence, no stupider, crass, or self-defeating than his own people, and he wanted that to be the basis for a lasting partnership. He didn't have much time for it, though, what with his work on the *Arrow*. He helped design new engines that melded Tsyfarian technology with human in ways no one had considered yet. Surprisingly easy to replicate, the advances he started could go on to revolutionize space travel for both races.

Bee split her time fairly evenly between retooling the *Arrow*, working mostly with Chellox and the *Ratzinger's* engineering team, and spending time with Bushfield. They'd met after the Tsyfarian Incident, as the records called it, and bonded, originally, over learning to deal with the cyclone of leadership and personality that was Jonah Madison, Mud's father.

That common point of interest may have been why they talked, at first, but it quickly became a tiny blip in what kept them together. They saw the universe the same way, most often, and enjoyed the freedom of their relationship, along with the closeness. It also amused them that, since the Madisons considered them both secondary family at this point, their relationship was greeted with a huge out-pouring of celebration. Two of their 'adopted kids,' as Bee felt sure they were thought of often, had found something between themselves, and it made Jonah and Shae happy.

Mud, though never less than happy with the relationship, did express some concern over Bushfield and Bee working together. Bee only shook her head at him, pointing out that his own parents were the founders of the first Insertion Team and since they, she laughed, were his parents after all, that maybe he could get over it.

The truth, though, which Bushfield and Bee knew, was simply that Mud considered them both to be his best friends, separately, and now dreaded anything happening to the relationship that would make everything strange for all three of them. Bee considered it sweet, and frustratingly selfish of him.

The *Arrow* came together over a few days, in plans at least. Full fabrication and design builds would take weeks, testing would be another few weeks after that, and, overall, a new ship wasn't going to just appear lovingly out of thin air.

The night they locked the new *Arrow* design down, Bee lay in bed with Bushfield, avoiding the party. "You sure this is OK?" she asked Bushfield, in their tangle of sheets.

"They want to throw a party for you, for doing your job and designing a ship that isn't even tested yet. And right after they also had to tell us all off in public? Feh."

"Speaking of," Bee said, "they're doing some kind of test based on your communications attempt?"

"All right," Bushfield said, sitting up, "first of all, how is that 'speaking of'? At all? Secondly, yeah they liked the idea and are setting up a bigger test of it the next time a comm blackout happens."

Bee shook her head. "That's not...it's not smart, Sarah." She ran a hand along Bushfield's back. "The risk of stress pulls don't go *down*. They're gonna get someone killed."

"Probably us," Bushfield agreed, "and then we'll have to save them."

"Wait, but in this scenario we're already dead, I thought."

"Since when does that abdicate our duty?"

"Only one of us is actually carrying a rank."

"You could sign up."

"And you could join the Insertion Team."

Bee sat up, and the two women looked at each other. They laughed together, Bee stopping only to glance at the clock that sat on a small shelf near the bed. "I really should put in an appearance at that stupid party."

"It has to be winding down," Bushfield said. "So might as well skip the whole thing."

"No, come on, it'll be fine. We'll go for ten minutes, steal a bottle of something, and come right back here." Bee got up and headed for the room's small shower.

Sighing dramatically for effect, Bushfield got up and followed her. "For the booze, fine. I'll go to the party. Ten minutes, though. I'm feeling selfish."

"Oh, trust me, I don't mind that," Bee told her.

CHAPTER 13

What Bee called a party was really most of the *Arrow* crew, some engineers, and Mills. Housed in a conference room, someone had made sure to at least move all the chairs to the walls and fold away screens and dismantle the center table to create space. Everyone stood around, mostly talking shop and milling about, sipping cheap alcohol out of disposable cups. A plate of random, small finger foods from the mess hall sat on a separate side table from the drinks, almost completely untouched.

"So you're running the test tonight?" Mud asked Mills as Bee and Bushfield entered the room.

"The blackout test?" Bee said, in a rush. "Tonight?"

"There's a blackout going on. We're not sounding alarms for them anymore because they keep increasing in frequency, and no one needs constant alarms dulling them to other problems. So, since you have the test ready—"

"But how are you doing it?" Bee glanced nervously at Bushfield, then at Mud, trying to will them to join her in stopping this.

"This isn't the place," Mills said. He looked around the room and shrugged. "Though no one would care and we all have clearance. Fine. It's the same thing Bushfield did, on a bigger scale. Hooked up a large-scale engine to a communications array, drifting off the ship, in the current blackout zone."

"Sir," Bushfield said, "that may not be the best idea."

"The engine isn't attached to the ship and is

floating free at twice what we worked out as a safe distance, just in case. We need the data, and can record this from outside if it goes sideways. If it works, then even better—we have a plan for now. What's the concern?" Mills waited, knowing these people weren't prone to needless worry.

"I'm thinking having the *Ratzinger* inside the same system as the test is the problem," Mud said. "Bee, back me up on this, but we don't know how wide the effects could be."

"We really don't," she agreed. "Bushfield's ship got torn apart—"

"And the ships near her were fine," Mills said.

"Yes, sir, but if you increase the power you're putting into the test, then the power coming out should increase as well," Bushfield said.

"Plus," Bee said, trying to do the math in her head as quickly as possible, "we don't know the conversation rate, in to out. The power of Bushfield's engine affected her ship and, let's say, a hundred feet away from it, the other ships wouldn't have been harmed, but if that scales exponentially and not linearly, then..." she trailed off, watching Mill's face carefully.

"We have no proof of that, and the engineers doing the test were sure that—"

"So they did a small-scale test first?" Mud asked, cutting him off.

"No, they said they modeled it, and—"

"Sir," Bushfield broke in, "they modeled it based on partial data from one data point. How could you approve this, sir?"

"Over my head, mostly. No, let's be honest here, I signed off on it, too. And I shouldn't have," Mills said, walking toward the door. "Come on, let's go stop this."

Mud, Bee, and Bushfield followed Mills. As he left, Mud waved off Steelbox and Olivet, both at the party, to stay behind. He also signaled them to make sure their comms were on, just in case.

They walked, quickly, a military march of a stride, through the ship to the science observation deck. Mills burst in, demanding the test be shut down. A number of people in the room, all previously splitting their time watching both their monitors and out the observation window, nervously informed him the test was already underway. The woman in charge hurried over, trying to settle everyone down at once.

"Lieutenant Commander Mills, sir, the test is going fine, as you can see." She swept her hand grandly, indicating the observation window. "Everything is proceeding according to plan."

"Except I'm telling you, Doctor..."

"Harrison," she told him, trying to not show how put out she was that he couldn't be bothered to remember her name.

"Right, well, Doctor Harrison, there's a new plan," Mills said. "Shut it down."

"It's an automatic routine," she said. "We can't just shut it down."

"Why not?" Bee asked, moving to one of the consoles and leaning over the person currently using it.

"Because it's automatic," Harrison said slowly, as if she spoke to a child.

"Automatic with no contingency?" Bee asked her. "No, never mind—Mills, fire her later, please? For now we do this dirty. Bushfield, get in a ship and blow that engine out of the dark."

"On it," Bushfield said, not waiting for Mills' consent.

"I can get there faster with a GravPack," Mud said.

"You'd have to get too close," Bushfield said, already at the door. "Sir, permission to launch?"

"Go," Mills said.

Bushfield ran out of the room. Harrison started to loudly proclaim how wrong this all was, who she would bring it up to, and how badly it would go for everyone. Mills looked at her, taking a slow, deep, breath. "Sit. Down," he told her evenly. "You've done a lot of good work, so no," he glanced at Bee, "I won't fire you, but no contingency? That's dreadfully negligent. We'll review your record later and deal with this when we're all calmer. For now, please, just sit and let me run the room."

Harrison sat, glaring at the three intruders to her space. Bee asked the person still sitting in front of the console she was standing over to move. They did, and she sat heavily into the chair, not sure what she felt most annoyed by: possible impending doom or the ruining of the remainder of her night. They tied, really.

Mud stood there, feeling useless. "Bee, Mills, what can I—"

"Get your team on standby," Mills said without looking. "I'll assume we won't need them, but if we do, we'll need them quick."

"For what?" Mud asked.

"If I knew that, I wouldn't need your team. All right?"

"Right," Mud said, and turned to face a corner of

the room. He spoke quickly into his communicator and made sure everyone would be at the *Arrow* and have it ready for quick launch, waiting for him and Bee, if the situation called for it. He gave them a quick update, sparse on details, and turned back to the room. "Bee, where're we at?"

"Deep Water launch in three. The test engine is still spinning up and will try to punch communications through in four, if I read this right. It's gonna be close. She'll take at least two minutes to get to the engine, another to destroy it. That's two minutes we might not have."

Her communications open but muted, Bushfield heard Bee's timetable and cursed, doing her systems check as fast as possible while still not being unsafe. No point in a gamble that left you dead. Then again, taking too long to launch...she cursed again and fired her engines bright. Crew ran, leaving the very last of the safety checks alone, and opened the hangar for her. Shooting into space, Bushfield turned wide, homing in directly to the engine.

Blaster fire would cripple it but not shut it down instantly. She checked missile stores, thankful the refuel and restock had went as planned. Pulling up a HUD target display, she sighted the engine carefully, had the computer's targeting system back her up, and fired three times, two more than should be needed. They wanted that engine gone, she'd damn well make sure it was gone but good.

The missiles headed to target, all three dead on. The engine used all of its power to push communications packets out. The missiles grew closer—a hundred feet, sixty, fifty—and at twenty feet to target, the engine...changed.

No one looking would swear to what the engine actually did. Explosion felt like the wrong word, implosion also sat wrong. It folded, was the eventual agreed-on word for what happened. The blackness of space lit up white, causing Bushfield's canopy to darken instantly as safety measures cut in.

On the *Ratzinger*, alarms screamed, flashing lights and blaring warnings. The science observation window darkened, same as Bushfield's canopy, causing a spate of cursing to erupt in the room. Mills demanded someone get the view back, as well as demanding to know what was going on. No one had answers. No one possibly could.

Outside, in the blackness of space, a Fold happened, and slowly split open.

Bushfield drifted nearby, flipping switches and trying to get her engines to cut back in. They'd switched off not long after the white light had hit her canopy. Physics still applied, however, and so she drifted at speed toward where the engine had been, with no engines of her own to turn her.

Her sensors gave off readings that she dismissed as impossible as they sputtered back to life. They'd gone dark when the engines had and were just now coming back online, which let her try her engines again. No luck.

The *Ratzinger's* sensors and engines still worked, but the readings they were processing made as little sense. Mills looked at the readouts, turning to Mud. "If that data is even partially correct—"

"*Arrow*'s gone as soon as step foot on it. Old ship's still in dock. Bee! Let's move!"

Bee looked from her screen to Mud and back

again, "Sarah's—"

"About to get a pick-up. Come on!" He nodded at Mills and spoke into his communicator. "*Arrow.* We're on the way to you. We launch the second we get there."

"Engines already cycling, Cap," Steelbox said. "Got your suits and packs on board."

Mud ran over to Bee, putting his hand on her shoulder. "Bee, we need to go *now.*"

Bee looked at him. "Two seconds, have to set up a message first. Sarah's comms will be down, everything will be screwy, but," Bee hit a button and stood, "she's smart enough to get this."

Mud nodded at Mills. "*Arrow* to launch and find out what the hell just happened."

Mills nodded, "Then go!"

Bee gave her monitor one last look, hoping her message would get through. "Don't touch this station," she said, to no one in particular. And I swear," Bee looked at Harrison, "if you *broke the fabric of space* we're going to have words when I get back."

"Punch her later, rescue mission now," Mud said, turning to run out of the room. Bee followed, leaving Mills with a last look.

The ran in silence, dodging past *Ratzinger* crew rushing to ready stations, all the way down to the hangars.

Out in space, drifting toward the Fold, Bushfield considered her options. She could bail on the ship, would have to soon enough. She didn't want to get so much as touched directly by whatever she'd seen. She also couldn't quite tell when it would be too late to bail. While she tried to work out her timing—

based on incomplete, and incomprehensible, data—she noticed a hollow, echo-filled thrum starting from her canopy. She went still, closing her eyes.

There was a pattern to the vibrations. Laughing, she rested her hand on the ship's canopy. Her communications array didn't work. There'd been no way to talk to the *Ratzinger*, but Bee'd be there watching. And she'd solved it. Bushfield grabbed the pencil and paper all pilots kept stored under the console for emergency use and made markings. The vibrations were in an old code pattern. Bee must've rigged up a laser, Bushfield thought, to vibrate her canopy with a message. How she'd worked out tracking to keep it going with her drift, well, that was Bee.

The message, decoded, read only, "Sit. *Arrow*," which wasn't really great, but gave her enough information to work out the rest. Stay in the ship, hold on, the *Arrow* was en route. Fine. She'd wait. And while she did, she would gather, look at, and back up all the sensor data she could.

The *Arrow* burst free of the hangar and headed directly toward the Fold. "How're we doing this," Mud asked the crew, "do we tow or just grab Bushfield?"

"That ship might have sensor data we can't replicate," Steelbox said. "I think we have to tow."

"If the Fold," Bee said, "I'm calling it the Fold, I'll show you why later but it's a Fold, I don't know how—"

"Bee," Olivet said, "tow or grab?"

"Right," she said, trying to focus, "if the Fold isn't growing and we can get close enough—"

"How close is safe?" Chellox asked. "It killed her engines, right? Otherwise she would fly free, so do we know that won't happen to us?"

"No," Mud said, "we know basically nothing. Right, then. We'll start a tow the hard way and abandon if needed."

"Mud—" Bee started to warn him.

"I know, but it's the best way. I'll go out and push. You scan the ship from a distance. If there's radiation, anything making the ship unsafe, signal me, I'll grab Bushfield and let her fighter go to hell."

"That's...Mud, that's not the best plan," Chellox said as they came within visual distance of Bushfield's fighter. "We scan the ship first and—"

"Quick, what state is Bushfield in?" Mud asked. No one answered him. No one could. "Exactly. We don't know. And until we do know, we assume she's incapable of helping herself. We take care of her first, worry about stupid plans later."

"And if it incapacitates you, too?" Steelbox asked.

"Then you folk come up with a second plan that's much, much smarter and rescue both of us."

"Cap, that's—"

"Mud—" Olivet and Steelbox said simultaneously.

"Yeah, I know it is." Mud said to his team. "I also know it's our best first shot. Chellox, stop here, safe distance. I'll be back." Mud started to cycle the airlock. "I assume."

Dropping out of the ship, Mud activated his GravPack, repelling against the *Arrow*, aimed at Bushfield's fighter. He zipped toward it, keeping an eye on his thinsuit's readings. Nothing odd, except for a big Fold in space that seemed to slowly grow like a glowing white maw against the darkness.

He knew his suit would darken his view soon, and if it went too dark, he wouldn't be able to see. He engaged a manual override and tried to ride the line between going blind and being able to see anything at all.

Changing his GravPack to attract to Bushfield's ship, he came up on it fast, hoping Bushfield was at least still conscious. He grappled up against the ship and set his pack to keep him there. Tapping on the cockpit, he fought against the urge to hold his breath. Quickly he felt the vibrations of her knocking back in reply. Now how to tell her to stay there. He knocked out code for "Stay." He had to assume she knew the code, since she'd stayed in her ship after Bee's message and seemed to be expecting him.

"Copy," came the tapped reply.

"Tow," he tapped, thinking. "I go," he added so she knew not to bother replying. Holding on to the front of her ship, putting himself between it and the Fold, Mud set his GravPack to reach out and attract to the *Arrow*. Getting underway took a moment, as the masses involved had to be slowed, stopped, and reversed from going the opposite direction. Careful to not accidently pull the *Arrow* toward them, Mud kept shifting his pulls. From the *Arrow* to a relatively nearby asteroid to the *Ratzinger* and then cycling back again, adding repelling strands to either the *Ratzinger* or the asteroid when he attracted to the *Arrow*. It was slow, tedious, even, and needed to be precise. Twice Mud stopped and rethought his plan, remapping everything while the ship drifted, holding tight. He wanted to give the ship some spin to point it away from the Fold, hoping Bushfield's canopy would turn transparent again, but adding the spin to everything else would make the math even stranger for him. So he concentrated on pushing, pulling, and generally cajoling the ship toward the *Arrow* as best he could.

With a final nudge to stop the ship drifting, he signaled the *Arrow* to release a tow line, attaching it to the back of Bushfield's ship. He moved back to the canopy and knocked out a simple message: "Out."

Bushfield blew the canopy, a rush of air explosively escaping, which Mud barely dodged, and she pulled herself out of the ship into open space. Mud grabbed her shoulder and targeted the *Arrow*, quickly reaching the airlock. One cycle later and they were on board.

"Get us back to the—"

"We didn't want to bother you and make you worry but did you happen to glance at the Fold out there?" Bee asked, cutting him off.

Mud realized that she'd stayed at her station, looking at her screens instead of greeting, or even checking on, Bushfield. He felt his adrenal system kick into high gear as his forebrain realized something must be very wrong.

"Of course not, my optics would've blanked and—"

"There's something coming out of the Fold," Steelbox said.

"There's...what?!" Mud rushed to his station to call up the data. Bushfield followed, moving to stand behind Bee, placing a hand on her shoulder warmly. "What are we looking at? Anyone?"

"Giant bug monster," Steelbox said slowly, "I

think? Or a multi-lipped dog, maybe, the size of a heavy cruiser? It could be a—"

"It's an incursion," Chellox said.

"All right. From where?" Bushfield asked.

Bee turned to look at her, covering Bushfield's hand on her shoulder with her own. "Where ever the Fold ends. So...not from around here."

"Another point in space, or...or...I don't even know what I'm asking," Mud said. "Are we sending this to the *Ratzinger*?"

"Of course," Olivet said. "And they're as stumped as we are."

"Right," Mud said, strapping in to his station. "Bushfield, your ship is dead for now. The fuel compartment looked burnt out. Something when the Fold opened, whatever energy it unleashed on open, did it in. Obviously it isn't still putting that energy out, my GravPack was fine, and you still had electronics so the battery stayed true, just rebooted. So why did it drain engine fuel?"

"Least of our problems," Chellox said.

"Not at all," Bee said. "Mud's right, if it did that once, it could kill the *Arrow*, or worse, the *Ratzinger*. We have to add it to our list."

"Bushfield, grab a seat," Mud said to her, "and strap in. I have a feeling about this." Turning to Olivet, he said, "Open communications. Let's try to talk to it."

"Copy that," Olivet said. He sent a series of generic, friendly greetings in every language the ship could manage, including binary and pulse code. "No reply, yet," he told Mud.

"Didn't think so, but we have to try. Steelbox, shoot the data on this to the following codes," Mud said, writing down a sequence of numbers, "and append this key to it." Mud wrote a second code under the first.

"Cap, long-range comms are out, remember?"

"Damn it, prep the message anyway and the second comms are back up, send it."

"Sure thing," Steelbox said, typing in the codes carefully. "Who're we shouting to?"

"Family code. They might know something."

"That the Gov doesn't?" Bushfield asked.

"I feel like if I say yes I'm incriminating a few people. So, I'm going to pretend you didn't ask me that."

Bushfield pinched the bridge of her nose. Of course the Madisons had their own files on everything they'd seen. And of course, she thought, they didn't fully trust the Gov with all of it. But something like this would surely be in official records. You didn't just ignore something this large and strange. She told that to herself a few times until she decided she believed it.

"It's attacking the *Ratzinger*!" Chellox yelled over his shoulder.

"Wait, it's what? Show me!"

Chellox fed the data to all screens, letting everyone look at what he was watching. Turned away from the Fold itself, their cameras showed some flapping piece of the thing reaching out and slapping at the *Ratzinger*. It didn't seem to have come further out of the Fold, just extended part of itself—that distance, it must be huge, Bee thought.

"Can we talk to them?" Mud asked, hopefully.

"We're in range for short comms," Bee said. "Opening channel to Mills now."

"Mills! You guys all right?" Mud asked as soon as the line went green.

"I have a...a what...space monster? licking my damn ship!" came Mills' reply. "That's about as far from all right as we could get today."

"I doubt that," Mud said. "Can you guys scatter?"

"Engines seem out," Mills told him, "but shuttle craft and fighters are reporting operational."

"Great. So don't touch the thing. Got it. Mills, scatter. Repeat, scatter."

"Sending nonessential crew now. Calling in the *Amalfi* now. Sending you coordinates."

"We'll coordinate evacs out here, but Mills, do not attack. Repeat, do not attack." Olivet and Bee nodded at Mud as he said it.

"It's attacking the *Ratzinger*, Arrow. We can't just ignore that."

"We don't know that it's attacking. We just know it's touching you. Your sensors are still online, right?"

"Only engines are out."

"Good. Keep collecting data. Bee and I will come to you."

"How's Bushfield?"

"She's good. Her ship is in the same situation as the *Ratzinger*, but she's fine. We'll bring her, too."

"Only long enough to get in a different ship," she said.

"Of course. Your fighter group will be needed," Mills said.

Mud turned to Bee. "Grab a GravPack and let's go."

CHAPTER 14

MUD AND BEE EXITED the *Arrow*, Bushfield in tow, and locked their packs to the *Ratzinger*, hauling themselves in quickly. They were about halfway to the larger ship when Steelbox caught up to them. He really wasn't a fan of the GravPack, but he used it fine, joining their group and getting safely aboard the *Ratzinger*.

"Steelbox, you're staying with—" Mud started.

"One less crew member on the *Arrow* means one more person we can ferry off. Sorry, Cap. I'm coming with."

"Fine," Mud said, not wanting to waste the time arguing, "but I don't want to hear about how I was mean and fed you to a space monster."

"Copy."

Bee and Bushfield said a quick goodbye, just on the air-filled side of the airlock, before Bushfield ran off to the hangar to find a ship and help evacuate the *Ratzinger*. Bee joined Mud and Steelbox as they ran the other direction, up to the main command observation deck.

With high, triple-reinforced windows and plenty of consoles and screens to record and check data, the command observation desk sprawled over a large footprint on the ship. Originally designed to be a research vessel, the *Ratzinger* changed focus as needed, not carrying a full compliment of scientists anymore, its hangar stuffed with fighters now instead of research probes.

"So what am I looking at?" Mills asked as the

three entered the room.

"We're not sure," Mud said. They all gathered with Mills, close to the windows.

The Fold hung there, not glowing as brightly anymore. Stretching out of it, protruding in every direction, vaguely indistinct shapes reached. They were hard to look at, seeming to pulse not with light but with existence. None of the four staring at it felt they were sure they even saw anything, even while they were utterly sure about what they saw. It made headaches blossom in each of their skulls.

"Any good scanner data yet?" Bee asked as she moved toward a console. She sat, combing through the data to date.

"Nothing that makes sense," Mills said, still staring out the window. "I've never even heard of anything like this. The bits of it touching the ship, they aren't tentacles, or hands, fingers—what *are* they? What does the rest of it look like?"

"Closest I can guess right now, they're pseudopods," Bee said, "not that there's data to really back that up. Still, look at them, changing shape, reaching out...and see how it flickers?"

"We all see that," Steelbox said, "and it hurts."

"Exactly," Mud said, moving to look over Bee's shoulder. "I'm not sure that the Fold leads anywhere at all."

"All right, you three work this out, I have to go manage an evac," Mills said, tearing himself away. He headed for the door, being careful to not glance back and catch sight of anything outside. "Keep me updated."

"Let's collate data and see if we can keep the *Ratzinger* afloat," Mud said, grabbing a seat and starting to scroll through data.

Mills stopped just outside the observation deck and considered going back in. He badly wanted to know what threatened his ship, but bigger problems took precedence. Calling out over an intership channel, he demanded status on all evac work. No one had spotted the *Amalfi* as of yet, and long-range comms remained down. Until then, all nonessential crew were being loaded into any ship that could hold people for a while and launched.

The move would buy them at least ten hours, Mills thought, but not much longer than that. People needed to eat, they needed to breathe, and both of those acts would require docking somewhere. If they couldn't return to the *Ratzinger* and the *Amalfi* didn't show in time, he'd have a large problem on his hands. A cluster of small scout ships, shuttles, and fighters full of the slowly dying.

Until then, until something actually happened, Mills knew the best he could do would be to manage the evac as speedily as possible. A list of ships, and crew counts, went on steadily in his ear as crew members read out status reports.

He adjusted resources in use even as they were read out to him, reassigning crew to different ships, trying to make sure as many as possible had a medic on board just in case, and not doubling up on them anywhere.

Mills made it to the hangar and grabbed a terminal, marking off the space as his new command center. He knew that, realistically, he could only bandage the problem until the *Amalfi* showed up, if it did. Until long-range comms came back online, he would have to assume the ship would arrive, running on hope and desperation.

Back on the observation desk, Mud, Bee, and Steelbox did essentially the same. The only data they could really count on made no sense. The rest was, as Bee put it, 'fuzzy at best.' Mud kicked his chair back from his station and looked at his teammates.

"I'm going to suggest something stupid," he said. They both looked at him, waiting. This wasn't the time for the cheap shot, and they knew it. "We need to find out what's in the Fold."

"You want to go into it," Steelbox said.

"I want to go into it," Mud confirmed.

"Letting go of the fact that from what we can tell, the best case is that it's a wormhole to an unknown part of space," Bee said, "how would you do it?"

"We could—"

"Take the *Arrow*?" she finished for him.

"Right, if that thing touches us we lose engines. So we dodge it."

"And if the energy in there, the energy closer to the Fold itself—what if it does the same thing?"

Steelbox looked at this terminal. "I don't think that's the case."

"And on the other side? If it has another side, or whatever it is?"

"We'll find out," Mud said.

"Well, you were right," Bee said, "you have a stupid idea."

Mud got up from his chair, shifting to sit on the edge of a console, looking at Bee and Steelbox. "If we launch a probe, it'll get caught by the long-range comm problem."

"So would we."

"But we could see," Mud said, "record things. The probe would just be useless."

"Looking at the data—" Bee pointed at her screen, "—no, really, come look at this," she said, and waited for Mud and Steelbox to come over to her. "This Fold is either a wormhole, which no one has ever gone through or even seen, or it's a doorway."

"To where?" Steelbox asked, reading the data as best as he could.

"That's the question, because it wouldn't be to anywhere in this universe."

Mud shook his head. "So it's a doorway to another universe?"

"To another something," Bee said, "quite possibly. Look, it isn't like I have any experience with this. No one does. Not that anyone's recorded. Nothing firm, at least."

"We think. That message still waiting to be sent?" Mud asked Steelbox.

"Yeah, the one with the strange code? When communications are back up it'll go. Until then..." he trailed off and scratched his chin, thinking it through. "No, wait, let me hook it to a probe and launch it. Once clear it'll send."

"And how will we get a reply?" Mud asked. Bee watched the exchange, wondering what they were even talking about.

"I'll append a request for reply and a note to keep replying until a confirmation is received on receipt," Steelbox said, smiling. "So where is this going?"

Bee looked at Mud, "You're sending the data we gathered home, aren't you?"

"You bet I am. If anyone has data that might help,

it's my parents."

"They need to learn to share more."

"They've been burned before. Anyway," Mud said, nodding at Steelbox, "go take care of it." Steelbox left quickly, opening a short comm channel to the *Arrow* and getting them ready to transmit the package of data to a probe once he got one lined up. They were busy, Olivet and Chellox, taking on evacuees from the *Ratzinger* and keeping their distance from the Fold.

The protrusions, pseudopods from the Fold, extended and glanced against the *Ratzinger* inquisitively. Slowly they worked their way along the length of the ship, expanding and trailing along the huge vessel. Eventually they would reach the hangars and evacs would be forced to halt.

The evacuation continued to move slowly, a fact that Mills despised. Normally, an evacuation would simply pile people into the escape pods and fire them off. Given the Fold, and whatever the thing reaching out of it was, they couldn't just fire the pods and hope. Under normal emergency evac procedures, the object would be to find a safe planet to land on, or a ship to hold the evacuated crew until they could get to a planet. Mills had something else in mind and still felt good about the idea, if not the execution.

Sending out the fighters with extra people limited their ability to respond to problems, but increased the number of people who could get off the *Ratzinger*, a metric off-set by Mills' stacking of the other ships with a good mix per department where possible. That management added time, but they weren't near a planet and the *Amalfi* still hadn't arrived. Plus, the incoming ship had been docked; older and being considered for retirement, it didn't have a steady crew anymore. Mills intended to rehome his people on the *Amalfi* and go right back to work.

All of which took planning, as file backups needed to be made, along with some bits of essential equipment and weapon stores to move as well—which managed, of course, to further slow everything about the evac down. Mills stood by his choice, though he wasn't exactly sorry that he couldn't be reached on a long-range comms and forced to defend it to higher ups just then. Instead, he continued to triage, waiting for the *Amalfi* to show up, and waiting for word from Mud and his team.

"What about GravPacks?" Mud was just then asking Bee.

"In the Fold?"

"Sure, why not? Look, the touch of that thing, the energy or light it put out when the Fold was being created, it seems to drain engine cells. But engines run off of different stuff than most of the rest of a ship uses, right? So electronics still work, sensors and so on are fine. But so is gravity."

"Yeah, but," Bee sighed, "then you have people with no better protection than a GravPack and shield going into who knows what. That's still not smart, Mud."

"A lot of our job is doing not-smart things," he said. "Someone is going to have to go in there. That's us. That's what we do."

"We have to be smart about it, even so. So we survive, and don't just throw away our lives because it seems to be what we do today."

"You're being overly harsh here."

"No," Bee said, stopping to take a calming breath, "I'm being honest. I'm all for half-baked plans and charging in where everyone else fears, sure. That's a lot of what we end up doing, and I get that."

"So then—"

"No, listen to me," she said forcefully, "this isn't going down to a planet and rescuing someone, this is leaping into a situation so unknown that physics doesn't cover it yet. That's not just some strange moment that other people are afraid of. There literally isn't enough data to make an informed choice."

"So how do we get better data?" he asked.

"We try a probe. Just try one. Attached to a GravPack so it has engines, hopefully, maybe. Just a quick test in and out." She turned her screen a bit so he could see it clearly. She'd been building plans for exactly the sort of probe she wanted.

"We send this and then we go in?"

"If we need to, if it's even a livable space. Then we go explore, and figure out who's doing this and what they want."

"Could be a natural occurrence, too," Mud said.

"Neither of us believe that though, right?"

"Not really. All right, get the probe up and out the door soonest. I'm gonna go brief Mills in person and see if I can relieve him. He must be driving himself to destruction down there."

Mud hit the hangar deck and pulled a wheeled terminal station over to where Mills worked. The two shared the job of managing the evacuation, speeding things up, and as they worked, they talked. They caught each other up at speed easily and moved toward working out the next steps on both sides. Mills only had one lingering problem.

"You can't send that data to your parents," he said, directing a group to one of the last shuttles.

"Too late, but what's your problem?" Mud asked him. He looked around the almost empty hangar, glad to be nearly done with this phase of the evac.

"Proprietary Gov information, the fact that they have nonsecured data the Gov should already have, using consultants without running it by me—I don't know, Mud, pick one."

"And you know the answers to all of them. I couldn't get them to hand over the family storage any more than you could. And in an emergency, even without one, since when do I check with you about using my own contacts?" Mud looked at Mills, smiling. "You just don't want the old man thinking we need his help."

"I don't want him coming out here and, I don't know...blowing things up."

"That's mom, and they won't come out here. I just need to check data."

Mills held up a finger, checking his console. "The *Amalfi* is close enough for short comms, so they should be here in about ten minutes."

"Surely that's close enough to start boarding people," Mud said.

"I want them on the other side of us, with the *Ratzinger* between it and the Fold. Then we can dock crews. There can't be a chance of needing to evac a second time."

"I'll start sending out notices, then," Mud said, typing quickly. He flashed notices to the ships, one after another, with instructions, putting them in text to save miscommunications and garbled read-backs of coordinates.

"Anyway," Mills said, sending the same messages as Mud to more of the ships floating and waiting, "send the probe into the Fold, but nothing else happens until the *Amalfi* is away."

"Where will you be?" Mud asked.

"Not sure yet. I'm going to leave a small security crew here, just to wait for a tow, but we're transferring everything else to the *Amalfi* and I'm taking it out as a replacement. Speaking of, make sure Bee sends all her data—"

"I've sent her terminal instructions already," Mud said.

"Good. You guys going into the Fold is incredibly stupid, you know."

"So I've heard."

"I'll realistically have to be on the *Amalfi* settling everyone in, but that means getting a good distance from the Fold. You won't have backup."

"Sure I will. The *Arrow* stays on this side with some of my team. Mills, we do stuff like this without you all the time. No offense, just...don't worry about us."

"You do *not* do 'stuff like this' all the time," Mills said. "No one does. This is—"

"Don't do it."

"What?"

"Tell me how this is different, more dangerous, whatever. That's what I mean. It's what we do. The unknown. You know this, hell, you *send us* to do it!" Mud pushed his terminal away and looked out the hangar into empty space. A gravity shield sealed them off from vacuum, phasing in ripples to allow ships to pass. "We're going, and no amount of warning or doomsaying will stop it. We both know it's our job, so don't feel guilt or concern and try to ease it off by lecturing me. Is this what having normal parents is like?"

Mills laughed, "Yeah, Jonah and Shae would just be annoyed you got to go first."

"They'd also," Mud said, shaking his head and laughing lightly, "trust me to take the right precautions and adapt as needed."

"All right, all right," Mills raised his hands, palms toward Mud, "I give. If the *Amalfi* is out of communications range, I expect that same probe delay message from the *Arrow*, though."

"Fair enough. Now go to a comm deck and get the *Amalfi* aligned. It'll be easier, I'll keep watch down here until loading starts."

"Thanks, Mud, and fly safe." Mills shut down his terminal and started off toward the ship's interior.

"And if my parents get back to you and say they're on their way, remind them I haven't sent an alarm yet. It'll make mom stand down and put them off."

"They're still going to demand to run the room remote, you know."

"That's your problem," Mud said, waving Mills out of the room. "Now get going, you need to keep the transfer running smooth."

CHAPTER 15

STEELBOX CAME BACK to the observation deck to find Bee working on a GravPack, attaching remotes and a sensor box to the bullet-shaped casing, muttering while she worked. He nodded at her and dug in to help.

"Probe?" he asked, looking at the components laid out across the table.

"Yeah. Hand me that wrench?" She'd gotten down to the crew storage and grabbed one of the spare GravPacks and as many sensor collectors as she could carry. The problem, as she saw it, remained figuring out and limiting what they needed to probe for. The probe needed to be small, which meant she only had so many options. But given the utter unknown on the other side of the Fold, she wanted to scan for literally everything that humanity—and everyone else they knew of—could think of measuring.

While they worked and Mud kept an eye on the hangar deck, reading scans from the waiting ships, Mills started running the reverse end of the evac. The *Amalfi* edged gradually into position, moving as slow as it did in hopes of not attracting attention from the thing in the Fold. No one knew if the creature cared, but they had to act like it might.

Around both giant ships, the fighters, shuttles, and extraneous vessels from the *Ratzinger* drifted like tiny minnow around whales. The cluster needed to stay close, but far enough apart to avoid collisions and to make sure none of the ships would cut off escape routes if the situation suddenly changed.

Mills kept requesting field information from Mud, who had an eye on the swarm of smaller ships. Everything looked good, and Mills gave him a pattern move that he thought should work before turning his attention fully to the *Amalfi*.

The *Amalfi* switchover presented interesting problems. A much older ship, Mills had to make sure its data stores could handle the load he'd put it under, transferring everything possible from the *Ratzinger*. That process started, Mills checked on the pseudopods crawling along the ship. They continued, slowly enveloping the *Ratzinger* foot by foot. No engines meant no way to escape their grip at all, except to try firing at the thing. Mills didn't want to go down that road just yet, not if he could avoid it. But that avoidance meant getting the *Amalfi* ready for his crew. As it stood, the ship arrived with a skeleton crew to fly it in. They were really just a docking crew who could pilot the ship.

Mud identified the ship's carrying bridge crew from the *Ratzinger* and Mills started working out a rotation to get the right people in board in the right order. He didn't have the hours it would take to do the job right, so he'd have to do it right enough to get by.

Mills caught a launch from the *Ratzinger*, unplanned and not on his list. Without thinking, he targeted it, locking onto the small shape quickly. "Damn it, Mud, did you guys just launch a probe?" He squinted at his monitor.

"Is that what that was? I caught it, too. Damn, let me confirm." Mud went silent for only a second before he came back on the line. "Confirmed. Probe is ours."

"We weren't supposed to launch it yet, I want my people safe before we—"

"I know, Mills. I'll yell at them later, let's get this done first."

"Mud, if they—"

"Mills! Watch your screen! You almost sent two shuttles into each other."

"Damn it, sorry," Mills said, sending adjusted coordinates quickly, "it's just distracting watching something eat the ship."

"If only we knew that's what it's doing."

"True enough. Mud, if you have this, I'm going to head over to the *Amalfi* myself and oversee from that end, get the place running."

"The *Arrow* is returning from dropping its load— I'll have them at the hangar for you."

"Perfect. I'm signing off the board. Bring them in for me."

"Got it."

Mills stopped by his quarters on the way down, shoving a few things into a bag to take with him. He looked around the room and sighed. The situation ate at him like utter failure. No crew lost, as of yet— no secrets given away, weapons stolen, nothing. But the downing of the *Ratzinger* hung in Mills' head as a giant sign he should resign, or at least demote himself, since he knew his superiors would side with a rational view and agree that this situation remained out of his control.

Zipping his bag angrily, Mills stopped and took a few deep breaths, pushing the feeling down and centering himself. He could feel like crap later—

for now he needed to go and ensure the continued safety of the people below him.

Mills walked through the hangar without saying a word to Mud, giving him a nod in passing while the lanky Hurkz kept working, speaking softly into a headset and typing furiously. The *Arrow* sat in the hangar, doors open for him. Engines still glowing, Mills picked up his pace a little. They took off for the *Amalfi* without Chellox or Olivet saying a word to him. They knew, he could feel, his sense of failure, and either agreed or didn't know how to defuse it.

The *Arrow* looped over the *Ratzinger* to bring the *Amalfi* into view. Mud's scheduled triage for the shuttles left a clear path, and Chellox guided them in swiftly. Mills departed without a word, not seeing Olivet trying to say something. Shaking his head inside his helmet, Chellox sealed up the ship and took off, opening up a hangar spot for other landing ships.

Mills hurried to the bridge of the *Amalfi*, swallowing his insecurities as he went. He needed to be, just then, a leader, and he couldn't let the hundreds of people counting on him down. He just hoped that if he faked it long enough, he would start to believe the mask. His bridge staff filtered in, one by one, as shuttles landed and they made their way directly to the bridge, dropping their bags next to their stations. Each one of them felt a duty to help before dealing with themselves, and it warmed Mills to see. Clapping his hands loudly once, he looked around the bridge, easily eighty-percent staffed already.

"All right, people, let's bring them home and set up shop." They got to work, checking their stations and bringing systems online.

Back on the *Ratzinger*, Mud considered an option. Protocol would be to land the shuttles with weaponry first, as the *Amalfi* had minimal stock in its weapons cache and what it did have sat badly outdated. The last thing he wanted, though, was for Mills to try attacking the Fold before they had good data. If he held back the supply ships, he could delay any sort of preemptive launch. Assuming you could really call it preemptive at this point. That itself would be the source of the debate.

Mills wanted to arm up—a standard, and rational, choice—but he'd be too busy to notice Mud messing with the order of ships just a little. A nudge here and there and he could have his way. Running his hands across his board, looking at ship positions, Mud decided to trust Mills rather than force his hand either way.

Switching one of his monitors to an external ship view, Mud realized how calm they all were about the Fold. What should've been a big, frantic event was unfurling almost leisurely, as if the slow pace of the creature engulfing the *Ratzinger* itself drove the speed of reaction.

Mud wanted to rush, to hurry in and deal with it, but everyone around him was pushing for slower reactions and careful maneuvers. He didn't blame them—hell, he found he mostly agreed with them, on paper at least. He glanced at one of the hull cameras again and felt his hackles rise. He agreed with them on paper, sure, but he needed to move on this now. Right now it was a slow invasion, a quiet attack, and they could take their time and do things with utmost care. That could change any second, and when it did, they'd be caught by it.

The *Arrow* landed in the hangar and Mud called Chellox over. Explaining the way the ship rotation needed to work—and with a reminder that the human pilots, with only human engines, couldn't fly like Tsyfarians—Mud left him in charge, letting Mills know but not sticking around for the reply. He knew what the reply would be.

He didn't care.

Grabbing his GravPack off the *Arrow*, he made his way quickly to the observation desk. "Probe back yet?" he asked, entering to see Bee and Steelbox staring fixedly at a screen.

"Yup," Steelbox said, not looking away.

"Good, so it could go and return," he said, "so let's—"

"Mud, you have to see this data," Bee said softly.

He walked over to the screen they stared at and gave it a look.

"If this is right—"

"It's right," Bee told him. "Upon entering the Fold, the probe accelerated from a normal insertion speed to something beyond the speed of light."

"The GravPacks can do that," Mud said, peering at the data thoughtfully.

"Sure," Bee agreed, "but not by themselves, generally. It maintained that speed, relative to this universe. But in the Fold, it seemed to still be going the same speed it entered at."

"This universe?" he asked.

"That's what hurts my head, too," Steelbox said. "Look at the data we got. That's kind of provably not this universe. The laws of physics seem slightly off."

"More than slightly at some points," Bee said, pointing at the screen. "It seems to be survivable for humans." She looked at Mud. "You know what I mean."

"Carbon-based oxygen breathers?"

"That's the one," she agreed. "So yeah, probably survivable, but definitely a different universe. Gravity seems to work, but differently, the speed of light is...off. I don't know what they use to see by, or what we would. There's a chance the gravity shield would manage to slow down tachyonic particles back to visible-light speeds? I think that's what this reading could indicate."

"So the camera didn't grab anything?"

"Sort of. The lens activated, it tried to capture photons, all normal. But the pixel translation went odd. I think. You know how looking at the Fold kind of hurts? This seems to be the same thing."

"Just...if we go in, could we see?" Mud asked.

"I don't know," Bee told him, "maybe. But only maybe."

"But we could also get back out," he said.

"The probe was set to repel against anything it could find, in the opposite direction of entry. And it did. So, yes. But Mud—"

"We're going in."

"We need more data," Bee said, poking the screen. "This is a start, but it's *only* a start."

"And when the Fold increases size, or shit comes out of it we can't deal with, or any of a hundred different problems?"

"Mud," Steelbox said, "none of that is happening. We should use the time we have."

"And we will. From the other side of the Fold,

working out what's actually going on, instead of waiting for it to come to us."

"Fine, but you're not going alone," Bee said, shaking her head, "and I'm bringing as much equipment as I can carry. Steelbox, too."

"Yeah," he said, stopping quickly to think. "Wait, I am? Oh, who am I kidding, of course I am."

"You both are," Mud agreed. "Get your equipment gathered and suit up. We breach a new universe in five."

CHAPTER 16

MUD, BEE, AND STEELBOX STOOD on the hangar deck of the *Ratzinger*, divvying up sensor equipment just outside of the *Arrow*. Olivet waved Mud over to the terminal he still worked at. Mud shook him off. Again.

"You know Mills is trying your comms, too," Steelbox said.

"Of course he is. And if I talk to him, this gets messy for him if anything goes wrong. So we're silent. It absolves him."

"Did you ask him if he wanted to be absolved?" Bee asked.

"That," Mud cocked his head to one side, like he was listening for something, "would defeat the purpose of not telling him, wouldn't it?"

"But at least he'd have a choice," she said.

"No," Mud countered, "he wouldn't, because by asking if he wanted to know, I'd be telling him, so even if he didn't want to know he'd know, which would implicate him, which...why are we having this discussion?"

"Because Olivet is going to have some sort of attack if you keep waving him off," Steelbox said. "I'll take care of it."

Chellox came off-board the *Arrow* while Olivet and Steelbox talked. "Mud, I should—"

"Nope, stay here, help them shut down the *Ratzinger* and start up the *Amalfi* with Olivet. Besides, I need you here in case someone needs to come rescue us," Mud said. "You and Olivet stay

138

here and get yelled at by Mills. He'll feel bad about taking it out on you, and it'll defuse him."

"Mud!" Bee punched his shoulder. "Are you seriously playing Mills like that?"

"A little. Maybe." Mud shrugged. "Look, can we just go?" He waved Steelbox back over, and the three of them finished their equipment checks. "All right, Chellox, we'll send a beacon back through when we breach. Past that...do your jobs, and we'll see you in a bit."

They walked quickly to the edge of the gravity shield that still closed off the hangar. A shared glance between them, a quick nod from Mud, and all three leapt from the edge of the hangar into open space.

They slaved their GravPacks to Mud's, who targeted the *Ratzinger* at three different points, creating an angle of entry that, he guessed, should avoid the pseudopods and drop them into the Fold. Remembering that the probe accelerated instantly on entry, Mud primed the GravPacks for max throttle, just in case. The light from the Fold had continued to dim, allowing them to look directly at it, to see where they were headed. It provided cold comfort.

They drew closer to the Fold, speeding toward it, accelerating the entire way.

One of the tentacle-esque feelers from the creature in the Fold whipped in their direction.

Mud held course, not wanting to target the creature itself. Instead he sped up, repelling the *Ratzinger* quicker, trying to skirt the angle and breach the Fold without being touched directly. The pseudopod drew closer to their side. Mud drew the others in closer to him and accelerated harder still.

The Fold itself sat only a few seconds away. Steelbox shuddered as he watched the gelatinous-seeming mass come alongside him.

The Fold was a few arms' lengths away.

Steelbox screamed as the thing from the Fold brushed against him, grabbing at his side.

They pushed through the Fold, tearing Steelbox away from the creature.

And just like that, they were through. Their GravPacks heated, the internal components going from a usual acceleration to acting as if they'd pushed themselves past normal physics and into faster than light territory.

Vision blurred, more so for Bee and Steelbox than for Mud, his Hurkz eyes adjusting faster to the strange way light behaved in the Fold. Clean lines seemed fuzzy at the edges now, blurring indistinctly, as if their shape remained only a firm suggestion. Colorwise, everything in sight shifted either red or blue depending on how it moved in relation to them. Open space, which Mud thought they had to still be in, didn't look like normal space at all. It glowed faintly, looking like an atmosphere without end, reaching into infinity. Which made less and less sense.

Bee keyed her comm and hoped. "Steelbox, are you all right?" she asked, glancing at him, still wincing in pain.

"I think so?" he replied, shaking his head. "You sound really odd."

"Never mind that," Mud said, "What happened?"

"That thing touched me. My arm feels...it isn't broken, I can move it," he waved his arm, showing them, "but it feels...soft."

"All right, important safety notice. Don't touch living things here."

"I feel distinctly unwell," Bee said, looking at Mud.

"Me too. And Steelbox is right, you sound...wrong. Sound is being affected too."

"For all of us. Look at this place, though!" They hung in Non-Space, gazing out into another universe, taking a moment to try to orient themselves.

The rear end of the creature from the Fold floated to one side of them, and Mud maneuvered them further away. They could see blurry, solid masses in the distance, but nothing that made concrete sense to them.

Mud shifted his GravPack's HUD display to a wide setting, targeting what looked like one of the possibly solid masses. He set an attraction thread to it and tried to direct them there, but the pull worked maybe half as well as usual.

Reporting that to the other two, they all started to deploy sensor gear while they moved toward the large mass. Steelbox worked slowly, obviously in more pain that he felt like letting on.

"We're sending you back," Mud said, "instead of a beacon."

"Cap, no, you'll need the help. I'm fine."

"You're not," Bee said, nodding at Mud. "Mud can shoot you out the way we came in and the *Arrow* will pick you up. The data from a touch will be invaluable anyway. Plus you can start to tell them what we've found so far. We won't be far behind, trust me."

"Yeah, this is a crap vacation spot. We'll do some recon and come right back."

"But Cap...Mud. I'm—"

"Going back, is what you're doing." Steelbox spun in space, realizing his GravPack was still slaved to Mud's controls.

"Come on!" he yelled, starting to switch back to free flight.

"You fight me on this and you're really benched," Mud said. "Now go."

Steelbox's GravPack, already heating, started to whine as Mud forced it to repel toward the Fold as fast as it could manage. Steelbox stopped fighting and took control when Mud gave it back to him, but he didn't stop his flight.

"You guys better make it back," he said.

"Promise," Bee said as her teammate and planetmate shot off toward the Fold. "And watch the reentry, you'll slow down really hard!" she yelled into her comm. "Brace for it, and just shut down the GravPack. Reboot it and you'll be fine."

Watching Steelbox go, Mud and Bee both noticed movement around them. They still flew toward the planet mass but watched carefully, trying to work out what they watched as they went.

The sky seemed full of pellets. Small, round objects moving quickly, cluttering the entire space. They hadn't noticed before, only now starting to be able to truly discern finer details as their eyes adjusted. Mud shifted his goggles slightly, wishing he could remove them.

Along the space above them, the pellets were vanishing when they hit the creature in the Fold. Other, larger shapes also moved around them, destroying pellets. The other shapes resolved, as they concentrated, into hexapedal forms—

obviously living creatures now that they could force their eyes to focus.

The forms wielded wide-sweeping energy beams, scouring the space of the pellets. They acted like, Mud thought, they were under attack. The pellets came far less frequently where they were fighting back, but outside of their range, pellets swarmed freely. Now they worked out part of cause of the fuzziness around them: pellets passing around them, making shapes seem indistinct. They realized the objects passed through them as well.

"It's like the worst case of air pollution I've ever seen," Bee said. "Do we help them?"

"We need to find out what the them is," Mud said, still aiming them at the large, solid-seeming mass their GravPacks were working on reeling them toward. "I think we need to get their attention."

"I thought we were doing just recon," Bee reminded him.

"We are, but that includes meeting the natives." Mud shifted the GravPacks to reel them closer to one of the Sweepers, as he thought of them. They drew nearer, able to make out not only six limbs, but that the creature possessed an internal spinal column, head and neck, eyes and a mouth. Obviously intelligent, it held a technological device to fire the wide beam. It seemed to swim along the strange, hybrid skyspace they floated in.

"How do we get its attention?" Bee asked. "No, how do we let it know we're not a threat?"

"First Contact rules apply," Mud said, "follow my lead." Mud held his arms out wide, hands open, fingers splayed. Bee followed suit, and they drifted closer to the Sweeper. "Hello!" Mud shouted, unsure of the sensitivity of the Sweeper's hearing.

It looked directly at them, bringing its weapon to bear. Opening its mouth, it spoke in what sounded to Bee like static being used as a whale song, or an unbalanced engine perhaps. Nothing close to any language she'd heard.

Mud didn't have a reference point for the language either, but he'd expected that. He kept still, showing no threat and no weapons drawn. "Mud," Mud said, slowly moving one arm in to point to himself. "Bee," he said next, pointing at her just as slowly. He repeated the process, still drifting closer to the Sweeper.

The Sweeper watched, holding its device at the ready. "Bee, record everything," Mud said, softly so only she could hear him, trying to not move his mouth much and confuse the name repetitions.

"I already was," she said. "Not sure we'll get anything usable, though."

"Need to try," he said, stopping their forward movement as he noticed the Sweeper start to back off. "Mud. Bee," he repeated.

A static-filled burst of notes emanated from the Sweeper. Instead of pointing at itself with any of its limbs, the Sweeper repeated itself, they thought, and jabbed the device in its hands toward them.

"Not a hello, then," Mud said. "A stop, probably." He nodded at the Sweeper. "Sure, we can do that." Holding steady, Mud went back to slowly repeating names.

"Mud, I don't think they care about our names."

"Trust me on this, all right? We don't have many other options just now."

The Sweeper jabbed toward them again with

its device, stopping to raise it and fire a wide flat beam, wiping out more pellets. It lowered the device—the weapon, Mud corrected himself—at them once more. Other large creatures, same as had poked through the rift, moved into some of the larger clusters of pellets.

"Mud—"

"We're fine," he said without looking.

"No, we're not, damn it, the Fold is closing!" Bee said loudly, reaching out to turn Mud to look back toward where they'd come. Sure enough, the Fold looked to be closing itself up, the creature that had been half in it moving back, and clear. Sweepers surrounded it, looking as if they were busy herding it back. Perhaps, thought Mud, the whole thing had been a mistake.

Either way, they needed the Fold to get home. Mud started to point at both himself and Bee and then at the Fold. "We go," he repeated over and over, as he started to work out where and how to use the GravPack to get them home before the Fold closed fully. The skyspace around them shifted as they went.

He wasn't entirely sure it could be done.

Another jab, and the Sweeper shouted something else at them. Mud couldn't remember if it matched what he assumed was a 'Stop' before. He also couldn't afford to stop, regardless. Lashing out with a few strands from the GravPack and starting to move, Mud pushed the pack as hard as it would go. He could feel the heat from it against his back, hoping neither his pack nor Bee's would actually burn them, much less fry their circuits.

Under them, the wide beam fanned out, the

Sweeper firing a warning shot. Mud kept going. Another warning shot, closer still. They pushed on. The Fold closed quickly, though, snapping shut without ceremony before they could reach it. Speeding right through where it had been, Mud cursed and brought them to a halt.

"Now what?" Bee asked, not trying to hide the frustration in her voice.

"We find another Fold, I suppose," Mud answered.

"That's your entire plan?"

"I'm working on it. But look," Mud pointed, waving his hand some to indicate the Sweepers. Masses of them moved away toward somewhere else, no longer firing beams to destroy the pellets, the rate of pellets far less.

"All right, what does it mean?" Bee aimed sensors at the area the Sweepers had left.

"Not sure, but something about this *feels* familiar." Mud held out his hands again as the Sweeper after them drew closer. "Here we go again."

The Sweeper started to gesture with his weapon, moving it to one side, pointing, and swinging it back toward Mud and Bee. They took the meaning and started to move, as smoothly as Mud could get them, in the direction requested.

"Hey Bee?" Mud asked quietly as they continued to go where the Sweeper led them.

"Yeah?"

"Notice that even when we move in tiny amounts, the GravPacks, they're acting...strange?" Mud set her to free flying. "See?"

"The probe did the same, from what I could tell. Strained like it leapt to somewhere above light speed."

"Sure, because this place is so different, it tries to compensate, but it's more than that. It's like distance doesn't match up."

Bee checked her readouts, then checked them again. "I believe you, but I don't follow."

"The GravPacks are straining, not just trying to keep up to a speed they're not going at, but they're feeling like they're burning miles they aren't. I think distance doesn't mean the same thing here as it does in our universe."

"But distance isn't a fixed thing, it's relative to speed," Bee said, looking over data as best she could.

"Right, which would mean—"

"Time isn't the same, either," Bee said, sounding vaguely horrified. "Oh, Mud, that's not good. That's potentially really not good. But if time works different, if space itself isn't the same, how are we—"

"Because the universe is stranger than we like to admit," Mud said, "and that might hold true across different universes, too."

"Really?" Bee said. "You're going to tell me your entire answer is 'sometimes things make no sense' and expect me to just accept it?"

"Until we have time to unpack it, yeah. For now just note it and file it away and shake your head at it."

"How's that plan coming?" she asked, glancing at the Sweeper herding them.

"So far they've done nothing to us. Could've shot us in the back. So we follow them for now and learn something."

"We shouldn't have come blazing in here, Mud."

"It'll be fine." The Sweeper gestured again and pointed them to a gathering of Sweepers. They all hung in open space, no visible suits or protection. Six limbs, but in no way insectoid in construction. The Sweepmeet, as Mud decided it should be called, allowed them to see more of the beings up close and start discerning differences between individuals. Head size and shape, limb length, and mouth size all varied in what he considered normal parameters.

They organized themselves carefully, he noticed. There was firm societal structure at work. Individuals were given preference in placement near the newcomers, and the staticky sounds of their voices rose and fell depending on who talked.

None of this helped him understand what was said, but the data allowed him to start working out how their hierarchy worked. Knowing that could let him, he thought, survive the encounter and get them both home safely.

Muttering to Bee to just follow his lead, Mud waved his arms to get the Sweepers' attention. He started to gesture wildly, trying to mime the Fold and their entrance. Reaching back to pat his GravPack, he mimed their flight.

"Bee, take over," he said, stopping his movements.

"Wait, what?"

"Mime the flight, and the Fold and all of it."

"Seriously?"

"We need them to know you are my equal. Trust me on this. Just go through it and add bits."

Bee shook her head and started to mime the flight and Steelbox's leaving, and so on. She felt ridiculous, but Mud could see it worked. Whereas the Sweepers only paid attention to him, they now split their focus, paying attention to Bee, but still glancing at Mud to see if he would join in.

He did, near the end of Bee's story. She looked at him and picked up his cues as he worked off what she mimed. Together they told the story of the Fold closing, and of following the Sweeper to where they were now.

"Do you think they understood any of that?" she asked.

"No idea," he said, "but they know we're a team, and that we're equals. It really is key. The last thing we want is for them to consider you disposable, or just an extension of me. We don't know how they view us, as organisms. Well, we do now. But we didn't before."

"You had the *strangest* upbringing," Bee told him. "I'm pretty sure the Gov doesn't have classes in First Contact."

"They do, actually," Mud told her, "but they're kind of...not great...at lower levels. And based off of the original Insertion Team's work, mostly, regardless."

The Sweepers conferred amongst themselves, the one who led them here speaking constantly to the others. It would point at Mud and say a phrase, then at Bee and say a different phrase. Mud grinned. He pointed at himself and said his name, then at Bee, saying hers.

The original Sweeper pointed emphatically at them both when that happened, and Mud looked at Bee. "Survival rates just went a lot higher. They know we have names, and they're learning them."

"Great, can they call us a cab, maybe?"

"Hey, once we get the Fold through to them, they

can maybe just...open another? We'll find out." Mud mimed the Fold again, pointing back in the direction where it had been.

The Sweeper who seemed to be in charge mimed at them slowly, using four of their six limbs. Good, Mud thought, they probably stood on the last two. He cataloged the info in memory and watched.

"Did they just say that the big beast thing...do they think we mean it?" Bee asked Mud, watching.

"Possibly." He mimed back, trying to make sure they understood the Fold from the creature that had poked through it. Back and forth they went, in circles, Mud worried. They distinctly did not want the creature brought over to them. Mud circled back and held his hands up, palms facing the Sweepers, trying to get the concept of waiting across. No go.

"We need to stop," Mud told Bee, "and define yes, no, and hold the hell on."

"Can't we just use math?"

"Yup," Mud said, looking at the Sweepers and holding up one finger. He lowered it, and held up his fist. Then repeated. A few more repetitions and he started to point at a single object when he raised his finger. One. Then he pointed at empty space when he closed his fist. Zero. Basic binary to get the idea of something and nothing established and agreed upon.

He stopped, hoping the Sweepers would get it, and they did, copying the motion and indication, raising one digit and pointing, then a closed appendage and pointing at nothing. That settled Mud worked on mapping them to yes and no, by building in a 'do not want.'

He threw his arms up as if to protect himself. The

Sweepers recoiled the first time, and he held up a closed hand. "Bee, try and hand me something," he said quietly. She grabbed a handheld sensor array and offered it to him. He held his arms up to protect himself again, and she lowered the device.

"Again," he said, lowering his arms. She offered it a second time and he took it. Then he handed it back. "Once more," he said, accepting it, handing it back, and then throwing his arms up the second time she offered it.

"That should do it, I think," he told her, looking at the Sweepers. They watched, no longer recoiling, and acting as if they understood him.

Now that basic terms were established, Mud let them know that they did not, in any way, want the creature brought to them and started again, trying to describe the Fold. The Sweepers seemed to understand this time, repeating no over and over.

They pointed at the creature and mimed a complex series of actions. "Are they saying the creature caused the Fold?" Bee asked. "Can it cause another just for a minute?"

"Yes to the first, but I think it's more complex than that. So no to the second."

They continued, trying to not get frustrated with each other. A bunch of the Sweepers chattered to their leader about something, growing impatient. They pointed, raising their voices. Mud began to understand they were upset about the pellets. Some of them moved off, angrily it seemed to Mud and Bee, gathering other Sweepers up to move along toward a large collection of pellets.

While they had been 'talking,' more pellets had started to appear from where they'd been destroying them previously, though nowhere near as many as other sections of their space.

Bee started to try to mime questions about the pellets, but the Sweepers left facing them would only point at Mud and Bee in response. "All right, let's focus on getting out of here, what do you say?" she asked Mud.

"For now it's the best bet, but I'm getting a feeling about this I don't like. I'll explain when we're back in our universe. I want more data."

"Agreed."

Mud tried to, with Bee's help, mime their need to leave. The fairly complex concept took a while, but Bee thought they'd made some progress. Sadly, if they had, the only answer they got was the equivalent of a shrug.

"I have an idea of how to get out, but you won't like it," Mud said. "They won't like it either, I think."

"So good chance we're going to die, then?"

"Don't focus on the downside. Look, the GravPacks think we're going above light speed, but we're not. So let's push them to above light speed for real."

"How," Bee said, trying to sound calm, "will that help? Except to show them what happens when a GravPack explodes? They're already whining like they're pinned on max, if we push them—"

"I know," Mud admitted, "that's why no one will like it. But, you have to admit, it should pop us out of this universe."

"Mud, what you're thinking may well pop us out of any universe. For good."

"It'll do something, and if we're both right about everything—"

"We haven't discussed what either of us think—"

"But I'm confident we're on the same page," Mud said, setting his GravPack to ask hers for slave control.

"So let's discuss this first, then the dumb plan."

"The GravPacks aren't acting like they're moving faster than light, they actually are. That map to what you've got?" he asked.

"Pretty much, but that doesn't make your plan any better," she said, watching the Sweepers that remained near them.

"I don't pretend to deeply understand it—you can science it to death later, but for now, I remain pretty damn sure that if we try to go faster than light when we already are, we should loop back."

"That's...that's not how it works."

"All right, how do the GravPacks go faster than light to begin with?" he asked. They still spoke softly, so they wouldn't alarm the Sweepers.

"Not knowing one thing doesn't mean you get to guess at the other." Bee glared at Mud, wanting to slap him. He did this, got ahead of himself, she thought, and though he'd slowly gotten better, he still wasn't good at listening too often.

"So what happens if we do this?" he asked, noticing the Sweepers that were left with them had started to drift closer. "Because I think we have a small window here."

"I don't know, no one knows." Bee clocked the Sweepers' advance as well and checked her urge to drift away from them. "And I don't want to find out, especially."

"If we're natively moving faster than light, Bee, we can't *slow down*. There's no mechanism for it. Our only choice is to go faster."

"I know."

"Yeah?"

"I got there a while back, but kept looking for an out. This is going to be ugly, Mud." The Sweepers kept closing in on them as they talked. More of them had wandered away to deal with pellets, or other business, leaving only a handful. Neither Mud nor Bee wanted a fight, though. They really didn't want a fight. Neither of them could think of a good reason to have one unless forced, and if forced, not only did neither of them have an idea how to harm the Sweepers, they were afraid to try.

If they did try, and managed to hurt a Sweeper, they would still be stuck in a different universe with no backup, no escape plan, and limited weaponry. This wasn't a fight they could win, if forced to have it. So running stood out as the only good option.

"I know," he agreed. "So tell me, how do we do it safely?"

"Honestly," she said, thinking quickly, "I hang onto you, we use one GravPack, not both. If yours blows or comes too close to it, we ditch it and hopefully we can get clear of the blast."

"Sounds good. Grab on," he told her, trying to work out a course that would allow them to attain the speed needed.

"Wait!" Bee shouted in his ear. "Hold on! Look!"

Mud looked to where she pointed and saw a harsh glow in the distance. "Is that a Fold?"

"It looks like it might be," she said. "Can we ditch this party and try for it?"

Mud tried to mime their intent to the Sweepers. To their credit they looked, saw the light, and looked back before giving Mud a simple 'no.'

"Not good," Mud said. Bee just muttered a nonverbal agreement. "All right, we're gone," he said, finding the nearest decent target for a gravity lock and setting his GravPack. Bee set her own coordinates and they launched forward.

Still moving far slower than they were used to, Mud suggested they try and push their luck and up the throttle. Both their GravPacks complained but complied, and they lurched forward faster still, if uncertainly.

The light they approached stayed dimmer than the light that had shone from the Fold they'd used to crossover in the first place, but they still made for it. No large creatures floated near the glow, at least. Looking behind them, Bee saw the Sweepers following and said so.

"Are they gaining?" Mud asked.

She looked again. "Nope."

"Are they aiming those guns at us?"

"Not yet."

"Then we don't care yet. Let them come along."

A wide blast of energy shot over their heads. "I thought," Mud said, "you said they weren't aiming anything at us."

"They weren't when I looked," Bee told him. She glanced back. "They are now."

"I noticed, Bee. Thanks. We need to push it. Stay sub-light...well, relative...shit, you know what I mean, but get close." They pushed their throttles harder still, changing anchor points and aiming themselves directly at the burst of light.

As they got closer, Mud realized his sense of distance here landed way farther off than he'd thought. Between the red- and blue-shifting light, the general unease, and everything else about the place, he hadn't pieced it together until they flew toward the light. From his normal judge of distances in the vastness of space—reference points and relative sizes that he'd learned when he was only a child—they'd come halfway to where the light should be.

Yet the light sat right in front of them, only seconds away. The fact of it hurt Mud's head and managed to make him feel nauseated when he tried to reconcile it. Right then he decided he hated other universes. He preferred the laws of reality and physics to stay where they were damn well supposed to be.

Either way, he decided he'd accept that their goal stood closer than he'd thought, even if it made him want to throw up a bit. "Bee, we'll enter the light in five...four..."

"There's no Fold," she said, bracing herself.

"Nope, so let's see where this goes. It seems like a pre-Fold, or maybe an unpopped one. Wait," Mud pointed, "is that—"

"Shit! Mud, that's a *planet*! Inside the glow! That's a planet!"

"Look at it, it's not fuzzy like the stuff we've seen here. I think it's on the other side. Either way, we're going for it."

"If we hit a planet," Bee said quickly, "at this speed...no shield in existence will help us."

"We're not going to hit the planet. Slave to my pack, I've had to do this before."

"You've what?!" Bee yelled, slaving her GravPack quickly, letting him take over controls.

"Not the other-universe part, but planet fall at

156

this speed. I think this speed. Whatever! Trust me! It was one of Dad's drills."

"Of course it was," she said, thinking again about how strange his childhood had been, and hoping that wasn't her last thought in life.

CHAPTER 17

THE LIGHT ENGULFED THEM.

A dizzying transition. The scalding fires of the edges of atmosphere. Mud and Bee headed toward a planet at a velocity so close to the speed of light they shared a mailbox.

As they entered the light, he called up his GravPack's HUD and selected the nearest large gravity well, building an arc away from it. He knew the selection wouldn't kick in until they were already in the edges of the planet's atmo.

Mud and Bee reentered their home universe, GravPacks screaming as they tried to shield away the heat of an atmosphere catching fire around them while calculating and compensating for the turn Mud had set up.

Neither of them could even consciously follow the curve as they slingshot away from the planet, pushing back out of the atmosphere and rocketing away from it. The extra speed, and the way the GravPacks adjusted for it, pushed them above light speed again for a few seconds, long enough for Mud to take stock.

Not dead. In what looked to be the right universe. Hurtling away from the planet at about a sixty-degree angle and traveling far too fast. Mud cancelled all ties from the GravPacks and then reestablished them back to the planet they'd avoided, this time with regular physics in mind.

"What did we just do?" Bee asked as they slowed and started to turn.

"The HUD selector software takes a tick or two to respond," Mud told her. "Normally it's a small enough lag in the system you won't ever notice it. But if you know you're going too fast to be able to react, well, you can plan for it. Sort of."

"I don't want to know how you drill for that, or what happens if you're wrong. But I kind of do, you know?" Bee checked her sensor equipment, making sure nothing had gotten damaged in their universe reentry.

"Set up someone below to catch, really," Mud said, as if that settled matters.

"At that speed? What if they miss?" All of her equipment checked out. She looked at the planet they had returned to, trying to place it from the stars nearby.

"Have you seen my dad miss with a GravPack?"

"No, Mud, I need you to realize this wasn't normal. For any child. At all." She laughed nervously, stopping suddenly when she realized where they were.

Mud saw her face and clicked his tongue, "Yup. Welcome home." Though born on Trasker Four, Bee had moved, with what survived of her planet's population, to Bercuser when the Tsyfarians invaded. With the matter settled, Bee knew of a group exploring a migration back to what remained of Trasker Four, so they could rebuild there. She didn't blame them.

They came in for a landing and stood on a small hill, mist gathering below them. Bee scanned the mist and compared readings with the other data she'd collected. "Bercuser must have been relocating. That's how it—"

"That's how it changes systems, yeah," Mud agreed, shaking his head at the unfolding of the universe.

"You knew?"

"No way!" he told her, laughing. "Not until I realized what planet we almost hit."

"And the mist," she held out a scanner and showed him the readings, "that's what the mist is. It's Other-Universe Stuff."

"Sweeperverse?" Mud asked.

"Excuse me?"

"We need a better name than Other Universe. But anyway, yeah, that makes a strange sort of sense."

"It does. The mist is a solid form of that glow, something in how the planet itself moves, a remnant. I mean, it didn't come fully into the other universe—"

"Sweeperverse."

"Nope, not sticking," Bee told him, setting her GravPack for free flight and taking off in a slow arc, lazily starting to fly toward her new home city. Mud followed, working the implications through with her.

"So they snort the mist, inhale it, and the difference in that stuff versus anything from our universe, it just—"

"It just totally," she said, nodding quickly, "interacts with their brains. Some of that stuff, at a molecular level, is moving faster than the speed of light, for a bit. While it decays, who knows what sort of tachyonic resonance it's exhibiting."

"The worst part of this," Mud said lightly, "is that we have to tell Olivet there's science behind his visions and we believe in them a hell of a lot more now."

"Poor Mud, having to admit when he's wrong." They landed at the edge of Bee's new home city, New Kromp, and walked to her apartment.

"Hey, this place is nice."

"Trasker encampment. For now. And it isn't like I'm ever here. When was the last time we had a total leave come up?" Bee let him in the front door and walked up a flight of stairs to her second-floor studio apartment. "I'm thinking of giving it up."

"Don't. Please. Hold me to better leave time, but don't let the Insertion Team be your only life." He looked around her small place and sat on the edge of her dresser. The studio was a room only a little bigger than her quarters on the *Ratzinger*, a ten-by-twelve space. A kitchen and bathroom both split off from the main room. Besides the dresser, she had a bunch of boxes, a bed, and a small table with one chair. "Find a nicer place, and take breaks."

"This from you?" she asked, laying out her sensor equipment on the table. "Since when do you have a life outside of the team?"

"I'm just saying, be smarter than me. Get a bigger place, hell, something big enough for you and Bushfield, maybe. Have a life."

"Now you sound like your mother."

"Great. So do we want to talk about the actual problem?" Mud tapped a few controls on his suit and read the results. Shaking his head, he looked back toward Bee.

"You mean that neither of us has used a comm to call home?" She took a small scanner from the table, looked at the readout, and flipped it to Mud, arcing it cleanly through the air.

He caught it and looked. "Sure, but before we knew long-range comms were out..."

"Sweepers," she said, darkly.

"Sweepers," he agreed.

"The pellets had to be communications, right?" Bee asked. "It lines up too easily."

"That's the only thing that makes me think it might not be—it lines up." Mud tossed the scanner back to Bee and hopped off her dresser, wandering into her tiny kitchen. "Except for the fact that our communications don't go through other universes."

"You know something?" she said, wandering to the doorway of the kitchen, leaning on the frame. "I don't know how long-range comms work. But they've always bothered me."

Mud ran some water, took off his goggles, and splashed his eyes. Blinking quickly, he settled his goggles back. "That's a new one."

"What? They make no sense. Mud, they're fairly instantaneous across distances that...the long-range comms have to be going faster than light."

"Of course," he agreed, pouring himself a glass of water, and then one for her. "How else could we keep the Gov together across entire systems?"

"And that," she said, taking the offered glass from him, "doesn't bother you?"

"Not really," he told her. He drained his glass and set it in the sink. "But I do think the comms are somehow what the Sweepers—"

"No, hold on," Bee said, walking back to the table covered in sensor equipment, "you can't just ignore that the communications we use break the laws of physics. You can't just ignore that."

"I really can," he told her, following her back into

the main room. "It's a piece of this, sure, but we should get back to the *Amalfi* and—"

"Mud!" Bee shouted. "We're breaking the laws of physics...again...and I think this other universe is paying the price. We don't get to ignore that."

"And we're not—"

"But you're saying you don't care how the comms work, and—"

"No, I'm saying the fact that they *do* work doesn't bother me. I agree we have to work it out *now* and see what's going on. If we're both right, then—well, if I had an answer, we wouldn't be here. So let's not be here. Let's hard burn back to the *Amalfi* and start finding answers."

Bee gathered up her sensor equipment again, having recharged all of it, and nodded. "Finally. Just sitting around here like this, what were we even thinking?"

"Bee," Mud said softly, "can I just say, from experience, that sometimes you need to pretend the world is small and normal and makes sense?"

She looked at him, eyebrows raised. "Really? I thought this was just another mission for us. Sir."

"Don't pull that," he told her. "When the strange builds too hard? Maybe not you, you can be the exception. But for me, when the going gets so strange that even the strange peel off for saner grounds, just pretending, for a minute, that this isn't my life helps me stay sane."

"Whatever you say. Captain Madison."

"Bee."

"Mud."

"It's all right to be freaked out by this."

"Oh, I am," she agreed, "but I want to do something

about it, not sit in my kitchen and pretend nothing is happening."

"That's not what...let's just get going," he said, "all right?"

"If you're sure."

"Hey, Bee?" he asked, as he checked his suit and GravPack systems carefully.

"Yeah?" She looked up from doing the same.

"Having a coping mechanism isn't a bad thing," he told her. "Promise."

"Stop treating me like I'm new," she said, trying to hold back anger. "I know I didn't grow up like you did, but—"

"It's just experience. You're getting yours now. No real difference."

"Can we just go?" she asked, finishing putting her sensor equipment away in various pockets and bags attached to her suit.

"Sure."

They left Bee's apartment without another word and walked out of the building, back onto the street. No one recognized either of them, or seemed to care that they were dressed in thinsuits with large, silver-bullet–shaped GravPacks strapped to them.

They took off slowly, drifting upward from the street. That, a few people took note of, watching them start to fly off. They allowed themselves to drift upward like that, lazily, until they reached a few thousand feet.

"Orbit then work out a flight plan?" Mud asked. Bee grunted a response and they both sped up, setting the GravPacks to repel the planet and switching their HUD displays to larger targets out of the gravity well in preparation. It left them unable to make small maneuvers until they got to low orbit, but they both accepted readings on their surroundings telling them they'd be moving fast enough and the sky would stay clear ahead of them that it was safe.

They broke orbit and drifted free in clear space for a minute, working to settle on a course back to the *Amalfi*. Pushing the GravPacks to go faster than light meant they wouldn't have to worry about most smaller objects, but large gravity wells could be a problem. Luckily their HUD navigation system had most planetary orbital data stored, so they could preroute a flight taking planets and suns between here and there into account.

Space, being mostly empty, presented far less problem in that regard than many people thought. Huge stretches of their flight would be through utterly empty space, their movement relying on momentum, out of range of anything for the GravPacks to latch on to.

Route plotted, they double-checked their data with each other, made small corrections so they would take exactly the same path home, and accepted the routes. The GravPacks strained a bit more than usual, needing, Mud knew, a teardown and rebuild after being in the other universe, but otherwise behaved normally. They shot off, gaining speed faster than anything had a right to, and before they could really notice it they were moving faster than the speed of light toward the *Amalfi*.

CHAPTER 18

THEY FLEW STRAIGHT and true, personal shields set at ten feet to deflect particulate matter and ensure they didn't arrive full of microscopic holes that would kill them along the way. Traveling fast enough that the normal laws of physics didn't hold saved them time dilation and still allowed them to cross the distances involved in a matter of hours instead of weeks or months.

They moved in silence, each lost in their own thoughts. Bee considered Mud's words and tried to be honest with herself about why she felt so angry. He wasn't, she knew, trying to be condescending, but he kept ending up that way. She needed to lay that out for him, to explain why he really needed to back off more and not treat her like a little sister as much.

She wanted to make excuses for him, knowing that overall it wasn't intentional behavior, but fought herself on continuing to brush it off. He needed to grow up, and on top of that, let her grow up as well and be the person she knew she already was.

Mud felt bad—he knew he fell back on old bad habits born of being treated like a kid, still, by his parents. They tried to correct that, and he tried to not fall into their patterns with his own team, but none of it came easy. He needed to apologize, and try harder. He knew his parents, both of them, would insist on finishing the job first and worrying about feelings second.

But he didn't want to be his parents. He respected them, admired them, even, but also saw the problems of their behaviors laid out for him in the way that all children can when it comes to their parents.

So he tried to balance the two, in his head. He would talk to Bee when they arrived at the *Amalfi*. He knew he could just talk to her as they flew through the emptiness of space, but he also wanted to give her time to think. No, he admitted to himself, he wanted to give himself more time.

While they flew, Mud decided to, putting bigger thoughts behind him, just fly. He closed his eyes and paid attention to GravPack, listening to it, making sure everything felt smooth and normal.

It didn't.

"Bee," he said, opening his eyes, "does this feel off to you?"

"I don't do that much hard travel like this, so I'm not sure. But yes," she replied.

"Something with the GravPacks, maybe from exposure to the Sweeperverse?"

"We're not calling it that."

"Bee."

"Sorry," she said, with a hint of a laugh, "but I don't think so. Still, if we're sure that going this fast ends us in the other universe—"

"It doesn't," he said, "it really doesn't. We would've noticed, just in how it felt—this isn't that, but it's like we're riding the barrier. Maybe that's what this travel is, riding that barrier."

"All right," she agreed, "then why is this different?"

"Baader-Meinhof phenomenon, if I had to guess," he said.

"Of course," Bee said, "sure, sure—now that we've seen the other universe we'll see it everywhere, the seams at least."

"So what happens if we kick the GravPacks a bit harder?" Mud asked.

"Are you suggesting we try it? I would assume we'd actually see the barrier for real instead of just feeling it."

"We should," he said, "wait to test it." He knew she'd want to wait and agreed. It was a dumb risk, even if it was the sort of dumb risk he liked to take at times.

"We should. But if we set the acceleration to last only, say, two seconds relative ..."

"We'd see something, or not, and drop back before anything could go wrong." Bee thought for a second. "Or we'd pierce the barrier again—"

"—and be in a lot of trouble," Mud finished. "Slave me to your GravPack, you have a better sense of the timing than I do."

"Is this some sort of apology?" she asked, not enjoying the idea that he could be soft-balling her.

"Nope, but one of us has to control the timing, and you know the science better," he told her, meaning it.

"You know the packs better."

"And they're fine," he assured her, setting his display to accept her control when requested. She slaved his GravPack to her control and set up some safety parameters. Pushing the GravPacks' throttles higher than they stood now set them into a dangerous place—they were already theoretically pinned at max. But you could go into an overdrive if needed. Too long there and the entire GravPack

168

would burn out. Neither of them knew of a case that overdrive had even been used, which should have counted as a warning. But then, they were also sure it had been, by the original team—they'd just never documented what they'd seen.

"All right, sensor arrays online," Bee said, "overdrive in three...two ..."

They felt a lurching as the GravPacks spun up to a higher speed, pushing against a passing gravity well quickly, harder than recommended. The light around them shifted, starting to gain the feeling of the other universe. A white light, the same as they flew into on Bercuser, started to glow softly around them.

Just as they each started to say something, as they realized the barrier laid right there around them, the GravPacks tried to drop out back to normal full-throttle conditions. But brushing against the barrier and pushing away from it confused an internal system.

Bee and Mud felt their packs shudder badly and grind as automatic systems detected a fault and cut all power, trying to bring them to a stop by pushing, repelling, and attracting strands against anything in range. Sadly for them, the only thing in range was the barrier between universes itself. Not being actually physical, the barrier couldn't be pushed against or pulled to, and the GravPacks turned off, but not before managing, somehow, to bring them to a complete halt.

"What the hell—"

Mud checked and double-checked his readouts before answering. "The GravPacks couldn't handle it. And we should've been right, just shot back to full throttle fine."

"I'm seeing the same thing," Bee agreed. "So how'd we dead stop?"

"That's what I need to know, because Bee, I hate to tell you this, but we're out of range."

"Out of range of what?" Bee switched her HUD back on and scanned. "Oh...oh, but...how can we be out of range of everything? There's not a gravity well the GravPacks can latch onto. But they can latch onto planets half a system away," she insisted.

"Sure thing. And space is really big, and really empty, and we're between systems, Bee. There's just...nothing of note. We're out of range."

"So how do we restart flight?"

"That's," Mud looked at the readings off his own HUD, "that's the problem, Bee. You solve the how we got here. I'll solve the how we leave here. Fair?"

"Fair," she said, pulling up the historical data and starting to parse it, running theories in her head. Bee held two facts steady to start: Momentum still worked in space, and if they had nothing in range to repel or attract to then they had nothing to stop against. Given those two facts, how could they have gone from faster than light to a dead stop in an instant? Furthermore, their small gravity shields couldn't compensate for that sort of change.

Even expanded to the size of a tiny ship, gravity fields started to have issues compensating for big shifts—it was why you shouldn't use the same tech as a GravPack to move a ship even as small as a fighter. The difference in space between the front and back of a fighter were enough to break a ship apart during a turn. Only a person remained small enough to allow the shields to act as a single

170

capsule.

That capsule though, given the relative speed change, should've collapsed itself. Mud and Bee, she knew, should've been reduced to small puddles of goo contained inside gravity bubbles if what happened had actually happened. Which was all well and good as far as the science went. Except for the fact that the event had happened and they were still alive.

She needed more data, data they simply didn't have. Bee realized she needed to look at the original specs for the GravPacks to work this out. Surely Mud had access to Doctor Williams' files, being his legal grandson and all.

While she worked through the data to that point, Mud focused on getting them out of this alive. They carried enough air to last a few days, and the small food and water stores in the suits could stretch as well, but a few days would be it. Meanwhile, they would float out here and die.

There was nothing in range. Nothing. At the very edges of his scanning for targets, Mud could just make out a possible point, but without some way of getting closer in time it didn't matter. Traveling at a speed substantially less than light speed would take them right to the edge of their air supply to get there, without enough left to get home.

At least, Mud thought, if he could get them moving at all in that direction, maybe he could make sure their bodies got back. A grim thought, but better than just vanishing in the darkness forever.

He shook it off and started over. They needed something to push against, or pull toward. More than that, though, whatever they used had to be big enough for them to gain serious speed. The GravPacks couldn't push you to interplanetary speeds by leveraging against a small rock—they needed a gravity well of decent size to throw things around that fast.

Mud searched with his HUD display again. Still nothing. Not that he expected a rogue stellar body to just wander by, but he needed to check, to keep distracting himself so his hindbrain could gnaw at the issue. There had to be a way to jumpstart their movement again. Mud just couldn't see it. He flipped through the GravPack's manual, something he hadn't needed his thinsuit to display for most of his adult life, and read through the still-familiar text.

Nothing. He wanted to knock his head against a wall, but if they had a wall they wouldn't be in this position. He flipped through settings on his HUD, looking for something, anything that could help. And then he saw a glimmer of hope scroll by.

"Bee, I got us a plan," he said, trying to sound far more confident than he was.

"So you're saying it's really thin and we're in trouble?" She knew his inflections far too well for his liking just then.

"Pretty much," he admitted.

"Thin is better than nothing. When we get back to some sort of base, can we dig out your grandfather's original research and specs on the gravity shell stuff? I can't work out how we stopped without it."

"Yeah, we'll need it to work out the comm issue, too. I'll get the parents on it. So, ready to go back to the *Amalfi*?"

"More than," she said. "How're we doing this?"

"Give me your GravPack," he said.

"Wait, seriously?"

"Yeah," he said, unspooling a length of heavy-duty tow cable from a compartment in the side of his GravPack.

"No, but," she said, seeing where this was headed, "having the GravPacks linked and pushing then pulling against each other would get us started, but the time it would take us to get to any decent speed would be far out of range of our air supply."

"Sure, if we were doing that," he agreed. "GravPack please?"

Bee took her GravPack off and pushed it across space to him. He grabbed it and sent a small strand toward her, pulling her over to him. He attached the tow cable to her GravPack and hooked the other end to himself.

"Wait, but even if whatever you have cooked up works, two people riding one GravPack at that sort of speed, is that possible?"

"It's been done," he said. "At least once I know of. But it isn't pretty. It'll work, though. I know that."

"There is no part of this I'm going to like, is there?"

"Bee, there's no part of this that I like, so...nope," he told her, opening her GravPack's access panel and messing with the wiring. "So here's the plan. We spin the stupid thing."

Bee's eyebrows rose slowly. "So an arc of repulsion on my GravPack at an angle to spin it on the cable?"

"While your pack has a strand of attraction to mine. We should be able to get the centripetal to something insane, then we cut bait and leave." He closed the access panel. "Better, the attraction strand should carry your pack with us. I've hotwired it a bit, so that it'll shut down and blow on a distance relative to us. We can't leave this tech floating and can't take it with us."

"So we have exactly one shot at this," she said, shaking her head. "But the centripetal forces involved will kill us. We'll have to be spinning at something that would, what, escape orbit on most planets?"

"Something like that," Mud admitted. He grabbed out the tow cable from her GravPack and hooked that to himself as well. Then he handed the other end to Bee.

"That sort of force, focused on us, even if the tow line holds—" She attached herself to the tow cable between them, making sure the line had almost no play. They couldn't afford to be separated by much of any distance for this to work.

"That, I'm sure of."

"Fine, so the tow line holds and we end up crushed to death."

"The gravity shields should be able to compensate. In a straight line it's fine, of course, otherwise we couldn't do the speeds we normally do. It's the constant vector changes from the spinning—I think the shields can compensate. They should be able to."

"See, Mud, that 'should' is my problem. 'Should' isn't a great measure for this."

"I'm open to other ideas, but this is all I got." He pushed Bee's GravPack away from them, letting it play out the tow line.

"I really wish I had a better idea," she said, wrapping an arm around Mud's side. "This is going to suck."

"I know," he said, setting up the angled strands in advance. "Even if the shields hold, given the angular momentum at play, and the fact they'll have to constantly adapt...there's bound to be some light crushing."

"Light. Crushing," Bee repeated.

"We might break a bone or two, is all I'm saying. Hopefully we won't pass out. If we pass out before we untether, we'll die."

"All right, can you give me back-up controls for your GravPack? Just in case?"

"You got it, shit, sorry I almost forgot that. That's... well, hopefully not necessary but, yeah."

"Just hit the button, Captain."

Mud activated the command structure and Bee's GravPack started to accelerate around them, spinning them in place as the tow line went taut. Mud's GravPack kept up with the angle shifts, pushing the other pack away even as it tried to pull itself closer. They were locked in a battle that spun them around the solo GravPack faster and faster. By making sure to start slow and center the movement against the outer GravPack, Mud ensured they wouldn't spin around each other, but that the rotation would happen according to plan, pushing them ever harder away from the solo GravPack.

Gravitational forces built around them quickly, causing Mud's GravPack to grow ever hotter against his back. He hadn't thought about the heat bleed—normally space is a good enough differential that heat just leeches freely, but the constant forces at play were trapping it against him and threatening to add a new wrinkle to their problem. If his thinsuit melted or charred through, he would be exposed to open space and die.

Then again, he reasoned, if he did, Bee would be fine and she could still control his GravPack and get home. So all wasn't lost, regardless. The forces continued to build, with their spinning happening ever faster. The tow line held, and Bee was glad they weren't in an atmosphere that could carry the sound of the cable straining. She knew that sound would drive her to utter distraction.

Though, she admitted to herself, a distraction from the forces pushing in on them might be nice. Their protective field started to strain, letting some of the force through. Bee felt her joints creak, cartilage compressing and allowing bone to touch bone in spots.

Mud felt his neck pop and tried to move it, slowly, to see if it was just a case of compression or if he'd broken his damn neck. Compression, thankfully, but the fact he wasn't sure left him uneasy. They were still only at about two-thirds of the speed they needed for this work.

Their speed continued to build. Bee's GravPack, at the center of the storm, sparked once that Mud noticed and he started to worry. If it gave out before they got up to speed, they were dead. If it, instead, exploded, they were also dead, just in a whole different way—and stranger still, to him, would then also fly off in a random direction.

Mud bit back a scream as his left shoulder dislocated. His head pounded, eyes feeling like they were going to explode in his head. He struggled to blink, his eyelids fighting against opening again, and activated his HUD. They were close to speed.

Close, but not there yet.

Mud's eyes closed again and he sank into darkness.

CHAPTER 19

MUD'S EYES OPENED SLOWLY, first noticing the lack of pressure against them. He looked and the starfield moved past him in a straight line. He exhaled slowly. Thankfully.

"Bee?" he asked sluggishly.

"Sir," she said, as lightly as possible. "I ejected us from spinning death in time. I think we have enough speed to reach the range of a gravity well before we stop breathing."

"Thanks."

"No problem, it was my ass on the line, too," Bee said. "What's your status?"

"Shoulder dislocated, vision blurred, and I think my toes might be messed up somehow, but I can't tell. You?"

"Dislocated all the fingers on my right hand," Bee said. "Which is surprisingly painful. I can snap them all back into place, no problem, but I didn't want to risk the pain. One of us has to be awake."

"Go for it, I can fly us for now," he said. "Actually, I can snap them back for you, if you want. It'll be easier."

Bee moved her hand over in front of Mud and he gripped her wrist firmly under his arm, pinning it with his elbow. Using his one good hand, he rotated and popped each of her fingers back into socket.

"Oh hell!" Bee yelled. "I wish I had passed out. Want me to get your shoulder?"

"Are you," he said, "asking as a form of revenge?"

"I will not lie, it'll make me feel better."

Mud rotated his body relative to hers, making sure she didn't let go of his side and drift clear of the single gravity field moving them both through space. "Go for it."

He inhaled and bit back a scream as she popped his shoulder back into its socket. His vision swam and he fought back bile, struggling to neither throw up nor pass out again. "We're even," he choked out. "Happier?"

"Not really, but I'm also not in more pain, so I'll take it."

"Great. I show a planet-sized gravity well in range in about an hour. We'll get closer than just on the edge of it and stop, adjust course, and hard burn home. Sound good?"

"Sounds good. Do long-range comms work?"

"I think so. Want to send a burst home, just a status and arrival time and that we'll fill them in when we get there?" he asked. He still didn't like the idea of using long-range comms when they didn't absolutely need to.

"Exactly my thought," Bee agreed.

Bee prepped the message and sent it, then shut her comms back off. It was about as far from protocol as you could get, but she agreed with Mud's feeling on the comm units just now and wasn't in the mood to argue with anyone at base over it.

They continued in silence, both of them nursing their pains, until they reached the nearest gravity well. Mud slowed them to a stop and they floated free for a minute, gathering themselves.

They used the remaining tow cable to redo Bee's anchoring to Mud, then set up a new route home. Before they launched, Mud unstrapped his

GravPack and opened it to space, insisting they both give it as good of a once-over as possible in their current conditions. The internals were lightly singed, but nothing seemed as if it would give out during a hard-burn faster than light for the amount of time they'd need it.

They hoped.

Shutting the access panel, Mud slung the GravPack back on and called up his HUD, triple-checking their route home. Everything checked out. He took a deep breath and accepted the parameters. The GravPack sprang to life and they shot forward, gaining speed until reality itself seemed to stop caring about them and they broke the light-speed barrier.

Up until just a few hours ago, he'd never given that much consideration, Mud thought. Going faster than light via GravPack was a quirk, a bonus feature in a world that often needed them to survive. It had never mattered how it all worked because it just worked. There didn't seem to be a downside, except for the scientists who tore their hair out wondering how it kept working every single time.

None of them, that Mud had ever even heard a whisper of, not even his grandfather, had seen the problem. Hell, Mud wasn't even sure he and Bee were correct yet, but everything pointed in that direction. They were seemingly messing with, in different ways, another universe. Mud tried to imagine how he would feel if something like that happened to his universe and then stopped.

What if, he thought, it *was* happening to his universe. How would he know? The entire thing would just be events that seemed completely normal for how things worked. Mud laughed to himself and tried to get off the paranoia train his brain was riding. Not an easy task, but he focused, instead, on how they would go about proving or disproving their theory, sure that Bee already stood three steps ahead of him on the plan.

He wasn't wrong. Bee'd spent the entire trip back so far working on what she'd need to discover the reality behind their guesses. She trusted herself, and Mud, but trusted actual provable facts more whenever possible. She had a plan. Now, she knew, she'd just need to put it in motion and gather the proper resources.

In silence, each lost in their thoughts of the future, they continued on through the darkness of space. They came around to where the Fold had stood, now long gone, and saw a large Gov ship, broken in two, dead, each half spinning, floating away from the other. Ragged edges exposed to space with spires of ice sprouting from broken pipping.

"Is that—"

"*Ratzinger,*" Mud confirmed. "What happened while we were gone?"

"And where'd the *Amalfi* go?" Bee asked. She turned her comms back on and sent a location ping request to both the *Amalfi* and the *Arrow*. They came back quickly, from the same location. "I have a location, so that's something. Here," she said, showing Mud the coordinates, "zero in and let's work this out."

Mud followed the readings and there, behind a relatively close rock the size of a small moon, hung the *Amalfi*. The ship looked fully operational, and they headed right toward it, thankful.

They remained that way right until they docked, landing on a hangar deck next to the *Arrow*, waved in with simple voice commands now that their short-range comms could take over. The Insertion Team, plus Bushfield and Mills, met them on the deck, all of them looking angry.

"Don't even try to explain yet. Follow me," Mills said, turning as he spoke and walking away. The team followed him and Mud and Bee trailed along, unhappily.

"Sarah," Bee asked Bushfield softly, "what's going on?"

"Your long-range comms worked," Bushfield told her, "but you turned them off. No data, no anything, after you vanish in the Fold? You got a lot of people mad at you. Including two you don't want angry in your direction."

"Oh no," Mud said, overhearing.

"Yup," Bushfield confirmed. "And thanks for that. We've been getting our asses chewed for a while now. Mills figures it's your turn."

They took a lift up a few levels, no one else talking, and moved down a hallway full of executive offices until they came to Mills' newest office. Larger than his old one—the *Amalfi*, in its day, treated staff well. A looming desk stood on one side of the room, with chairs in front of it. Against the far wall, a good fifteen feet away, an oversized screen hung. Bee realized Mills' office might be larger than her little apartment on Bercuser and sighed.

"All right, you two," Mills said, moving behind his desk, "you have a lot to explain."

"Yeah, look, Mills, there's a reason for everything. But how's Steelbox?" Mud asked, looking at the man in question. His arm seemed fine, no cast or sling or even bandages visible. "And what happened to the *Ratzinger*?"

"Hold on," Mills said, typing on a control pad on his desk, "let me just...there."

The screen at the end of the room sprang to glowing life. On it were two people, both with tight-buzzed haircuts. In their sixties, they both still seemed more active than people a third of their age. Lines creased their faces but their eyes shone, currently flashing with anger and worry.

"Mills, thanks, son," said Jonah Madison from the screen. "This is your op and all, but mind if Shae and I take a whack at this first?"

"Oh, Jonah, it would be my pleasure," Mills said. He stood behind his desk—the Insertion Team stood in front of it, making sure Mills could be seen. Mud and Bee stood off a bit to the side.

"Uhm, hi, Dad. Mom," Mud said, feeling suddenly like a ten-year old caught shoplifting.

"Newt—" Jonah started, using Mud's childhood nickname.

"Soldier, no," Shae stopped him, a hand on his arm. "Mud, be grateful Mills is letting us run this show. You went on an illegal op, disobeyed direct orders on timing, and then willingly turned off communications after? This should be a full-on inquiry right now."

"Do you have," Mud asked in reply, "Granddad's gravity research? All of it? The GravPack testing and more?"

"What does that have to do with—"

"Jonah," Bee cut him off, "it has everything to do with everything." Mud and Bee looked at each other, and Mud nodded. "Long-range communications use gravity tech, don't they?" she asked the room.

"Yes, I'm not sure how, but yes," Mills said.

"Sure," Jonah agreed.

"That's the problem," Bee continued, "somehow they cross into a different universe, and the other universe is sick of it."

"You broke the barrier?" Shae asked quickly. "That's not...you should never—"

"You pulled it off?" Jonah asked, cutting his wife short. "We never could figure out how to safely." He went from angry to impressed and curious as if a switch had flipped.

"Yeah, we did. That's what the Fold was," Mud said. "So we did our job and investigated. Mills," he said, turning, "the Fold was an active possible threat. So we went in. That's what you pay us to do. I'm sorry it wasn't on your timetable, but the universe doesn't allow us to work that way sometimes." He turned back to the screen. "Mom. Dad. Quick question. Hell," he looked at his team, bringing them into the conversation, "all of you, tell me. If you found out that long-range comms caused problems for an innocent culture, if they seemed to be possibly harming them, would you continue to use them?"

Everyone stood silent for a few seconds while they digested the concept.

"Well," Steelbox said, "no, of course not."

"All right, so let's move past that and solve this."

"Now hold on," Mills said, "you can't just wave a wand and make this vanish, this was a mistake on every front."

"Maybe," Shae said, "let's work through it. I'm not

184

sure anymore. Jonah?"

"I'll get the plans and shoot them over. But Mud, if long-range comms are a problem, should we come down there instead of this?"

"No," Bee said, almost too quickly, "we understand we have to use them sometimes, but we made a call out there and both stand by it. So let's move on."

"We can't just move on," Bushfield said, "you might've been dead, or in trouble, or—"

"Or doing our jobs," Bee said softly. "Let's keep doing them." She looked at Bushfield and the two spoke without words for a moment, settling their anxiety about each other. "Because this is bigger than even that, possibly."

"Oh, right," Mud said, "Olivet, we solved the Bercuser mystery and know what the mists are."

"Wait, what?" Olivet said, shaking his head.

"Dad, get those plans and let's find a better space to work in, and we can go over everything. All right?"

"Sounds good," Jonah said. "Mills, we'll wait for a call. Say reconvene in thirty?"

"Thirty is good. And thanks, guys," Mud said, turning away from the screen as it went dark. "So, Mills, got a workspace for us?"

CHAPTER 20

THIRTY-SEVEN MINUTES LATER, in a workspace best described as 'cluttered,' Mud and Bee spread out their sensors, each hooked up to a terminal to display findings. Along with that, a set of cameras ringed the table, showing the view to Jonah and Shae, who were visible on a screen at one end of the large table. A two-screen display showed the original gravity research and notes from Doctor Williams.

"Where's Steelbox?" Chellox asked, even as the one missing member of the team came rushing into the room.

"Sorry, I had to find where I put them in all the evac rush," he said, laying out the two star charts he'd been studying.

"Bee," Mud said, "it's your show."

"I haven't had time to really dig into the Williams research," she said. "But I can already see that Mud and I were right. Long-range comms work by wrapping packet data in small gravity shields and accelerating them, the same as GravPacks, so they can move at highly insane speeds."

"Wait, but then how does that work?" Olivet asked. "If that's true, then they'd have to all be point to point, but multiple ships can pick up, even intercept, long-range comm traffic, which would indicate they're broadband, not focused."

"Sure," Bee agreed, "if normal physics applied. But they don't, the same way they don't apply to the GravPacks. It turns out that if you can accelerate

186

something fast enough, it can slide out of our universe—either just a bit and ride the barrier, like a GravPack does, or, if it's even smaller, breach completely. It's that total breach that allows the impression of broadband. Doctor Williams didn't actually solve long-range instant communications, he faked it. The other universe runs on slightly different rules. Space isn't the same, and neither is time. I'm not entirely sure how this all works, and I don't know that Doctor Williams was either, honestly. But it does, and this is a large part of how."

"The problem starts," Mud said, looking at Bee for her approval to continue—she nodded and he went on, "with the realization that the packets, when crossed, are flooding the other universe, which we're going to need a name for. Anyway," he continued, "they're fighting back. They have these guns, or something, that cast a wide beam and destroy the messages."

"I've been thinking about them. Look at this data," Bee said, calling up one of her sensor's readings. "The beam from those guns disrupts gravity—well, our version of it, at least. Which is off from theirs, which is why the GravPacks stuggled over there. Similar, but not quite the same. The guns disrupt it, and the packets either pop back into our universe or are dispersed, I'm not sure. Either way, those weapons pose a serious problem for us. If one hit us square, it could destroy a GravPack and, like the packets, I don't know what happens next."

"I think the beings on the other side are natural disruptors of our version of gravity," Mud said. "It'd explain what happened to Steelbox when he brushed against that creature. A localized disruption of his own internal gravity along one arm? It'd hurt like a bitch but cause no lasting harm if contact was brief enough."

"But then," Chellox said, "wouldn't it have been in extreme pain when it was sliding along the *Ratzinger*?"

"Yup," Bee confirmed. "And we saw a few of those larger beasts on the other side. My guess is that the Fold wasn't planned. The beast was in pain, probably from so many packets hitting it, and it breached at a soft spot and tried to work out why the *Ratzinger* kept hurting it."

"All right, then why did it," Mills asked, "decide to break the ship in half later, just before the Fold closed?"

"Dumb beast, caused itself more pain trying to stop the pain, so it lashed out?" Mud guessed. "There's still a ton we don't know."

"But the barrier, you saw it?" Jonah asked.

"We breached the Fold and ended up in the other universe. Then, once we came back, we hit overdrive while at full throttle on a GravPack and could physically see the barrier around us," Mud told his father.

"Which seems to be why," Bee said, calling up a section of gravity research, "Doctor Williams capped the throttle where he did. He knew the barrier existed and found the line to draw."

"We knew there was a barrier," Shae said, "and to stay away from it—except that one time, remember that?" she asked her husband.

"With the really tall pink scaly things?" he replied.

"Yes," Shae laughed, "and you had to overdrive us out because they could latch on, and—"

"Mom, come on. Dad, let's stay on topic," Mud said, trying to not sound annoyed.

"Sorry," Shae said, "anyway, yes we knew there was a barrier, but all my father would say was that getting too close to it would destroy us."

"Which, it turns out, isn't quite the case," Mud said. "But I see why he wanted to keep you all away from breaching."

"I'm not even sure a full breach can just happen anywhere," Bee said. "I think there are soft spots where it's possible, but otherwise...think of it as a wall, all right? There are places in the wall where the surface has worn down, and you can get through those easily with some force. Breaking the wall where it's still strong, though, would take a lot more force."

"And you don't even need to fully breach for some strange things to happen," Steelbox said. "I think you're dead on about the soft spots." He pulled over his star charts. "I had been working on the Bercuser problem myself, just in my spare time, right? And I noticed this," he pointed at the maps, overlaying each other. "See how the two systems Bercuser inhabits line up when you overlay them, but flip one totally? Just one hundred and eighty degrees and suddenly..." he made sure one of the cameras pointed at the maps, while his team looked on.

"They match," Jonah said.

"Perfectly," Shae added. "How did not one ever catch that?"

"Because," Steelbox said, "they didn't used to." Everyone stared at him, confused. "These star chats are recent, around fifty years old. But if you go back before that, they don't line up, not enough to be spooky, right? But when you take a few hundred years of charts and stack them all, flipping the same set the same way...the systems have drifted into a reverse-identical layout."

"How?" Mills asked, flipping through star charts.

"I couldn't begin to guess," Steelbox said, "until Bee and Mud handed it to me. If the other universe has a different concept of gravity and Bercuser breaches—"

"I don't think it fully breaches, though—" Mud pointed out.

"Even if it slides along the barrier," Steelbox said, "it's going to cause hell for nearby space that just gets exposed and washed in that crap, right? And over enough time, I think the gravity differences have been trying to stabilize as best they can, orbits and all just matching up."

"Are we sure this is how Bercuser moves?" Olivet asked. Everyone looked at him and fell silent. One by one they realized they'd been discussing his home world, revealing a secret no one knew. They couldn't predict how the planet's population would react to such a revelation, much less this one man. "That's it, all of our myths, our history, and relationship to the mists, our culture, everything is just an accident of nature?"

"Accident, yeah, probably," Mud said, "but not of nature. Chances are—and this is a guess, I don't know where we'd find records—but if someone else, someone from Bercuser, tried to build a gravity engine, before Granddad did, and pushed it too far, it could've taken the whole planet and upset things."

"And the mist?" Olivet asked. "Just all in our

heads?"

"The opposite, really," Mud told him, smiling. "It's particulate matter moving at strange speeds both faster than light and—I don't know how to make this make sense—faster than light but still slower at the same time. The mists are strange stuff, and given the particles involved, they could easily, if you'd adapted to ingesting them, allow you to see possibility waveforms before they collapse. Sometimes."

"They're real?"

"They are," Mud agreed. "And stranger than we could've imagined. It explains why any scan of them made no sense. Because they make no sense. We just know why now."

Olivet looked around the room, then back at the star charts and data on the screens. "When this is over, I wish to go home and explain the new truth to my people."

"Of course," Mills told him.

"Thank you. So, these soft spots—the accident on Bercuser, or whatever did truly happen, you think that caused a soft spot to form?" he asked Steelbox.

"Maybe? Or maybe the soft spot already existed in both places and the accident, or whatever, just pushed through. I mean, if there's a soft spot near here, I don't know if an accident caused it."

"But, circling back," Bee said, "I do have to wonder, if we're all right on the soft-spot-being-the-only-place-to-breach concept. How do communications packets breach fully every damn time?"

"Size, or maybe that they're not physical objects," Chellox offered. "But more to the point, what are we going to do about it?"

"Go talk to them," Jonah said. "Make sure the problem is what we think it is. Bring them in on this. They know more than we do about their own universe, I promise."

"Jonah's right," Mills said, "so how do we talk to them?"

"I recorded them, along with everything else. Mud got them to understand us some through sign, but we mapped it to words as well, so we might have some translatable data. But their language is so unlike anything we've heard."

"Bee, that's what humanity has said after each new race we've run into," Shae told her. "How about you, me, and Olivet work on that?"

"May I join as well?" Chellox asked. "I can offer an angle on this that you humans will not have, being from one of those other races."

"Great," Bee said, "we'll set up a small war room for translation efforts."

"And the rest of us will work up an insertion plan," Mud said. "We need to find a way in that can cover us when we get out, since we can't take ships."

"Why can't we?" Mills asked.

"Something in that universe kills engine cells. Specifically, whatever is in the mix there. When the Fold opened wide enough, that's what did Bushfield's engine in, and then the *Ratzinger* when the creature touched it." Mud switched one of the screens over to a display from a sensor showing what he meant. "See there? That leeching, that's what I mean. We send a ship in, it'll deadstick instantly."

"Then how do normal craft land on and leave from Bercuser?" Mills asked.

"They," Olivet stopped and looked at Mills. "Wait, how do you not know this? We allow normal ships landing graces so long as they empty or load cargo and passengers quickly and leave. We have long established that ships caught during transition would not be able to fly. We thought the fuel loss was a side effect of the...I guess it really is."

Mills shook his head. "Then what do you do for fuel cells on Bercuser?"

"We have special shielded packs that can survive the planet shift." He stopped again, realizing what he'd just said. "Yes, but we won't be able to get our hands on the technology quickly. The adapted packs are not compatible with normal-use fuel ports and carriages. There would be an entire retrofit exchange needing to be built. Questions would also be asked, and we'd have to answer them. Those answers...I do not yet know how my people will take this information."

"So we're back to GravPacks only," Mud said. "Let's go and work out an insertion plan that includes extraction and retrieval, all right?"

Mills laughed. "Both groups are going to use a different space? Guys, one set of you stay here? We haven't finished moving into the *Amalfi* yet. You don't get all of it. Translation group, come with me. The rest of you stay here and work. I'll run go-between for both groups."

"Thanks, Mills," Mud and Jonah said simultaneously. Father and son eyed each other through a monitor. Jonah ran a hand through his short hair and laughed. Mud shook his head and pulled over star charts. They got to work.

CHAPTER 21

CHELLOX, BEE, AND OLIVET set up a smaller room, flipping on a monitor and relinking Shae in. Bee called up translation data histories while also queuing her recordings of the Sweepers. She played the recordings for the room.

"That static, is that in the recording?" Shae asked.

"No, that's part of their vocalization."

"Many nonhuman species use sounds you can't replicate," Chellox said, "which is why, I assume, almost no one speaks Tsyfarian but we learn your languages all right. Your vocal ranges are *tiny*."

"They really are," Olivet agreed. "I worked with Chellox on my Tsyfarian and at best I sound like a small child with a dislocated jaw."

Chellox laughed, "Close, yes."

"All right, but we can replicate it digitally," Bee said. "We just need to translate it. These sections here," she chose a selection of recording, playing it for the room, "is Mud saying our names and the Sweepers repeating them. We think. At least, they seemed to repeat the same sounds each time. So we have to go down that road."

"The problem is," Shae said as Bee ran the recordings through a program designed to break speech down and translate it, "your names have no sounds in common, so I'm not sure what we can really claim here."

Bee frowned and thought for a minute before brightening, "Fold! I'm sure we had them repeat Fold as well! That will tell us at least one letter, one sound length. We can average and see if the math works from there."

"It'll give us a guess," Chellox said, "but this is thin, frankly."

"It is, Bee," Olivet agreed. "But it's what we have, so let's try it."

"One thought," Shae said. "Listen to Mud's voice here. What's wrong with it?"

"Their...atmosphere? Whatever it was that allowed sound to carry in what should have been space, it made us sound like that."

"Right, sure," Shae said quickly, "so modulate all the recordings back until Mud sounds normal. We need to hear how they would sound in our atmosphere if we except a computer to speak, in their universe, and have it sound right."

"Wait, what?" Olivet looked at Shae in the monitor.

"Whale calls. Sound moves differently in water than air. So a recorded whale song sounded deep and thick to us, but if we adjusted for how the sound would move in air, they were completely different. Now, if you play a whale song recorded underwater while underwater, the water would slow the sound waves down *again*, see?"

"Of course," Bee said, shaking her head. "Thank you." She set about restructuring her program to take medium into account.

They continued to work, deep into the night.

Back in the other meeting room, Mud and his sub-team worked out a tentative plan for insertion and extraction. There remained one major sticking point in the plan.

"If your mother and I leave now and hard burn, we can be there in time."

"Dad," Mud said with a sigh, "stay home. Please. We have this under control."

"We really do, Jonah," Bushfield added.

"This one is big," Jonah said, "it's damned big, and the more hands on deck the smoother—"

"Nope," Mud insisted. "I need you and Mom as backup. If this entire thing goes sideways, you'll need to come to our rescue. But until then, until Mills calls you in, you need to stay put."

"Shouldn't we at least head to the *Amalfi*, and—"

"And what if another creature comes out of a new Fold and attacks this time? Or a hundred other things. Like you said, you're not that far. So the best thing is to stay put."

"You just don't want your old, annoying parents sticking their noses in and taking over," Jonah told his son.

"You want me to deny that's a part of it? Of course that's part of this, Dad. This is my team now, and if you guys jump in every time something big happens, how will you ever enjoy being retired?"

"Who said I enjoyed it?"

"You did, a few weeks ago."

"Jonah," Mills cut in, "hang back. I promise I'll call you in the second I need to."

"This is what you all want?"

"It is," Mud said. "And it isn't personal. But we have a team that's used to working together." He wished he was as fully confident in his team and his skills as he forced himself to sound. "Shaking that up in the middle of a mission never works out well. You taught me that."

"Fine. But, Mills?"

"Jonah?"

"I expect regular updates."

"Of course. Now," Mills said, "about the deployment areas—how many ships are we really talking?" He pulled up the star chats they'd focused on and started marking them up, working out how he could swing the manpower needed for the operation to go smooth.

They kept working, determined to get this right—and to not risk lives any more than was actually needed to get the job done.

When they finished, they shut off the monitor connecting Jonah and went for food. Most mess halls and commissaries in giant Gov ships were simple grey affairs, all industrial footprint and no personality. That night, Mud's team brought personality with them. They drank, they partook, they reveled. If not quite as heartily as they might have liked, given a mission launching the next morning, they still made sure to attempt a memorable evening of friends and teammates.

An hour or so into their evening, Bee's translation team joined them, settling deeply into chairs. Exhaustion draped over the table, and yet they enjoyed themselves. Most missions they stayed away from any sort of preassignment quasi-party. Not out a sense of decorum, but because throwing yourself a little party before you left made the mission feel doomed. The celebration would feel funereal, even if only accidently.

This night, however, that was intentional. Each one of them felt it. A pall loomed over them, and they fought it back the only way any of them could think of. Denial, fueled by laughter and mostly decent food. Mud and Bee had only survived an insertion into the other universe by a shade of luck. That time, nothing had even tried to attack them. This time, they couldn't be sure that would hold—and worse, they had exactly zero idea of what an attack would honestly consist of.

None of them could even be sure that communication beyond basic hand gestures sat in the realm of the possible. No part of their plan felt secure. But still, they planned departure times. They laid out resources and goal markers. They did their jobs and never gave voice to their concerns, seeing as how they were shared and unsolvable.

Late in the night they departed, each to their own restless sleep.

CHAPTER 22

THE INSERTION TEAM STRAPPED on GravPacks and stood around the hangar of the *Amalfi*, waiting. Bushfield and her fighter unit loaded into their ships and performed system checks. They needed to leave first, for the plan to work, but the *Amalfi's* older infrastructure proved hard to deal with and the ready teams rushed, trying to make sure everything actually worked before they launched ships.

Far later than Mud would have liked, Bushfield led her team out and they broke off, still in visible range, heading in different directions. Each fighter trailed a small environmental enclosure, neither fancy nor comfortable, but designed to keep living creatures alive.

Bee looked at a time readout along the arm of her thinsuit and resisted the urge to tap her foot. The longer it took to get underway, the worse the mission felt. She shifted the gear strapped to her, and then went and helped Olivet recheck his own gear, the two acting as the translation team for the mission.

Mud also checked the time and looked around the hangar. "Insertion Team mission status green," he said into his communicator. "Off and hot in five."

"About time," Bee said, patting herself down and checking suit seals one final time.

"Are you sure we can't take the *Arrow* to the soft spot, at least?" Chellox asked. "The GravPacks are just annoying."

"They're all we have," Steelbox reminded him, "so hey, we'll be fine. We've all logged enough hours by now."

"You guys have been briefed on what breaching felt like and how the GravPacks performed in the other universe," Mud told them, "and you're ready for this. Just remember," he looked at each of them in turn: Steelbox, Bee, Chellox, and Olivet, "no one can predict what's about to happen. We do our best, we watch each other's backs, and we survive. Above all, we all come back safe. Understood?"

They all nodded, prompting Mud to nod in return before he walked toward the edge of the hangar. A thin gravity shield stood between him and open space. The team walked up around him, meeting him at the edge. "Go in three...two ..." Mud stepped off the edge and walked out into the blackness, followed by his team.

One by one they activated their GravPacks and flew in light formation around the *Amalfi*, doing a systems check. Satisfied everything worked, they got down to it.

"Soft spot should be where we remember it," Mud said.

"If it's still there," Bee added.

"Only one way to find out," Olivet said, trying to sound confident.

"Right. We'll loop the *Amalfi* again, head over to the wreckage of the *Ratzinger*, then switch strands and build to full throttle. Stay in formation and on target."

As they completed their loop, they fell into a V formation, with Mud on point, and headed to the *Ratzinger*.

They switched as planned and started to accelerate hard away from the wreckage, toward the location of the Fold. Open space loomed in front of them and they rushed right toward it. Their speeds crept up through percentages of light speed, and they logged distance quickly. A final coordinated push and—

Breach.

No Fold spun in space to give them access. No tear in the fabric eased their transition between universes. The soft spot, such as it was, allowed them to breach and tumble into the other universe, but the reality they'd started in fought back.

Their atoms belonged to one universe, and that universe wanted to keep those particles for itself. Each member of the Insertion Team could feel their molecular mass struggle to keep cohesion as they slid roughly from one universe into another.

To reduce the sensation to the simplest terms: It hurt. Luckily for all of them, their consciousness also shattered briefly, along with their atomic structure, and so much of the memory of exactly how much breaching hurt drifted off of them like an oil slick. The small slice of pain that did stay in their conscious minds wrenched screams from all of them.

Technically none of them actually passed out during the flip between universes, but they each felt as if they had. Struggling to regain cognizance, they drifted along in the other universe for precious seconds. The change in light, blurring hard edges, didn't help any more than the constant color-shifting as everything they looked at either red- or blue-shifted depending on relative direction.

"You could've warned us—" Olivet said sluggishly.

"Man, trust me," Steelbox said, "it wasn't like this last time. I wouldn't have come back if it had been. Cap, what the hell?"

"No Fold, no light, we had to punch through," Mud said, his eyes adjusting quickly. He'd been here before and could at least remember what feeling normal passed for in this place. "I'm guessing the universe doesn't like that."

"Universes," Bee corrected, "that, I agree, don't like fraternization." She looked around, checking readings from her thinsuit. "But we'll have to adjust quickly. Sweepers incoming."

She pointed subtly, the others following her direction, seeing the Sweepers for the first time. As they focused in on them, the Insertion Team started to notice the pellets in the sky—for the space they floated in still didn't look or behave quite like open space, but more of a swimming sky. The pellets, long-range messages, were scarcer around them than in the distance, but still strange to look at. Chellox tried counting them and gave up, wondering instead how he would feel if his precious flight routes were busied up with that much raw noise.

"Remember, don't touch them, or let their beams touch you," Mud said softly. He turned toward the Sweepers and raised his hands. They stopped and he tried a few of the gestures they'd worked out last time, but these weren't the same beings, and word apparently hadn't spread yet.

One of the Sweepers spoke to them, and Bee, having grabbed one of her translation devices, watched the readouts closely. "I think... no, wait, hold on."

"Do we have 'hold on' time?" Steelbox asked. He felt ill being in the other universe, physically.

"We have to," Mud said. "Bee, what do we have? I can rebuild hand signals if you need."

"No, let's see ..." she hit a few buttons and put a small mic up to her throat. Their voices already sounded odd to them. Hopefully, if nothing else, her device could compensate and reproduce the correct frequencies.

"We mean no harm, come to solve problem," she said. Static came out of her translation device, followed by a few halting sounds as the computer system parsed data slowly, by design. Messy translations worked better slowly, she reasoned, giving everyone time to tweeze out meaning.

The Sweeper who had taken charge waved four of its limbs in what Olivet judged to be excitement. Speaking again, it jumbled a mass of static and sounds out quickly, and Bee had to wave her hands and mime stretching to try to get across the idea that too fast would make the translator trip up. Seeming to understand, the Sweeper spoke again, slower.

"You (untranslatable) the space (untranslatable) noise yours remove," came the translation, after a few seconds

"Well that works," Mud said. "Amazing job. It'll learn as we go?"

"That's the idea," Bee agreed. "So let's get to work."

They started by trying to find a good term for the pellets, and then took blame for them, on behalf of their universe. They didn't equivocate or try to dodge it—they simply accepted it and tried, then, to explain its importance.

The Sweepers started to argue amongst themselves. The leader wanted to do something with the Insertion Team, and they weren't quite sure what that might be, but it didn't sound promising. Other Sweepers disagreed and thought the team could help them with the problem. Obviously, the team backed this plan. Still, the Sweepers' leader seemed unconvinced.

"Stay and (untranslatable) until (untranslatable)," he said.

"Too many blanks for my taste," Steelbox said.

"Agreed," Chellox said. "Should we leave, come back with better data to show them what we mean? Maybe with a plan to reduce communications?"

"That sort of plan could take weeks, and if they ramp this up the way they have been, I don't know if we have weeks," Mud told him. "We want to help," Mud said into Bee's translator, "to work with you, not against you. We desire a peace treaty to work together going forward."

As the translator chewed through that, Bee shook her head, "I feel like there's something not getting across right. An idea. Something."

"No, we're getting our ideas over," Mud said, "But this guy wants to be Leader so bad he's willing to strut for it."

"Could we bring him to our universe and maybe that would help?" Olivet asked.

"We can offer, we should," Mud said, "but right this second, that offer would sink fast. They want to keep us here, possibly lock us up or worse. Suggesting we just abscond with their leader..."

"Not abscond, go with of their own volition," Olivet said.

"Yeah," Mud said, "I get that. You get that. Will they? It's risky. I think we make the offer but we can't push it hard."

"Also," Chellox said quickly, "remember, we don't know if the move would kill them. We're wearing environmental suits. Are they? What happens in our version of hard vacuum?"

Mud nodded. "And of course we didn't bring anything. But we wouldn't know what to anyway. Right. All right. Let's try and discuss it with them."

Mud turned back to the Sweepers. "Does your leader wish to come back to our universe? To discuss peace with our other leaders?" he said, and waited. Bee's translator burst out the message, and the Sweeper who seemed to be in charge recoiled physically. The Sweepers spoke quickly amongst themselves, gesturing at the Insertion Team with short, sharp jabs.

"They're going too fast, we can't get almost anything," Bee said, watching the readout. "Not putting it to audible, no point, just words—but none are good."

"Angry, hostile, or both?" Olivet asked softly.

"Both. Mud, we might have to move," Bee said, glancing between readouts and the Sweepers. "This could go south fast."

"Not yet," Mud said. "Let's translate this." He thought for a moment. "Together. No harm. Peace." The translator did its job and some of the Sweepers seemed to calm down, but others, including their leader, did not.

One of the Sweepers raised a gun. Mud held a

hand out toward his team, holding them where they floated. The other Sweepers noticed the weapon being raised and started to fall silent, watching.

"They're not stopping him," Chellox said.

"Get ready to scatter, but we can't react early," Mud said.

"Cap, if we wait, we get shot first and then react—not a great plan," Steelbox said.

Mud shifted himself, aligning the team subtly until the gun pointed directly at him and wouldn't get a clear shot at anyone else. "I know," Mud admitted, "but if we move now, trust me, this blows apart."

The Sweeper with the raised gun pushed his way through the ranks of his own people, making sure he was next to his leader, weapon still aimed. Mud floated, hands up and palms out, facing down the Sweeper. Mud tried to remind himself that life varied enough that he couldn't actually come close to reading the Sweeper's expression. Cultural differences, not to mention biological ones, meant the physical cues he knew, even from other races, simply couldn't apply here.

He knew that, deep in his bones. He still floated, convinced he could see desperation, layered over a desire to prove something, in the eyes and face of the Sweeper. The look of a being ready to kill to gain an inch of status. He decided, instead, to shift focus. Mud stared at the gun pointed at him, identifying the trigger mechanism and the digit of the Sweeper resting against it. The business end, a flat, wide opening, pointed right at him. He kept watch on it.

The expression, the intent, of the Sweeper didn't matter against the digit on the trigger and the angle of that barrel. Those became Mud's world, even as he continued to gesture surrender and peace. "We want only peace," he said, letting the translator work for him, "no anger. Peace."

A tightening on the trigger.

A spark of energy along the barrel of the gun.

Mud moved without thinking, shoving hard into his team to get them out of the way, even as he rotated his body to present a larger target. The shot hit him in the legs and Mud screamed, feeling disruption wash over his body. The shot felt like the needles of his suit ramped up by a hundred. His legs went numb, and he felt thankful for it even as he hoped it wasn't permanent.

"Extract," Bee yelled.

"How?" Olivet asked.

"Run first, plan on the way," Mud said, fighting to keep his voice level. "But do *not* return fire yet."

The Sweepers advanced on them, and Mud couldn't be sure their intentions. None of the others raised a weapon, and the Sweeper who had shot him lowered its weapon. They talked quickly again.

"What are they saying?" Mud asked Bee, while trying to focus on a plan. They could run, and would, but slower than normal, and they had no good direction to choose.

"I'm just getting confusion," Bee said. "I don't think they'll attack again?"

The Sweeper's leader signaled to his people and they stopped advancing. Taking a device from his back, a pouch or some other holder that Mud couldn't see, the leader held it aloft and spoke slowly.

"(untranslatable) false leave (untranslatable)

(untranslatable)."

"All right, they want us gone," Steelbox said, "I agree. How?"

The Sweepers gestured at the leader, and the box in hand. They seemed upset, from the speed of their movements.

"Brace yourselves," Bee said, "This doesn't look..."

Her words were cut off as the Sweeper did something to the box and it exploded in a blinding white light. The Insertion Team felt the light touch them like a physical thing, a hand slapping at their molecular structure. The sensation was utterly different than the gunshot had been—not necessarily as painful, but utterly disturbing in different ways. They felt ripped apart, but almost peacefully.

The sky around them in the other universe dimmed. Olivet thought he might vomit, and tried to catch his breath but couldn't breathe deeply. Chellox passed out from the dislocation, and Bee slapped at sensors along her suit, doing her best to record the event.

Breach.

The Insertion Team fell into their home universe hard, without ceremony. The transition seemed quicker than their last breach, and far more memorably painful. They fought to regain internal balance and coherence. Steelbox noticed Mud floating, seeming to be far more out of it than anyone else. "Cap?" he said, drifting closer with his GravPack.

Mud remained unconscious, even as the rest of the team shook off the effects of the forced breach.

"Did they just toss us out of a universe?" Bee

asked, checking her data. "How could they even—"

"Bee, not now," Olivet said, cutting her off. "Something's wrong with Mud."

"Chellox, locate us and call us whatever pickup team is closest," Bee said, using her GravPack to get to Mud's side quickly, "and tell them we need Medical."

Bee and Steelbox studied Mud, careful to not jostle him. They made sure he was breathing freely and still protected by his suit and gravity field. Past that, they waited while Chellox and Olivet arranged for location and pickup. Mud's plan had worked, if messily and partly by accident.

Bushfield and her team had deployed to Bercuser as well as leaving a small transport ship near the location of the Fold. On top of that, they'd made sure they could get to several points between the two locations quickly, Mud figuring they'd track along the same path that he'd taken with Bee before. Mud's team hadn't gotten far from the Fold, but still far enough from the *Amalfi* that one of the mid-pickup ships arrived to grab them.

They returned to the *Amalfi* at hard burn, docking and meeting medical staff. Mills met them and went with Bee as they rolled Mud to a medical unit. She briefed him as they walked and Mills sighed, breaking off to make a call he dreaded.

Mud came to about half an hour later, foggy and confused. The Insertion Team, as a whole, sat around, and each stood as their leader woke up.

"Cap, you all right?" Steelbox asked quickly.

"I dunno?" Mud said thickly. He looked around. "Are we on the *Amalfi*?"

"All right, I have to ask, I'm sorry," Olivet said, "but

how could you know that? You've never seen the medical bay on this ship."

"Yeah, as of last service," Mud said, shaking his head. "The pipe conduit layout along the wall. It's a design flaw if you wanted to cut power."

"Yeah," Chellox said, "I think he's fine."

"Seems so," Bee agreed. "Are you fine?" she asked to make sure.

"Not sure," Mud admitted. "That blast did me in. Damn it, Steelbox," he said, looking over at the large man, "you never said it hurt that bad."

"I just got grazed, Cap, and it didn't hurt me as much as it seemed to you. But human versus Hurkz, maybe?"

"Maybe," Mud admitted. "Maybe. Still," He struggled to sit up, looked down his body, and tried again. "Hey guys, I'm going to say this as calmly as possible, but I can't really feel my right leg, at all."

Bee patted Mud's right leg gently. "It's right here. Doctor said there didn't seem to be damage, but they were running some final tests."

"Well the doctor's wrong, and their final tests are about to show that. Because I really can't feel it almost at all. A distant sort of hum, maybe, but that's it."

Chellox hmm'd to himself. "We theorized the beams from the weapon disrupted our local gravity concept, correct? So it hurt for Steelbox, but then was fine once his molecular structure reestablished itself. Perhaps you just need more time."

"Or the forced breaching right after interacted," Olivet said. "I don't want to think it, but it has to be possible."

"All right, the doctors can do what they can do,

but we need a work up of possible scenarios they can't imagine," Mud said.

"Mud, we need to let them figure this out," Bee said, shaking her head. "I know this urge—you need to do something, to figure it out, but let's see what they say first."

"Fine," Mud said, dragging his body up the medical bed until he was sitting. "Then get Mills in here and let's do a full debriefing while we wait."

"On it," Steelbox said, turning to talk softly into his suit's communicator. "Mills is on his way, he says."

"Good," Mud said. "Now, Bee, wrestle up some speakers and something to process the translation data. If we use the *Amalfi's* core, we should be able to get much better translations next time."

"Next time?" Chellox asked.

"We can't just sit and do nothing. We still have a mission to complete."

"Of course," Chellox said, "but—"

"But nothing," Mud said. "I think Olivet is right, the gravity disruption followed by a hard breach just made the effects linger." Mud wiggled the toes on his right foot. "I already have more feeling than I did."

"And maybe you'll get more back," Mills said as he entered the room, "but they're still working out what happened. I told them to cross-reference Steelbox's scans and to localize for gravity and molecular problems. Plus they're digging out the old Hurkz biological scans, from when we had to test the cryogenic chamber on you."

"Thanks, Mills," Mud said. He ran a hand over the top of his head slowly, feeling relieved that they were working on the problem. He could wiggle the toes on his right foot—he could even sort of feel the leg, but it didn't respond correctly—that much he knew. He pushed the concern down deep, straight into the valleys of the back of his mind, and tried to focus on the mission again. "So, let's talk what happened."

CHAPTER 23

MILLS CALLED FOR A CONSOLE to be brought in and the team debriefed, going over every point they could remember and had recorded, combing it for deeper truths. The problem, Mud felt, lay in resolution options. Yes, communication stood in their way, but they were, even now as they talked, finding paths forward. The *Amalfi's* processing power dwarfed Bee's remote rigs a thousand times over without stressing. The next time they could talk to the Sweepers they would be able to truly talk.

Mud didn't know what they would say. Everyone had ideas, of course. They played around with each idea in turn, twisting them and braiding them to see if they might hold weight, but in the end, they frankly didn't know enough. Culturally, they didn't have data about the Sweepers, and that would make all the difference, Mud knew. A solution that humanity, that the Gov, would find acceptable for both sides might not begin to come close to viable for the Sweepers on a purely sociological front.

"We're getting nowhere," Mud said, his frustration plain.

"That's not true—we're building a bunch of good cases here, Mud," Bee said.

"Too many, maybe," Mills put in. "We should let it sit for a while."

"We can't," Mud said. "If we let this continue too much longer, Mills, your bosses will decide it's been lingering and take it over themselves. And we know what happens then. Dumb things."

"Hey now," Mills said, "let's not just decide all Gov decisions are bad and only you know the good choices, all right?"

"You guys do seem to want to blow things up first, write a paper about it later," Steelbox said.

"You're just being—"

"Mills, relax," Chellox cut in. "Our point stands. We have a better chance at solving this than someone else does using our data but not our experience."

"If you all hate the Gov so much then why do you work for it?" Mills asked. He couldn't quite tell if his anger lay at feeling forced to defend his bosses or at a sense of betrayal from a team he defended to his bosses constantly.

"Enough," Olivet said, "from all of us. We're all on the same side. Mud, you need to rest. The rest of us can keep working the angles. We'll reconvene in a few hours."

"Fine," Mud said, shaking his head, "but we really don't have much time."

"Agreed," Mills told him. "But we'll make some out of nothing if we have to. I promise, doubts about my superiors aside, I won't let this get kicked out of your roster yet."

"It'll do," Mud said, "since it sort of has to. Fine, get out of here."

The team left with Mills, taking the console and equipment with them, leaving Mud theoretically to rest. He lay there, admitting his own exhaustion to himself but unable to really wind down, spending much of the time trying to move his right leg and wondering what the future held.

A while later, Mud woke up, not remembering

falling asleep, to familiar voices.

"The only thing that'll wake him up is if you insist on keeping me from seeing him."

"Baby—"

"Oh, you're going to side with some military rule, Soldier?"

"No, I'm siding with a medical professional."

"You do that, I'm going to see our son."

"Mom, Dad," Mud said, raising his voice, "I'm awake. Just come in, and don't hurt anyone doing it."

"Mud," Shae Madison said, shoving past a nurse and rushing to her son's bedside, "we came as soon as we heard."

"Mills called us," Jonah said, walking in slowly. Mud noticed, looking at his father, that he was working to hide his limp. Mud wanted to laugh. Did his father think that seeing someone limp would somehow affect Mud himself? Probably did, but that was his dad.

"I figured he would," Mud said, patting his mother's hand where it laid on his shoulder.

"Which is why you didn't call us yourself?" she asked pointedly.

"Mom..."

"Shae, leave Newt be."

"Dad..."

"Sorry, Mud," his father said. "Old habits and dogs and tricks and all that noise. Look, what do you need? Want us to take over the Op?"

"Nope. I just need the latest report from Medical and then we can get back out there."

"I'll get them in here," his mother said, "but Mud, I don't know if you'll be—"

"Let me talk to them," he insisted.

His parents shared a look, making Mud sigh. Of course it wouldn't be good news—he knew that from how his leg felt. But he resolved to find out for himself.

A doctor came in not long after his mother left and returned. The doctor kept her serious face on, the expression a professional wears when they need to deliver bad news to a patient who they can't be sure won't find a way to go irrational.

They exchanged pleasantries, perfunctorily, both Mud and Doctor Henbough sounding as if they'd been issued cue cards for the conversation. Another minute or two of that and Mud ran his hand over his head slowly, then locked eyes with the doctor. "Just hit me with it, will you?"

"A lot of the damage is permeant," she said briskly. "You'll never recover full use of the right leg. However, with time, we think some of the effects of what happened will fade. You'll be back on your feet, within a month, but lingering issues—we just can't be sure yet. Best case, you'll need a cane."

"And worst case?"

"The leg won't support your weight correctly again, and the range of motion will be severely hampered. Either way, field work isn't going to be an option."

Mud closed his eyes and breathed slowly. "That's not going to work for me."

"It's not up to what you want," Henbough said.

"I don't know, Doc," Jonah put in. "I've been working with a bum knee for decades. Your idea of what's acceptable for field work is all paperwork and forms."

"It ignores," Mud said, "that I'm not less capable of anything. I just have to think around it."

"That's my son," Shae said. "We—"

"Were worried I'd be pinned down by this and spiral?" Mud asked. "Are you forgetting who I grew up with? This won't be easy, I know," he told Henbough, "but my job isn't easy to begin with. What I need now is a hip and leg brace that'll let me get moving in a few hours."

"Impossible. I can't sign off on that," she said.

"Then we have a problem," Mud said. "Dad, go force them to work something up for me?"

"Sure thing, Mud." Jonah stalked off, steering the doctor out of the room by force of will.

"And Mom?"

"Mmm?" She was trying to fight the smirk on her face as her son gave them orders.

"Can you wrangle my team back in here? We have work to do."

"They left your comm on the table," she said.

"Oh," Mud laughed, and he grabbed it, calling everyone back. "I *am* going to get through this, right?"

"Are you asking me or telling me?" his mother asked softly.

Mud thought about it and flexed his toes slowly. "Telling you."

"There you are, then."

Neither of them, of course, felt certain the other believed either themselves or each other.

CHAPTER 24

THE INSERTION TEAM, along with Mills, Shae, and Jonah, assembled in Mud's medical bay. Everyone worked to seem properly motivated and optimistic, each of them convinced the others were faking.

"Mills, do they have clearance?" Mud asked, pointing to the draped screen that shielded the right lower side of his body. Doctor Henbough worked there quietly, along with two nurses, attempting to adjust and fit a device to Mud's leg.

"Not really," Mills said, "but they'll be done soon, right, Doctor?"

"Even sooner," Henbough said, "if you continue to talk about us like we're not in the room, I'm sure."

"Sorry," Mud said, "but how is it going?"

"Fine, and I'll be out of your way soon. I don't think this is a good idea, though."

"I get that," Mud told her, "but it needs doing."

"When you come back in worse shape, I won't be surprised," she told him. The rest of the room just watched, not sure what to do while Mud and his doctor fought.

"I won't be, either," Mud told her, "and we'll get there when we get there."

"Well, you're done for now," she said, and moved away from the bed. "The harness and brace combination will allow you to move the leg with mostly normal range at about half the speed you would normally be able to. But," she warned, "it'll hurt after a while. The more it hurts, the more damage you're actually doing to the leg, so just be aware of it."

"Got it."

"Also, I added the power adaptor your friend asked for," she said as she left the room. "But they wouldn't tell me why."

"Clearance levels," Mud told her. "Thanks, Doctor."

Henbough left, her nurses right behind her, annoyed at yet another useless patient. One day, she hoped, she might get a patient who decided to listen, and actually heal. One day.

"We don't," Olivet said as the door closed, "have enough shielded power supplies from Bercuser to equip the *Arrow*, say, but I thought—"

"Yeah," Mud told him, testing the brace and swinging his legs over the side of the bed to stand, slowly and unsteadily, "and thanks for that. When we re-breach I'll need it."

"Also," Bee said, "you might need this." She grabbed a metal stick from where it rested against a corner in the room and passed it to Mud.

The staff stood shoulder-height on Mud, and just about an inch in diameter. Dark, matte black, the staff gave off the coldness of solid metal. Mud gripped it in his hand and lifted it, studying it close.

"I compressed some hull metal into a staff," Bee told him. "Shaved it down to get the weight to about twenty pounds for you. I hope the next version will be able to interact with your thinsuit, and color shift with you. But for now, it'll help you stay steady."

"And club anyone I need to," Mud said, tapping it on the floor. "Thanks, Bee. And that, I think, concludes the injury show, if we can get to work?"

"Sure thing, Cap," Steelbox said. "So the translation database has a much deeper understanding now.

We still need a better word than Sweepers for them, but their name is unpronounceable by us, so we have to set that straight."

"Also," Shae said, "you'll need to figure out how they pushed you out of their universe. If they have tech like that, just laying around—"

"Right," Chellox finished, "who knows what else they have. Any strike from us would be possibly catastrophic, Mud."

"We have zero plans of a strike. Zero. Mills, that's true for your end, too, right?"

"So far. I won't lie," he said, leaning against a wall, "there's word upstairs that, while they don't think they should take over, they want me to take a more direct approach and declare this a military operation. I'm not sure what they would do if that was the case. But I can't imagine it would entail invading a universe. But they're getting worried, and more so all the time."

"That ends well. They know your engines won't work, right?" Jonah asked.

"I've made sure of it. They're looking into solutions but are starting to edge around more."

"All right, so we go back as soon as possible," Mud said, "same retrieval plans as before, but I think we have to have two goals this time. First, we find one of the two groups we spoke to before and get a sense of their society. If it's just a bunch of unaffiliated clans, we're about to have a real problem."

Chellox hmm'd, tapping his foot on the floor. "We can't unite them, either. Worst case we hope there's a giant council or something."

"Or that they inter-community communicate by sneezing," Steelbox said. "Whatever we end up with, there'll be something."

"All right, so let's assume we can get a consensus of any sort from them. We still need to bring a leader, a small delegation at most," Mud said, "back here to really get this moving—plus find a way to get our people there that doesn't, hopefully, at least, involve pain and GravPacks. I can't see a lot of the brass going for it."

Mills nodded, "That sounds—"

An alarm cut him off, followed by flashing red lights. Everyone reached for comms and screens to try to figure out the problem. Mills spoke into his comms in a hushed tone, demanding to know the emergency. The *Amalfi* was only technically in service, not a hundred percent spun up yet. An emergency big enough to set a ship-wide alert meant they were either being attacked or something simply *that bad* was going on.

Looking at the assembled people in the med bay, Mills spoke slowly, with the calm of a man living in a totally unbelievable moment. "Claudia 64-TU is... imploding."

"There's a star imploding?" Jonah asked quickly, "at speeds we can witness? With no damn warning?"

"That's what they're telling me," Mills said, already moving to leave the room. "I have to—"

"Go!" Mud said, knowing everyone else intended to follow. As a group, they rushed the best they could. No one waited for Mud, and he understood. He tested out the brace, and with his new walking stick to lean on, he could hobble fast enough to at least keep visual on them as everyone else hurried to the bridge.

On the bridge, Mills took command quickly.

Officers pulled stats up on screens and showed him the best video they could of the scene. Claudia 64-TU did seem to be shrinking, frighteningly quickly for an early-stage yellow sun. "Anything inhabited around it?" Mills asked.

"Only Claudia Seven," Shae replied quickly. "Claudia 64-TU runs a bit cool still."

"We're going," Mud said.

"To do what?" Mills asked. "You intend to fight a sun? Or fix one?"

"Doubtful," Chellox said, "But I think Mud's point was more one of evacuation. Who's near Claudia Seven?"

"Nothing big," Mills admitted, "but even if you guys went, the *Arrow* can't hold that many people and—"

"Mills, I helped organize a planetary evac once, remember?" Bee said. It wasn't strictly true—she had left right before the Trasker Four evac started, but she and Steelbox had helped draw up plans while building the first ship she'd left planet on, the *Hang On*.

"Bee's right," Jonah said, winking at Bee. "They have the skills to run this on site."

"Given how fast Claudia 64-TU is going, I don't know if you can get there in time," Mills told them all, reading data.

"Then we're gone," Mud said, and he turned to leave the bridge. His team followed him. Outside of the bridge, Mud looked at them, realizing his parents had joined him. "Bee, Chellox, guys, don't wait for me, prep the *Arrow*." They nodded, and the Insertion Team hurried ahead to the hangar. "Mom, Dad, stay here and help Mills. He's going to need it.

So will I."

"Good luck," Jonah said, nodding at his son before he turned to head back to the bridge.

"Make yourself proud," Shae told her son.

"Don't you mean make you proud?" he asked her as she turned to follow her husband.

"You do that already," she said over her shoulder.

Mud took a deep breath and tapped his walking staff on the ground. The hum and whirr of his leg brace distracted him as he started to push it harder, hurrying as best he could to the hangar.

He boarded the *Arrow* and sat in his seat heavily. "Sorry that took so long, I—"

"Cap, end it. We're good to launch. Mills has us on deck and green lights across the board."

"Chellox, make us regret having you pilot," Mud said, strapping in.

Chellox looked back at Mud, his birdesque helmet already in place. "Hold onto something, everyone."

They launched, pushing the engines as hard as they'd go, turning and twisting in space to find the angle Chellox wanted so they could gain velocity straight to Claudia Seven. On a hard burn it would normally have taken them a day, but Claudia 64-TU looked like it could collapse completely before then. Chellox decided to get some help from the universe for the trip, swinging them by the first big gravity well he saw and skimming it to gain speed off a slingshot.

The internal gravity fields couldn't keep up with Chellox's moves as he kept finding them gravity wells, small and large, to continually increase their velocity. Bee and Olivet moved to secured seats near the engines, keeping an eye on them as various components and motors whined and creaked under the strain. They complained like children who don't want to do the dishes, and who thought that if they only caught fire, they could escape work.

They held, regardless, for the moment. "Bee," Mud said from the main cabin over ship comms, "I need you working on a plan for Claudia Seven."

"Mud, you know I didn't really—"

"Yeah, except you did. I remember the briefings after. The ship rotation and schedules were mostly your design."

"Steelbox—"

"Did a bunch of it with you, sure," Mud continued, "and as he can spare brain power away from navigation, he'll work on it, too. So both of you, double up."

"You got it, Cap," Steelbox said. "Bee, I'll patch us to a private channel, I have the specs on ship deployment and planetary capabilities on a screen here."

"We should be done with the worst of the maneuvers," Chellox said. "I could push it harder, but I don't think the ship would stay in one piece."

"All right," Mud said, thinking. "Bee, Steelbox, get your GravPacks on, go ahead and start work. We'll catch up in a few hours, but right now every minute counts."

"But the engines—"

"We can put out fires, Bee, go."

Reluctantly, Bee slid on her GravPack and watched Steelbox do the same. The idea of going flat out with a GravPack remained low on both of their lists. Steelbox just didn't trust the devices fully—he felt pretty sure he never would. Bee felt differently.

She didn't enjoy the GravPacks, but also had never gotten around to hating them. She basically nothinged them. But ever since the Breaches, she'd felt guilty using them. While she knew they weren't causing the problem, the technology remained the same, and that alone bugged her.

Regardless, they cycled the *Arrow*'s airlock and leapt into open space, selecting strands along the *Arrow* itself to gain speed. Chellox's route slid them past enough gravity wells, in case he needed them for a boost, that they were able to accelerate quickly, gaining super-light speeds within minutes.

"Bee," Steelbox said, "where are we evacuating the planet to?"

"I have *no* idea," she admitted. "The whole system will be dead without a sun. We can't just planet hop them."

"No, and finding enough ships to get everyone to another system...this doesn't end well, does it?"

"Probably not," Steelbox agreed, "but we'll get it as close to decent as we can." They flew on, running through data and considering options as they went, selfishly hoping the trip would take longer than they both knew it would.

On the *Arrow*, Mud went over the data as well, having shifted to sit in the navigation seat, leaving Olivet to stand watch over the engines. Chellox flew comfortably, not needing active navigation, his flight plan established and locked in. Mud watched his pilot, his friend, fly with a natural ease Mud would never know.

Chellox seemed to only gesture toward the controls and the ship would respond. Constant tiny corrections, the softest of touches, to keep their path optimized. He paid the flight the sort of attention parents reserve for their children. Mud forced himself to stop watching Chellox's hands flick over control surfaces and cycled back to the problem at hand. It loomed.

An entire sun being destroyed out of nowhere sat as the stuff of nightmares. A tale told to children so they would behave. Total instant solar collapse simply didn't happen. Mud chuckled to himself silently. His entire life, his job—his calling, it seemed—was dealing with things that "simply didn't happen." Until they did.

Back before he'd taken his parents' old job over, he'd been lost, in a sense. Some light troubleshooting on a per-contract basis, but never for the Gov— stupid retrieval jobs to secure enough funds to keep going, sure, but no real direction. He'd been raised for this job, for the Insertion Team, and had instead struck out anywhere but, trying figure out what he wanted. All roads, though, lead right back. He'd admitted that truth to himself and taken up the job happily, thinking that would be the end of it.

Now, as they raced toward a huge unsolvable problem, the uncertainty threatened to come back. An entire planet of people was about to die. His team were the first responders. Realistically, no one wanted that pressure settling on them. But here he sat, he knew, offering himself, and his team, for the job and the weight of it.

And maybe, he thought suddenly, that remained the point, at the end of everything. No one wanted the job, no one enjoyed it, but someone had to do it. And if you could stand up and be that person, why wouldn't you? Because of the fear, the chance of failure? Everything that existed came with those ingredients, but you couldn't let people suffer for your own inability to face forward. Mud stiffly flexed his right leg and felt a soft vibration from the brace. Better, he decided, than needles all over your body pushing down and injecting you.

CHAPTER 25

BEE AND STEELBOX SLOWED down as they reached the Claudia 64-TU system. The star, even from the edge of the system, could be seen to be in trouble. From their distance, the star stood out only as a small disc of light, but one that seemed to shake in ways that stars never did in normal situations. They sped back up to get in-system rapidly and approached Claudia Seven as fast as possible. The planet's orbit was full of ships. The problem, they could both see quickly, stood out in that the ships had achieved orbit but didn't look to have a destination in mind. They floated, directionless, generally just pointing away from the star.

"Steelbox, run some quick math for me. Rate of star decay against mass left. We need to know when the gravity will dip low enough that Claudia Seven's orbit will actually cease."

"Got it. Yah, I'm going to need to shoot that to the *Arrow* to have them run the rest of the system as well. We need to see where this all hits."

Bee nodded, and Steelbox started the calculations. They both knew that once Claudia 64-TU's gravity well dropped below a threshold, every rock in the system would fly off like its strings had been cut.

Though only Claudia Seven held life in the system, the planet wasn't alone as far as planetary bodies went. Six other large rocks spun in orbits around Claudia 64-TU, and each one of them became another problem for the math. Steelbox loaded all the orbital data he could collect, added the solar data, and fired it off to the *Arrow* for them to work on. They needed to know when the sun would lose its grip on the planets and where each one would go after that. Hopefully, best case, none of them would hit Claudia Seven. That scenario would only mitigate the damage—but then, they would happily take any lessened degree of problem.

"I'm calling up whomever thinks they're in charge," Bee said, "or trying to. There's a bit of panic, you can imagine."

"Yeah," Steelbox agreed. "We're first on scene, and no heavy cruiser nearby yet, but there must be a Gov building on the surface we can talk to, no?"

"We'll have to go down there," she said, jerking a thumb toward the planet, "and find someone. Let me get Mills to clear some red tape and find me a name."

They started to drop into the planet's atmosphere, slower than usual as they needed to keep changing vectors to avoid panicked launches coming right for them. No one seemed to be in charge of airspace currently, and they both knew it would only be a matter of time before collisions started and everything got even worse. But, for now, they could only wait for the data and start triage as best they could manage. A tone from her wrist told Bee the information from Mills she needed had arrived, and they started down to the planet's surface, nervously watching the sky.

Aboard the *Arrow*, Mud and Olivet crunched numbers. They ran them a second time and then a third, hoping for better results and never turning them up.

Mud slapped the keyboard in front of him in

frustration. "Is there at least a sign of what's causing it? A way to stop this?"

"Not without deep solar scans, I don't think," Olivet said, "which we won't be able to get until we arrive."

"Six hours," Chellox said over his shoulder, "and even that should be impossible."

"No one is blaming you for the size of the universe, Chellox," Mud said.

"Good, because any faster—"

"And we won't have a ship to get us there," Mud finished. "No, you're doing the impossible, Chellox. No worries."

"But, Mud, what can we even do?" Olivet asked.

"Bee and Steelbox will rough out a plan," Mud replied, trusting in his team. "But we have to get them this data."

"Sending now."

"Six hours, huh?" Mud asked.

"Size of the universe, Mud, not my fault," Chellox said briskly.

"I know, I know." He stretched his leg and set a timer on his thinsuit so he wouldn't ask Chellox again.

Steelbox landed in front of a Gov building, Bee alighting by his side. A mass of people crowded outside, demanding entry from the four guards who stood in front of the gate. Trying to be as gentle as possible, Steelbox worked his way to the front of the crowd, Bee following close.

Holding up ID for the guards, Steelbox waited. The guards weren't inclined to let anyone in and didn't seem to want to call inside for authorization.

As they waited, Bee's communicator went off and

she looked at the data stream coming in. "We don't have time to wait," she said, as much to the guards as to Steelbox.

"Ma'am, you'll have to—" the guard stopped midsentence as Bee cursed softly and took off in her GravPack, going over the fence.

Steelbox followed her within seconds. "Bee, we can't just—"

"I meant it when I said we don't have time."

The guards yelled after them and Bee turned long enough to yell back, "Shoot if you think it'll help." She landed at the doors and yanked them open hard. They went inside, finding it less crowded but no less chaotic.

Bee made straight for the office Mills had told her to look for. Resisting the urge to break into a run, she still pushed people aside and ignored their yelps of surprise. Steelbox, normally the crowd shifter of the two, followed her, apologizing to people as he went. "I get you're channeling your inner Madison, Bee, but—"

"Four hours," Bee said. "The *Arrow* won't be here for six, we have four until lights out."

"That's—"

"Not nearly enough time. So to hell with nice." Bee found the door she'd been told to look for and yanked it open without knocking.

"Excuse me!" General Bennet said, looking up from his desk. Around the wide, wooden desk stood several aides, all showing him various printouts.

"Insertion Team, General," Bee said quickly, moving across the dark olive carpet to lean her hands on the desk. "You should have a notice telling you to expect us and that we're here to run

231

extraction."

"Run extraction, is it?" Bennet shook his head. "We don't have the ships to evacuate a whole planet and we aren't even sure what's going on."

"We're aware of what you *don't* have. We're here to use what you do," Bee told him.

Steelbox linked his thinsuit's data comm to a wall screen facing the desk. "As for what's going on, sir," he said, "Claudia 64-TU is collapsing in on itself."

"I know *that*, you—"

"Then you also know you only have four hours until the sun's completely gone?" Steelbox asked.

"What?!" Bennet looked at his aides. "Why haven't you told me that?"

"We didn't—"

"And," Bee added, "you must know that there's a twenty-six percent chance that once it blinks out, Claudia Seven will hit one of the other planets in the system as it flies free."

"That high?" Bennet looked at his desk, the color draining from his face. "Where did you get—"

"We're very good at what we do, sir," Bee said, softer, easing into gentle, knowing how wretched the General must feel. "We're here to help. Let us."

"What do you need?"

"Everything you have," Steelbox said quickly. "A command post, full auth codes for everything going on in or out of orbit, and command auth to direct traffic."

Bee sat on the edge of the desk and got to work, calling up data feeds on the wall screen. Another set of screens were brought in, and quickly they established their command post. General Bennet felt his ire rise as these strangers took over his office, but he tamped his feelings down, knowing they were rushed to the point of not caring.

Steelbox worked up a constant display, rotating and showing the decaying orbits of everything in the Claudia 64-TU system. The smaller the star got, the less of a dent in the universe it made, the less gravity. When you're on a planet, you don't often realize, but they move fast. Very fast. And small changes in the gravity well they rotate around cause big changes in orbital paths.

Bee worked out flight paths for any ships leaving orbit, adjusting paths in real time to compensate for the widening arc of Claudia Seven's orbit. She also relayed the info to all ships still too close to the planet. "Where," she asked Steelbox, "are we putting these people?"

"Into whatever can fly, I guess," he said. "We can try to put people here into bunkers and keep them warm once Claudia 64-TU goes out, but—"

"No, I mean, where do we land them? These ships are packed. They don't have proper supplies or fuel to make another system with passengers alive." She shook her head. "How do we *save* them instead of just prolonging their suffering?"

"We hope the others have a plan, and we just get this done," he said. "This is your Op, Bee, you call it."

"Don't put this on me, I can't—"

"Really?" Steelbox asked. He barked a few course corrections to an assistant standing near him, the room milling with people rushing in and out to deliver status updates. While Bee directed ships, Steelbox directed resources on the ground as best he could, all while keeping up star charts and pattern guesses.

"Really!" Bee shouted. "I can't be responsible for this many—"

"Right up until you stared at it, you were running this operation," he said. "So stop thinking about the weight of it, maybe. You're as bad as Mud, sometimes."

"Ha! He's been trained forever in this." Bee forced a launching freighter to adjust course. The ship made the correction, but sloppily, causing a cascade of issues. Bee and Steelbox lost their conversation to work for a while, both of them muttering under their breath between frantic communications.

An hour passed, and then two. They were brought drinks and bits of food that they picked at. Closing her eyes as the second hour ticked away, feeling them burn with exhaustion, Bee cracked her neck. "He really has been at this since birth, you know?"

"Mud?" Steelbox asked. "Sure. And he still doubts himself all the time and tries to hide it. The both of you."

"Fine," Bee said, grinding the heels of her palms into her closed eyes, trying to rub away the tiredness that had settled on her. "Hey, you doing new solar scans?"

"Trying to," Steelbox said, "but I keep getting interrupted by other fires."

"Prioritize it. I got most of what could carry people into orbit and I'm just arranging paths at this point, for a while at least. I'll take point on ground resources. But we need to know what's causing this before it ends."

"You think we can save Claudia?"

"Not at all. Even if we did, we can't exactly reignite it to size, and it's already to a point where we'd have to manually shift Claudia Seven's orbit to sustain life long term. No, but I want to know what did this."

"Sure, and then?"

"I'm going to find a way to hit it, I think."

Steelbox laughed and set up a new set of solar scans. He added a few other, deeper scans of the area around Claudia 64-TU as well, just to see what he could see. Bee shifted screens around and took over the ground operations while he worked. Not much remained on their list. Bee knew that if she didn't find something to do, she would spend the rest of their time fretting about the countdown.

She started to work, instead, on the bunker plans. A lot of the personnel on the base, and across the planet, simply couldn't leave. Claudia Seven contained nowhere near enough ships for an evacuation on that scale. But once they lost Claudia 64-TU fully, a deep freeze would start, even as they spun off into the universe. Their atmosphere would stay put, mostly. Should. It'd be thin, and they'd trail a bit of it behind, but the lack of a sun would remain the biggest instant problem. Within a week, the surface of the planet wouldn't be habitable.

Of course, finding space to house the large number of people left on Claudia Seven proved its own challenge. Even with the population seriously decreased and in space at the moment, nothing served as a long term-plan.Bee shook her head and took a deep breath. Long term wasn't her issue, it was the rest of the team's. She just had to hold on to that and put the stress out of her head as best she could.

They continued to work, trying to hold back death for as many people as they could, trusting in their teammates to find a way to shut the door.

CHAPTER 26

THE *ARROW*'S CREW knew they were fighting time and would lose. They couldn't arrive before the sun went out, but they could, hopefully, be prepared for when they arrived. Mud worked with Mills over comms, amassing a truly heroic number of large cargo ships and transports. They recommissioned a bunch of ships, spread staff too thin, and had everything underway, or close to it, in record time.

Assuming Bee and Steelbox could keep much of the population of Claudia Seven alive for a few days, they could be transferred and rehomed. Where they would be rehomed still remained a big, glaring issue. In the current human circles of space, there simply didn't sit an empty habitable planet. That did not happen.

Mud ran some math to pull up a list of sparsely populated planets that were in a few days' range. There weren't any. Temporary rehoming could be achieved if they scattered the population of Claudia Seven to enough planets. Mud got Mills on board with the plan and started him working on getting the appropriate approvals up the chain of command.

Knowing the pressures Bee and Steelbox were under, Mud resisted the urge to check in with them, knowing they'd burst in with a call if they needed help. Until then, Mud knew, all he could really manage would be to distract them.

While they were still about three hours out from Claudia Seven, the comms lit up. "Data burst from

Steelbox," Olivet said from the back of the ship, where he was still keeping an eye on the engines. "This is a lot of data."

"They'd be able to crunch it faster where they are," Mud said. "Toss it to my screens, too?"

Olivet shared the data stream and they both looked over the results in front of them. "All right, so why send it to us now?" Mud asked.

"Look at the surrounding scans he did," Olivet said, "he isn't sure about this bit." Olivet let the engines watch themselves for a moment and walked up the ship, leaning on the back of Mud's chair. "It looks familiar, but I don't know why."

"We could just ask."

"Let's," Olivet agreed.

"Steelbox," Mud said, opening the channel, "we got your data. What's up?"

"We're in a holding pattern here, got as many evac'd as we could, getting as many into bunkers now as possible. Hoping you have a long-term plan."

"We're working it," Mud told him, "but the data you sent, what's the score?"

"Right," Steelbox said. "Olivet, check the surrounding scans. It looks familiar, sort of like Bercuser. Can you verify that one for me?"

"Oh," Olivet said, looking over the data again, trying to match it up with memory. "Don't we have good scans of Bercuser?"

"Not really," Mud said, "at least nothing reliable. Because of the—" he trailed off, seeing the pattern.

"Yeah, that was my thinking, too," Steelbox said. "Olivet?"

"It could be a nimbus of the same breaching that Bercuser does," he admitted, "but I can't be sure."

"It'd look different," Steelbox said. "Suns work different than solid planets, to be sure, but if we're all right on all this—"

"This is a Breach event?"

"Inside the sun, I think," Steelbox said. "It would explain why the sun is vanishing and at the speed it's doing it. Think about it."

"I am," Mud said, "and that's the problem. So the breach opens in a sun, sucking it into the other universe, but why? And how do we stop it?"

"The second part's easier," Olivet said. "We don't. I mean, the physics difference between the two universes works like a heat exchange. Open the door and stuff goes from here to there, but not the other way."

"We've moved between them," Mud said.

"Sure," Steelbox agreed, "but we can't push a star. And I think we'd have to."

"But Bercuser flips back and forth," Mud said, chewing the problem over.

"That would be the worst case," Olivet said. "Imagine Claudia 64-TU just reappears somewhere else with no warning. A sun just popping into a system. I hope it can't."

"I don't think it could. If Bercuser was an experiment with gravity engines gone sideways, something in that caused the constant shifting. Claudia won't have that," Steelbox said. "I hope."

"None of which answers the how," Mud said. "And we need the how."

"Those big creatures, like the one that broke the *Ratzinger*," Steelbox said, growing excited. "They've been near every breach and soft spot we've seen, right?"

"Sure," Mud agreed.

"All right, so what if they're doing it? By accident—they didn't seem malicious, they don't attack, just seem to want the energy from fuel packs."

"The light from breaches does the same, though," Olivet pointed out.

"But the tentacled beasts, they seemed to want more," Steelbox said. "Let me call you back, I want to run some tests with Bee and be sure about this."

"We can—"

"No, the data I need will be right here," Steelbox insisted. "Just get here and have a plan in place to get these people safe long term."

"You got it," Mud said. "We're still just under three hours out."

"We know. Sun goes in one. We'll be fine, but let me send you the coordinates for where we think the planet will be when you get here."

"Copy," Mud said, "and get back to us when you work the rest out."

"Copy." Steelbox broke the connection.

Mud and Olivet sent the data to Mills and confirmed their end of the plan was well underway.

On Claudia Seven, Steelbox pulled Bee from her work and caught her up quickly. She sighed, nodding as he explained, and asked him for the same data he was already calling up.

"Look at it," he said, pointing at the screen. "Communication spike."

"Massive one," she agreed, "a day or so before the sun breach started. They reached out to the central Gov outpost about a host of issues and had to transmit reams of data. Way above normal for anywhere. What happened here?" Bee tasked one of the assistants still rushing in and out of General Bennet's office to find the General himself and get him in there.

"General," Bee started as soon as the man entered the room, "a few days ago you had a huge communications spike. What happened?"

"A few days ago?" he said, thinking. "Ah yes, of course. We'd been running some data testing for the central offices. Large A.I. stuff, huge amounts of data. A few days ago we sent it all through. Why?"

"Just confirming a theory," Steelbox said, smiling. "Thanks."

"That...that will fix he sun?"

"Not at all," Bee admitted, "but we have to focus on why, now. So we can prevent it from happening anywhere else."

"Not," Steelbox added quickly, "that it would. Don't go saying that, please. Please."

"Of course not," Bennet said, sounding insulted, "I would never—"

"Great," Steelbox said, giving him another smile.

"We need to work the math out on this, General, sorry," Bee said. "We'll let you know."

"Uhm...all right," he said, leaving his own office, still not quite sure why he accepted that so easily. An aide went with him, taking notes as the General started to list recipients of a memo so he could update people along the chain of command.

"So the pseudopod things eat certain types of energy," Steelbox said.

"And when really large bursts of communication come through, they can cause a soft spot—but then why haven't they until now?" Bee mused.

"This is where I desperately want to say it's above

241

our pay grade."

"Yeah, sadly it's our job."

Steelbox sighed and tapped his fingers along his leg, "You know, I joined up thinking it would be more punching and less thinking."

"Ha! I agreed to join hoping it would be the reverse." Bee called up the data on her screen and started running through it again.

"You win, then."

"Do I?" she asked. "I'm the one talking about punching more, remember?"

"I suppose," Steelbox told her, switching the screen in front of him to current readouts of the bunker plan. "We should finish saving these guys either way, huh?"

"Might as well, right? Mud said they had a plan."

"He said he was working on it."

"They won't be here for another few hours, so he'll work fast." Bee looked at Steelbox's screen. "Hey, reach out to that bunker on the night side of the planet, something looks off."

"Which?" he asked, looking where she pointed. "Oh, damn it, yeah, let me get them on comms." They both glanced at the clock but didn't say anything about it. Instead, they got back to work and adjusted how people were filtering into the bunkers, calling for troop deployments to settle small scuffles and outbreaks of chaos as best they could. The job needed at least six other people, but they dispersed the responsibility, trusting local members of the Gov forces to report in regularly.

They worked, and they waited.

CHAPTER 27

AN HOUR OR SO LATER, Claudia 64-TU finished vanishing into the other universe, winking out of sight completely with a final flicker and burst of white other-universe light. The light didn't bleed out far enough to hit Claudia Seven, thankfully, so their fuel packs weren't drained. In the mayhem of the final hours, Steelbox and Bee had missed the possibility of this surge—only when the light shone forth, as the last embers of the star left their universe, did they realize they had dodged a much bigger problem.

Claudia Seven's orbital path vanished fully as Claudia 64-TU did, and the planet wobbled before heading off into space at large. As it did, giant windstorms erupted around the planet, followed by earthquakes. Those, at least, they'd remembered to plan for, and kept damage to minimal amounts for anything with people in it.

They kept working—checking, then double- and triple-checking, everything from the status of the launched vessels to the bunkers, making sure to contact each one themselves. They were in the final throes of their third check when the door to General Bennet's office flew open forcefully.

"Someone called for a pickup?" Mud said, working his way into the room slowly. "You guys found a nice workspace."

"Someone," Steelbox said, not looking up from his screen, "tossed a General out of his office and never looked back."

"Seemed like it would be quiet," Bee said, then held up a hand as she pinged another bunker. "Sorry, still finishing a check. You have a plan for the rest of this?"

"We do," Mud said. "Did you work out what caused it?"

"We did," Bee told him. "Let's trade."

Mud patched Mills in and he briefed the Insertion Team on the fleet of resuscitated ships already underway. They'd cut it close, as far as supplies in bunkers and ships went, but the margin would work out for them as best it could.

While the plan continued to spin up, Bee briefed the rest of the team on what her and Steelbox had discovered: that the pseudopod creatures seemed to be pushing through and making soft spots.

"We have no good choice, then," Mud said, after making sure Mills and his parents were patched in. "We have to breach and find a way to explain."

"Agreed," Mills said. "I can spare the same routes for pickup. Go. Before another sun gets yanked in."

"We can't use this soft spot," Bee said quickly, "there's a sun on the other side—we don't want to breach right into it."

"Right, so we head back to the *Ratzinger* site," Mud said, "on GravPacks. We don't have time to waste. Mills, get someone to follow us in the *Arrow* and set up other pickups." He looked around the room at his Insertion Team. "Let's move, people."

They hurried to the *Arrow*, Mud keeping up as best he could, which, he noticed, was faster than when he'd walked in. He hefted his walking stick and tapped it on the ground hard. This would work. It had to.

Aboard the *Arrow* for long enough to strap on GravPacks and gather supplies, Bee resynced her translation devices, stuffing them in carry pockets along her thinsuit. "Mud, if this doesn't—"

"If this doesn't work, we find something else— but Bee, this will work."

"How can you be so sure?"

"Because all the alternative options are terrible."

They finished suiting up and left through an airlock without ceremony. Before he could request it, Mud saw the team activate slaving to his lead, and he pushed their GravPacks hard, staying just clear of the boundary.

"Brace yourselves," Mud said hours later, the team having flown back to the wreckage of the *Ratzinger* in silence. None of them knew how they could pull this off, but they each went over their jobs in their heads. There was nothing to say, no overall plan to go over. The mission remained simple on the surface of it: breach, find a way to get the problem across, find a solution, get out.

The details left them each frustrated, if only because there were none. Mud felt the worst about it, considering it a failing of his that he couldn't see the angles needed to get the job done. He tempered his own annoyance with an acceptance that no one could see what lay ahead enough to predict how things would unfold. There wasn't enough data available to any of them, to anyone at all.

As they approached the wreckage, Mud sped them up, recalling data to find the exact point of their previous breach. He aimed them straight on and felt his own GravPack shudder and whine a little. His staff, strapped along his back, made his jaw ache with its vibration—but better to have it than not. Just in case.

Breach.

CHAPTER 28

HOW DO WE FIND the same group?" Olivet asked, shaking his head to try to clear it. Breaching still sat low on their collective ideas of fun, and it didn't seem to get easier with repetition.

"Do we even want to?" Steelbox asked. "They weren't the friendliest."

"We need someone," Bee said, pointing at a group of Sweepers who had noticed them, "and can build from there."

The Sweepers swam over and Bee activated her translation devices, hoping the newest data would let them work faster. "We need to talk about the breaches," Mud said, and waited. A series of static and noise came from Bee's thinsuit and one of the Sweepers stopped, tilting its head.

It opened its mouth and spoke to them, and a few seconds later the translation came through. "You are the strangers, from the (untranslatable) side."

"Can we pin that to 'other'?" Mud asked Bee. She nodded and he considered his phrasing carefully. "We are from the other side, yes. The other universe. We need to solve both our problems."

The Sweeper waved two of its arms toward the packets that filled the sky. Steelbox made note of the large creatures starting to slowly converge along a particularly large mass of packets, and he fought back a wince. "You send these, they fill the (untranslatable). You must stop."

"At least the translations are better," Chellox said. "Can we ask about a leader?"

"Good idea," Mud said, then spoke toward Bee's translator again. "Is there a leader we could discuss this with?"

The Sweepers listened and then spoke amongst their own in hushed tones the translator couldn't pick up. Mud tried to be patient, giving Steelbox a shrug. They kept still, otherwise, waiting.

The Sweeper who had been speaking to them turned back to the team and waved three of his arms excitedly. "Our (untranslatable) does not speak for all of us, but many. We will take you to them."

"Did we just manage a 'take me to your leader'?" Olivet asked.

"Jonah did the same, once, with my people," Chellox said. "Surprisingly, it works more often than you would think."

They followed the Sweeper across the open skyspace of the other universe. They were lead to one of the landmasses that still looked soft-edged, if not actually blurry, to Mud's eyes. "Can we actually stand on that?" Bee asked.

"I think we're about to," Steelbox replied as they landed. Their feet sank an inch or so into the soft ground, and they noticed that the blurriness of the landmass wasn't a mere visual problem with how light worked in this universe. The ground itself seemed to fray, loose edges of spongy matter waving in some sort of cosmic breeze. "This place makes less sense the more time I spend in it," Steelbox said.

"Except that I agree, I would point out that I often feel the same about you," Chellox said.

"Yeah, fair enough," Steelbox told him.

Lumps of the landmass, mounds of it, sat in front of them. One of them opened up, a curtain of mass acting like a door—or possibly a curtain, Mud couldn't be sure. Three Sweepers came out of the opening and talked in hushed tones to the one who had led them to the planetary body.

"You are in charge of the other side?" one of the three asked them, at length.

"We can speak for it, yes," Mud said, knowing that to be enough of the truth to pass muster right then.

"You will stop this invasion," another of the three said quickly.

"We need to discuss that, with you and with our people," Mud said slowly, considering how to approach this. "We need your scientists and ours to meet."

"Your technicals," the last of the three Sweepers said, "need to stop. There is no talking."

"Your animals? The large beasts," Mud pointed to one in the distance, "are breaking into our universe, pulling things through. A sun, for example, most recently. This needs to stop. We must have talks to find a solution."

"You stop, then no need for talks," the second Sweeper said. Their guide backed away as the exchange continued, entering the building the three Sweepers had emerged from. Bee wanted to follow but couldn't.

"There is danger to us both," Mud said. "Please, let us return with some of your scientists."

"No need," the second Sweeper repeated.

Bee leaned over to Olivet and Steelbox. "Can either of you go follow that Sweeper who led us here and talk to him?" She handed Steelbox a smaller translation unit. "It's my backup. I think he might be helpful."

"I don't know how we can break away," Olivet said.

Steelbox nudged Mud. "Cap, let's go on a walk with them, have them show you around and try to get through to them, but Bee has a plan, so some of us need to vanish a few."

Mud nodded, never taking his eyes off the trip of Sweepers. "Show me, if you could, how this affects you." He swept his hand across the horizon line slowly and started to walk away. The Sweepers followed quickly, clearly upset. "This area, for example, is it bad here?"

The team trailed behind the Sweepers, and after a few feet, Steelbox and Olivet snuck away as one of the Sweepers said, "This area, no, our sky is affected. You must stop."

"We can stop it if we can discuss with your scientists," Mud insisted.

Steelbox and Olivet pushed the entranceway of the building, finding the soft door easy to open. Inside their contact Sweeper sat, seemingly in meditation. Olivet fired up the spare translator and cleared his throat. "Scientists. You know where they are?"

"These leaders will not help," the Sweeper said. "They want stop and will not give to help."

"But you will?" Steelbox asked.

"Our technicals will help you, help us. All. With yours," the Sweeper agreed. "But leaders see short and (untranslatable)."

"All right," Steelbox said, relaying the information to Mud softly through his comms.

"How do we find them, and how do we get back to our universe with them, without your leaders noticing?" Olivet asked.

"We will need to (untranslatable) and (untranslatable)" the Sweeper said, reaching into a small structure near him and coming back with a box. "This makes the other easier to reach."

"A breach box?" Olivet asked.

The Sweeper tilted his head, not understanding, but Steelbox looked the box over. "It looks like the thing they used to shove us out last time, so...that wasn't a great trip."

"No, but if it could breach the other way, we should at least take it and study it," Olivet said.

"No hurt, use second flip," the Sweeper said.

Turning the box over, Steelbox saw what he meant. There sat two switches. He pointed at one and the Sweeper nodded. "All right, so the first switch breaches and the second makes it painful? Who builds that?"

Olivet laughed, "Sorry, no, I bet it's just a speed issue. Not an intentional pain thing."

"I hope so. No," Steelbox corrected himself, "I take that back. You better be right. If these people built this specifically to...no, that changes things for me, I think."

"We have weapons, too," Olivet pointed out.

"Sure, but not ones that throw someone out of a universe," Steelbox said.

"If we could, we would," Olivet insisted. "But that's not the point. We don't know why they have this set the way they do. We do know that we need it."

"Fine," Steelbox said, turning back to the Sweeper.

"How do we find the scientists?"

"I will bring them here," the Sweeper said, and it walked out of the building. Steelbox and Olivet just looked at each other for a second, wondering what the catch would be.

"They're going to bring scientists to us, and we have an exit plan," Steelbox said over comms. "Have they noticed we're gone yet?"

Mud walked, the rest of the team following, as he continued to ask the three Sweepers about their lands. "Do the large creatures ever land here?" he asked, pointing toward what seemed to be a crater.

"They do not sit on our lands," Sweeper Two said. "They fill the sky, mighty beasts."

"Mighty indeed," Bee agreed. "They are strong, and yet seem peaceful."

"Unless angered," Sweeper One said.

"Of course," Mud agreed. Then: "We're still getting a tour," he sub-vocalized so his comm would pick it up.

"We're stuck here while we wait," Steelbox said. "So keep buying us time."

"We'll try," Bee told him, before nodding at something Sweeper Three had said that she hadn't heard.

They continued to walk, asking questions. They dug out information on the Sweepers' habit of floating in their skyspace (unless they needed shelter or production, it calmed them, apparently), their low use of technology (they didn't like using it but had needs), as well as their seemingly high level of the same technology (once they had tools improved, they simply stopped using the old tools—though the levels of different factions within their race would be different) and, most of all, their societal structure.

The universe the Sweepers inhabited sat much smaller than the one the Insertion Team originated in. Still vastly large, the other universe seemed older, with far more of its matter having been converted to energy—the Sweepers and their large, whale-like creatures both capable of digesting that energy to live on. To further Bee's thoughts along the age of the universe, diversity of species would tend to happen early on—a vastly old universe, such as (probably) the one she now walked in, had seen enough collapse that only a few species remained.

Given the millennia upon millennia involved in such a process, it remained unlikely the current species even recalled, or had records of, prior ones. So for the Sweepers, everything stood as it always had.

Their society seemed to be made up of different clans, varied in size, across bands of their universe. Some regions were uninhabitable for reasons Bee's translator couldn't get a lock on. The clans communicated, as best they could given the insanely vast distances and time to travel, but for the most part they left each other alone.

Which presented one of the biggest problems, to Mud. They realistically didn't have a governmental body set up to deal with a problem of this scale. They needed it dealt with, to be sure, but any one clan could agree to a solution that another would reject. This, he told himself, was why they needed to get the scientists back to their universe and hash something out that would manage to actually solve the problem.

253

Far easier said than done, Mud knew, assuming that level of solution could even be achieved. Though he had seen—and heard stories of, of course—attempts that moved the needle simply by having been attempted. People could fail, but the act of trying as hard they could would, on occasion, shift the balance. It would be something to hope for and fall back on, if the time came.

While Mud, Bee, and Chellox continued to learn about the Sweepers, Steelbox and Olivet waited nervously. When, after what seemed like hours, the Sweeper returned, it gestured wildly at them. "Come, come now, to the technicals you need," it told them.

"You were going to bring them here," Steelbox said.

"This is easier."

"No, we need to collect our people as well." Steelbox looked at Olivet for support. "You said you would bring them here."

"We must go now," the Sweeper said, gesturing for them to follow.

"We're being led to a second location," Olivet said into his comms, "so this might get strange."

They followed the Sweeper out of the building and across the surface for a while, where, without warning, the Sweeper leapt and swam upward into the skyspace. Steelbox and Olivet followed, using their GravPacks, glancing back nervously.

"Do you have a name?" Steelbox asked the Sweeper.

"(Untranslatable)," came the reply.

"Helpful," Steelbox told Olivet, who shrugged. "How far are we going?" he asked the Sweeper.

"Not far now, small land around this one."

Sure enough, a smaller landmass lay in the shadow of the one they had left, and the Sweeper landed there, the humans not far behind. On the springy land mass stood several small buildings like they had seen before, and from one came four Sweepers, all carrying various devices—Sweeper technology.

"They will go with you," the Sweeper said.

"Yes, we will help you," one of the Sweeper scientists said, "but we must go now."

"We need the rest of our team," Steelbox insisted. "Let me arrange to meet them, up there." He pointed toward the skyspace between the two landmasses. "Guys," he said into comms, "we have the scientists, they have a bunch of their tech. We need to get out of here. We're in the skyspace above the landmass now. Home in on me."

"So what," Mud asked Sweeper One, "can we call you, individual names or as a race?"

"We are the (untranslatable), and I am (untranslatable)," came the reply.

Mud nodded, and he listened to Steelbox's message. "Well, I guess Sweepers it is, for now. Anyway," he looked at his teammates, "we should get back to our own universe. We will continue to find a solution."

"Yes," agreed Sweeper Two, "you must solve."

"Unless," Mud said, "you want to help? Let us talk to your scientists?"

"No, you must solve," the Sweeper insisted.

"All right," Mud nodded, "we will go. Our friends have already started off, so we will meet them," he said, using his GravPack to begin to rise off the surface. Bee and Chellox followed, as did all three Sweepers.

"We need to ditch them fast," Bee said softly.

"I know," Mud told her.

"How will you move back to the other?" Sweeper One asked. "We can assist."

"Oh, no, that's all right," Mud said, "don't worry. You go back. We'll be fine."

"We can assist you back to other," the Sweeper repeated.

They rose higher, and Mud could see Steelbox, Olivet, and the four Sweeper scientists. "Slave your packs," he said softly. Bee and Chellox did as asked, and Mud linked an attracting strand to Steelbox's own GravPack, reeling them over to the other group quickly, leaving the three Sweepers behind.

"What did they say?" Mud asked Bee as they got to their teammates.

"Out of range, no idea."

"Right, OK, fine. Steelbox, you have an exit?"

"I have it," Olivet said, pulling out the box the Sweeper had given them. "We were told it wouldn't be as bad this time."

"Well," Mud said, glancing behind them, "let's hit it. Those guys have noticed us all." He saw the three Sweepers, the leaders they'd been introduced to, coming angrily at them now. They'd spotted the scientists and probably, Mud thought, the box Olivet held, and had easily worked out the plan. From a strictly political angle, this mission had gone about as far south as it could go. Still, it would get the job done, he hoped.

They huddled closer together, the Insertion Team and their new science quartet of Sweepers.

"Quick," Bee said, "Mud, throw a gravshield around them." Mud did as told, and before he could ask why, she nodded, "Not sure what they need to breathe, but this should trap some of what's around for a while."

"Good call," Mud said. "Olivet?"

"Right," Olivet said, and he hit a switch on the box in his hand.

Breach.

CHAPTER 29

SPACE SPAT THEM out a good distance from the wreckage of the *Ratzinger*. The Sweepers floundered, waving their limbs and making struggled sounds. Mud extended his shield, and Bee merged hers with his, checking on them.

"Are you all right?" she asked, worried they'd made a giant mistake.

"Yes," one of them answered after a few seconds. "Switching to your side is not pleasant."

"We feel the same in reverse," Mud said. "The feeling should ease soon."

While Mud and Bee talked the Sweepers back to calm, Chellox comm'd for a pickup. They'd emerged from the other universe only a few hours hard burn from where they'd entered, so the *Arrow* could swing around and get them sooner than later.

While they waited, the scientist Sweepers helped feed Bee's translator with basic words and building blocks, as well as some of their grammar, improving it far faster than it would otherwise. They seemed in good spirits once they recovered from the initial breach.

"Won't your people want to get you back?" Steelbox asked. "We didn't exactly leave on good terms."

"(Untranslatable), who brought us to you, will calm them, and explain. They would agree eventually, but we felt no time left."

"We agree," Mud said, "but what convinced you of the time concerns?"

"The (untranslatable) events—"

"Breaches," Mud said, and Bee nodded, tapping something into the translator, which repeated the phrase in the Sweepers' language.

"Yes," the Sweeper agreed, "the breaches, they became more dangerous with each time."

"A star from our universe just got pulled into one," Bee said.

"Yes, but also the between," the Sweeper told her, "weakens. Too many more and both sides will become one. Neither will survive."

"Wait, what?!" Steelbox said loudly. "Did you just say both our universes will collapse into one?"

One of the other Sweepers waved its limbs quickly. "And we are low on time. The between grows weaker. Your small crossings agitate."

"The large creatures get angry and attack the walls of the universe itself," Bee said, "and every time it gets worse, are you sure?"

"We would like to look at your data as well."

"That will be easy," Bee told them.

They continued to discuss matters loosely while they waited. Shifting to work out what the Sweepers could survive in, they discovered that open space would not do, nor could the Sweepers propel themselves in a void.

Chellox bottled some of the skyspace they'd brought over with them, carefully storing it and hoping they could replicate it back at the *Amalfi*. Olivet just hoped that what they were floating in currently would last long enough for finding out. The team played with thin margins often, Olivet knew, but this one seemed recklessly so.

Not that he had a better idea. Which was,

historically, the problem. Not with the team itself—none of them really thought that, at this point—but more with the need for the team. The problem of the universe, Olivet supposed, remained that things broke down without warning.

They continued to wait, and to learn about each other. Bee felt lighter working with other scientists. When a word or phrase wasn't understood by the translator, they worked at it, finding expansion points to help overall instead of just coping in the moment.

And then there came the problem of names. Building an alphabet proved difficult given that neither language used the same sonic frequencies, much less similar building blocks. Bee, Olivet, and the scientist Sweepers built something rough, though. Once the name 'Sweepers' could translate, they agreed it would do for their race, for now. Individual names, however, were transcribed as phonetically as possible.

Traksit, Jomin, Wokha, and Pelith were as close as human languages would come to the Sweepers' names, and both sides agreed on using them. Bee wondered how far off their own names were for the Sweepers, not that it truly mattered.

Chellox hung back while language translation went on. He wanted to point out that Tsyfarian names didn't quite translate properly, either, but decided it would only muddy the waters. Still, the general hubris of humanity never failed to surprise him in little ways.

The *Arrow* arrived at last, and the team boarded quickly, keeping the shield around the Sweepers so they could breathe. Inside, they tested the difference for tolerance to a general air mixture and found it closer, but still not right.

Chellox and Steelbox headed to the pilot and navigation seats and relieved the crew there. "Thanks for taking good care of her," Steelbox said, clapping the temporary pilot, Joanna Klein, on the shoulder.

"No problem," Klein said, "but they should've warned me—those engines handle strange, I've never flown anything like it."

"We get that a lot," Chellox said, smiling. "Tsyfarian tech. Catch me on the *Amalfi* sometime, I'll give you a run down."

"Oh hey, thanks," she said, moving to the back of the ship with her navigator. They both stopped dead at the sight of the Sweepers, floating in a small gravity shield. "What the—"

"Our honored guests," Mud said, "so let's make sure to treat them that way, all right?"

"Yes sir, Captain Madison," Klein said quickly. She moved further down the ship and sat down before he could sigh, or correct her on what to call him. Bee noticed, laughing, and buckled herself in.

"It won't be long," she told the Sweepers, "until we are at our base."

"Mills," Mud said into comms, "what's our status?"

"In the *Amalfi* closing in on a midpoint between Claudia Seven's last address and you. The evac is still going on, as planned. We saved the majority of a planet today."

Mud closed his eyes and let his head fall back. He hadn't wanted to admit the worry to himself, but at its removal he let it wash over him and away. "Great to hear. We have our cargo. Four in number. Bee's going to send through readings on a sample of what they breathe. Work it up for us?"

"We'll get on it. See you soon, *Arrow*."

Wokha and Bee worked together during the trip to start running numbers on breach probabilities, their data merging with what Bee and Steelbox had worked up so far. They discussed the long-range comms issue, Bee showing Wokha and Jomin how they worked. Adding the Sweepers' data to their own, Bee saw a larger issue. It wasn't just the large creatures from the other universe causing breaches. The amount of small breaches from communications itself weakened the barrier.

"Mud," Bee said, calling him over, "this is both bigger and worse than we thought."

"Isn't it always?"

"I want to disagree, but I can't," she told him. Pointing at the data on her screen, she circled some results with a finger. "But. We might have to reduce long-range comm use, across the board."

"That's...what does that even look like?"

"Not for us to decide, I think," she replied. "I just know it's not going to go over well."

"Keep looking for alternatives," Mud said, and he sat back down heavily. He mirrored her screen and told Olivet to do the same.

"I don't think there are any," Bee told him softly.

"We look regardless. You know they're going to ask. Hell, insist. So we show them every dead path we can."

The *Arrow* and *Amalfi* met and started to address the problem of breathable atmosphere for the Sweepers. Mills and his teams tried a few solutions, the Sweepers gamely trying each one, if warily, until they found something that worked. A spare GravPack went with them, creating a shield to keep the strange mix close to the Sweepers and away from everyone else who needed to breathe.

Bee and Mud caught Mills up with the problems they faced. Mills looked at them, a twitch at the corner of his mouth as if he were about to burst out laughing.

"This isn't funny," Bee said. She studied him, wondering if he'd snapped under the strain of being pulled in so many directions at once. If so, she felt she couldn't criticize him for cracking up—she'd often wanted to give in and curl up in a dark corner herself.

"At this point, it's a *little* funny," he said.

"Not really," Mud put in, "and if we have a double breach, a total collapse of both universes—"

"Because we use the radio too much to talk to each other," Mills said. "And there's the funny. There it is. Humanity, entire universes, destroyed because we played a big game of 'No, you hang up,' which...I guess I get to explain."

"Are the Brands still on board?" Mud asked suddenly.

"Yeah, I think they...yeah, they are, we decided to rehome them in a cell here for now. Why?"

"Let's get them up here. They might be a help."

Mills called down to the brig and spoke quietly to the guards there. Mud caught Bee up with his ideas and they moved to discuss them with the Sweepers. "Oh, hey, Mills," Mud said, as they left, "grab my parents, too, will you? We'll meet in the lab the Sweepers are using."

CHAPTER 30

BEE WAVED HER ARMS at Wokha, who waved arms back. "We can't just stop using long-range communications," she insisted for something north of the third time.

"But you must," Wokha replied.

"Surely," Traksit added, "your universe is more important than speaking quickly to each other."

"Here's the thing," Mud said, resting a hand on Bee's shoulder in an attempt to tag himself into the conversation. They'd been going over the idea of reducing comm use for a while now and had gotten nowhere, despite trying to stay only technical. "We can't just cut long-range communications. I mean, we *can*, obviously, but there are impacts you don't see."

"So then," Jomin said slowly, "explain."

"In this part of the galaxy, and frankly a bit further than that, we have what we call the Gov. It's humanity led, though not exclusively human at all. It protects our planets. It also helps make sure trade is run smoothly, and fairly. Without the Gov, each planet fends for itself."

"You would not be able to remain peaceful, if not for this overseer?" Jomin asked.

"Oh, sure, for a while," Mud said. "Possibly years, even. But eventually, some idiot on some rock will decide he wants someone else's stuff. Now with long-range—instant, I might add, that's key— instant communication, that idiot starts something stupid and the Gov hears about it. There's a ship, like the one we're on now, hopefully close, and the problem is resolved before a major loss of life."

"So a peacekeeping force," Traksit said, nodding.

"Trade is also key," Mud said. "I admit, at this point, some days, I wonder if trade isn't more important than peacekeeping, or even just another word for it. All the major planets have a voice in the High Council. They work together and trade allows an economy to work across the realms of human and known space."

"Your species runs on trade?"

"We really do," Mud agreed. "That might not be noble, I know it really isn't, but it's what we do. An economy this vast needs oversight, and it needs instant communication. I'm not sure how we remove one without removing the other."

"But maybe," Bee suggested, "we don't have to remove communication fully."

Mud looked at her and nodded.

The Sweepers considered in silence for a moment, looking at each other before Pelith spoke. "At first, the intrusions were small—"

"Was this in your lifetime?" Mud asked. "How long do you live?"

"Our time is quicker than yours, but yes, I was young then," Pelith continued, "and the intrusions started, minor, odd, unknown." The translator Bee had installed in the room kept updating, growing the translations' accuracy using the *Amalfi*'s computing power. "This showed us the existence of your universe. But they grew."

"Sure," Bee said. "We used more and more communications as we expanded."

"Yes, but the amount grew, quickly, and weakened

the space between. Perhaps if you went back to the start it would be delayed. But the need is for this to stop."

"Getting to full stop from here will be a process," Mud said. "But Bee is right—if we can reduce communications, it can buy us time. We've been using long-range communications for decades now. Scaling back while we find a new solution might just be the only answer."

The room was overcrowded. They'd had to move much of the lab equipment to the side to make room for the atmospheric shield the Sweepers stood in. Mills entered the room, followed by Sybil and Tiago Brand. Behind them walked Shae and Jonah. Already close, the lab now felt full to bursting. The Brands looked confused, seeing the Sweepers, unsure of the moment. Mills waved them off and sighed.

"The Gov doesn't like any of this," he said.

"Not that anyone's surprised by that," Jonah added.

"Why are *we* here," Sybil Brand asked, "and what are they?"

"*They*," Mud told her, "are our guests. And you're going to help us, them, and all the people of two universes."

"In exchange for pardons," Tiago said bravely.

"In exchange for me not kicking you in the head," Shae countered.

The Brands turned to look at her and managed to not cringe openly. They understood Shae didn't joke. But they also knew the law, and that Mills would uphold it. "Why should we help?" Sybil asked.

"You live in this universe, too!" Bee said. The frustration of the mission, of the impending doom and her inability to get around it without outside help, burst out of her, directly at the Brands. "Stop being dumb. You're not stupid, not if you actually came up with half the tech you supposedly did. So was it you, or the people who work for you?"

"It was Sybil," Tiago said.

"Thank you for selling me out, brother," Sybil said, shaking her head. "Yes, fine, but we don't work for free."

"You really do," Mills told her. "You're being pressed into service, emergency protocols."

That sat even worse with her. "You come out of nowhere and invade our home," she raged, "kidnap us—"

"Arrest you," Mud said.

"—and now you expect us to do your work for you? What kind of—"

Sybil Brand hit the floor suddenly. She laid there, a hand on her back, rubbing at the fresh pain. Shae stood over her, lowering her foot to the floor slowly. "All right, I lied, I didn't kick you in the head. We need your head. Get up, and get to work."

"This is illegal," Sybil said, standing slowly.

"You can't—"

But Mills cut Tiago off. "Can we just get past this and do the work and leave the bullshit aside? Please? Fine, look, I'll reduce any sentencing and put in that you helped save the universe. Just work."

"That," Sybil said, glaring at Shae, "is better. Now what do you need?"

"Do you have a way to use long-range communications that don't go faster than light?"

Mud asked.

"No, of course not," Sybil replied. She rose an eyebrow and gave the Sweepers another look. "Do we need one?"

Mud and Bee caught everyone up on where the problem stood. As they spoke, Tiago started to write various mathematical formulae on a nearby pad, grabbing it from a workbench. Bee kept glancing at him but didn't stop telling the tale. Even so, she let Mud handle most of it, finding herself paying more and more attention to Tiago's ever-expanding equations.

After a few more minutes, Sybil joined him, grabbing a second pad and sketching out designs for some sort of tech, reading over the math Tiago supplied.

"Are we boring you?" Mud asked the siblings.

"If I answer honestly, will I get kicked again?" Sybil asked.

"Possibly," Shae said, and Jonah rested a hand on her arm.

"No," he amended.

"Tiago might have half a solution," Sybil said, trying to not look at Shae.

"I thought he said you came up with the tech," Bee said, "not him."

"I do," she said proudly. "He is much better at the math, though. Why do you insist on thinking you understand us, our lives, what we do?"

"Brand," Mills said, not seeming to mind which of the siblings he addressed, "stop thinking we even care. This is about survival. Get it through your heads, all right?" He looked at Mud. "Bringing them in might have been a bad idea."

"Nope," Mud said, looking at the sketches the Brands drew, "they've already started on a solution. They're worth the annoyance."

"We are right here," Tiago said.

"Oh, I know," Mud told him. "I said you were worth having here to work. Stop being a pain and you'll even be worth talking to. Seriously, just work with us, not against us, and this all goes smoother."

"We *are*." Sybil said, handing Mud her pad. "You say these larger beasts eat at the barrier, yes?"

"They do," Traksit replied.

"Because of the communications," she continued. "Lessening communications alone will not help at this point. They reflexively go for them now, and if you lessen the amount, they will possibly push through the barrier just to search for the rest. Tiago's math, though—we could send a single, larger communication at a different frequency and spin."

"You want to use quantum spin on a communications burst? But that would render it useless," Bee said.

"For communication, yes," Tiago said.

"But not for bait," Sybil finished for her brother. "We use these...breach slingshots at different locations, always moving them, at random extended intervals. They should provide a much better meal."

"How does that solve the communications issue?" Jonah asked, peering at the sketches.

"It doesn't," Sybil said. "That isn't a thing that will happen. Tiago's math proves it—I assume your own studies show the same."

"They do," Bee admitted.

"Then a reduction is needed, but as we've

269

explained, that alone would not work."

"Are they right?" Shae asked Bee, who nodded.

The Sweepers also nodded, waving limbs as they did. "This may work," Wokha said. "If we understand what you are saying correctly."

"I think you are," Mills told them. "But the problem will still be convincing the Gov of a communications reduction. I'm not even sure what that would mean for...anything."

"I can help there," Jonah told Mills. "They'll hate it, but they can blame me, and yell a whole lot," he shrugged. "Wouldn't be the first time."

"You can't just shelter me from my own job, Jonah," Mills told him.

Jonah smiled. "We'll discuss later. But for now, can we even build these cannons?"

"Breach slingshots," Tiago corrected.

"And yes," Sybil said, "they should be easily buildable for a trial run."

"Then," Mud said, "this should be—"

The lights went out. Emergency lights flashed on and then sputtered themselves. In darkness, Mud said only, "No one move," sharply, and checked his thinsuit's readouts. The *Amalfi* hung dead in space. He cursed and considered their options.

CHAPTER 31

NOISE FROM OUTSIDE the room forced Mills to work his way to the door and slap the sensor to open it. Nothing happened and he sighed, flipping up the manual override and pulling the door open.

"Mills, hold on," Mud said, placing his hand on the man's shoulder. "I'm pretty sure this isn't natural."

"Could be another breach and creature attack," Mills said, then reconsidered. "No, everything is out. All right, what've you got?" Mills felt the engines stop. Any ship, even one as large as the *Amalfi*, could be counted on to pick up a subtle vibration from the engines running. You stopped noticing it quickly, until it vanished.

"Nothing yet," Mud said, "just suspicions."

Mills stopped an enlisted woman going by the room and talked with her quietly. Nodding, she left, and Mills moved to follow. "I have to go to the bridge," he told Mud. "What's the plan?"

"Have everyone get into emergency positions, but hold there for now. I'll wrangle my team."

Mills hesitated. The Insertion Team weren't the only people on the ship, far from it, and Mills knew he could call security and have a well-armed team in minutes ready to sweep the ship. But Mud's instincts tended toward good, so Mills backed his play, running a countdown in his head for when he would resume control. "You've got mission ops for now," he said, leaving the room.

Mud looked around quickly. "Mom, Dad, stay here and guard the Sweepers. Good thing their air shields run on an external source. Keep the Brands out of trouble, too. Bee, call the team on internal comms and have everyone meet up at the *Arrow*."

"Without any power, that won't be quick," she told him.

"It has to be," he said, stepping out of the room. "I'll meet you guys there, I just need one thing first." And with that he went down the hall, his staff clanking loudly along the floor.

Bee slid the door shut as she left, giving Jonah a final nod. Calling the rest of the team to meet them at the *Arrow* was the easy part. She still needed to get down to the hangar herself—but then she remembered something. Electric access tunnels.

They were equipped to run through the entire ship, and it was assumed by default that if you were servicing the conduits there, power problems would be happening, so ladders were always used to shift levels. She slipped into the nearest maintenance access room and started making her way to the hangar as quickly as possible.

Though the lights, and most emergency lights, had remained off, the *Amalfi* still had a final set of independent lighting that allowed the ship to take on a dark, gloomy, shadow-filled air.

Mud worked his way as quickly as possible, which was nowhere as fast as he'd have liked, to the *Amalfi's* Document Cold Storage room. A little-known place, the DCS kept records for the vessel, as well as maps and certification backs printed out. Too many local governments wanted hard copy, still, as well as maintenance workers, in case of power problems like this. He grabbed a handful of maps and pushed the door closed behind him.

Sweating, Mud rested against a wall. The leg brace still hadn't been quite fully calibrated, and even with his staff, this much walking, at speed, hurt. A deep breath, followed by another. Mud pushed himself off the wall and cracked open a maintenance door, heading for the hangar.

A short while later, as he stepped out into the hangar, Mud could see his team gathered around the *Arrow*. "We got power on board?" he asked as he closed in on them.

"Yeah, seems the *Amalfi* was knocked out, but just that," Olivet said.

"I thought so. This was targeted," Mud said as they climbed aboard the ship. "I think they're after the Sweepers."

"That's a pretty big leap," Steelbox said. "This could just be some electrical problem."

"That took out the main and back-up generators, not to mention the engines?" Mud asked.

They each considered that for a moment. "So," Chellox asked, "why do you think it's someone after the Sweepers and not the Brands? Never mind who is even here doing this."

"Could be a team on the Brands' payroll here to bust them out, sure," Mud said. "I'm open to it. But we saw those other Sweepers chasing us. Plus we know they can get to our universe."

"That's still assuming a whole lot," Bee said.

"Is it?" Mud asked. "The Brands would have had folks here already."

"They'd need time to plan," Steelbox said.

"I'm still open to it, but I'm assuming this is Sweepers. It just feels like it. Worse, and more worrisome, so far their plan fits with what I'd do if

273

I were them."

"Regardless," Bee said, "we need to find whoever it is and stop them."

"Right," Mud said, laying out the maps of the *Amalfi* he'd brought with him along one of the *Arrow's* consoles. "We'll use GravPacks to get around faster—we have no way to know what they're using or how well they know the ship. Whoever did this knows at least enough to cut power and engines, though."

Bee traced a line along hallways from the engine room to the main power junctions, and from there to the lab where the scientist Sweepers were. "So if they came in and took care of the engines—"

"Power first," Steelbox said. "Lights went out, then the vibration stopped." He traced the same line beginning from the power junctions. "Which tells me they may not have known the ship too well. Your way is quicker," he said to Bee.

"Power first so everyone is rushing for that in confusion, then engines, even if it costs a bit of time," Mud said. "While they're working out the power drop, you take care of engines. But either way, the Sweepers and Brands are in the same room. So from that lab—"

"We go here," Chellox said, pointing, "along this corridor. Even if they use the access shafts it would take them right along it."

"Right," Mud agreed. "Chellox—you, Olivet, and Steelbox take that route. Bee and I will come at it from the other side."

"You think they doubled around and are looping the ship?" Chellox asked, tilting his head to consider routes.

"It's what I would do. Whoever makes contact first, shout." Mud strapped on his GravPack and checked the charge on his Acadian blaster. "Shoot to stun only, and keep a shield up. We don't know how they're armed, and we can't risk the ship or any crew."

Mud and Bee left first, both hovering slightly, using their GravPacks to propel them through the ship. Chellox, Olivet, and Steelbox followed soon after, splitting off at the access corridor. Once both teams had entered, they accelerated, shooting through the tunnels quickly to intercept the intruders.

"Why'd we really split?" Bee asked Mud as they rose rapidly to the engine level of the *Amalfi*.

"Nothing odd here, Bee, tactics," Mud insisted.

"We can go fast enough that it—"

"I think they split up," he admitted. They made a harsh-angled turn along the maintenance corridor and then went up another level, leaving them on the far side of the ship and three levels below the lab.

"Because that's what you would do?"

"Call it a gut instinct." He slowed, and Bee followed suit. They hovered, upright, a few inches above the ground. The darkened corridor left Mud uneasy. Too easy to hide, for anyone, and if they were Sweepers, Mud didn't know how their vision worked. They could have, he thought, far better luck seeing in the murk.

A blast spanged off the wall near him, missing by inches. "Contact front," he said softly, reflexively, firing back with a wide, stunning shot from his blaster, even as Bee fired her sonic along the corridor.

Steelbox looked at Olivet as they heard Mud over comms. Before they could react, though, Chellox echoed him. "Contact front!" he yelled, firing his sonic three times in rapid succession, aiming at the walls of the corridor to ricochet the shots. Olivet followed suit, but Steelbox held back, sonic blaster held out, waiting for a clear shot. Wondering what they were shooting at.

"What'd you see, Chellox?" he asked, drifting forward. They hovered, same as Mud and Bee, along a corridor that fed from the engine room.

"Movement," he said, "and an obvious weapon."

Olivet nudged Steelbox and slid forward, taking point. "There's a junction ahead," he said. "If we go single file, maybe we confuse them."

Steelbox nodded, taking middle position, and Olivet drifted slowly toward the junction. He vanished around it, the others waiting for an all clear. Instead, they heard shots fired and rushed forward.

Mud and Bee rushed forward as well. Mud in front, pushing out his gravity shield to a good five feet in front of him, using it like a battering ram. The shots kept coming, arcing through his shield, and he made contact before he could even fully see what he rammed. "Sweepers," he said into his comm, turning around. Bee floated on the other side of them, boxing them in. Four of them stood in the corridor, wearing oddly bulky suits and clear helmets. They each carried the same weapons they used to clear communication packets.

"We know," Steelbox replied, "contact here, too. Six."

"We've got four," Bee said. She waited, aiming at the Sweepers. If she took a shot with the sonic, some of the rebound could hit Mud. He floated, too, waiting.

"Let's talk this out," Mud said.

Bee repeated the sentence into the translator still attached to her thinsuit. The Sweepers didn't reply, and instead ran directly at Mud without firing a shot.

Mud started to move toward them in response, setting his shield out to push them aside a second time.

The Sweepers jumped and dove around the cone of the field, having worked out the dimensions of it from the first ramming, and made for a door back into the main hallway. Mud turned to follow, with Bee closing in.

The Sweepers ran down the hall, Bee's sonic and Mud's stun blasts not stopping them at all. Mud landed and braced himself with his good leg. Switching focus on his GravPack, he set a strand to one of the Sweepers and attracted it, yanking it backwards. Bee landed next to Mud and grabbled with the Sweeper, punching and kicking him as if it were a test. She probed areas to find weaknesses, dodging the strikes coming back at her as much as possible. Four arms and two legs made that an extra challenge and Bee gave up, ducking and charging at the Sweeper, tackling it and driving them both to the ground.

Mud, at the same time, reversed the pull and flew right at the remaining Sweepers. Swinging his new staff in a wide, flat arc, he caught one of them across the waist. Shoving that Sweeper to the ground, Mud brought the tip of the staff around and planted it firmly in the gut of another Sweeper, using the leverage to flip that Sweeper up, slamming its body against the ceiling before dropping it on the prone Sweeper struggling to stand.

The final Sweeper kept moving, not engaging at all, turning a corner just as Mud spotted it. "Secure these three, I've got the last," he called back to Bee and took off. "Guys, what's the score?" he said into his comm as he turned the corner, seeing the Sweeper slide past a door.

"They turned and made a break for it. They're *fast*," Steelbox replied.

"One of ours did, too," Mud said as he pushed the door open further to glide through. "I think they're all headed back to the engine room. They either docked there or think they can cause more damage before we stop them."

"Sonics don't—" Olivet started.

"Nope," Mud said quickly, "and the stun on my blaster doesn't either. So we punch them. A lot." Mud sent a soft tone through his comms to let the others know he would be dropping radio silent while they converged on the engine room. The same tone came back over the comms at him and he smiled. The team really could work well together. A swell of pride, followed by worry. The current enemy needed dealt with, and fast, so they could get back to work.

Mud snuck toward the engine room, refusing to rush, sensing a possible trap. He weighed the options in his head. They could simply be trying to get off-ship. No clear way to tell. Mud ran the numbers in his head again as he came to the door for the engine room.

The rest of his team was already there, trading blows with the Sweepers. Seven of them, swarming over Chellox, Olivet, and Steelbox, arms swinging. Mud took in the painful dance of violence and hefted his staff in hand. The Sweepers noticed him, and one of them ran for Mud, arms out. Mud swept his legs quickly, looking around the large engine room. Over in a corner he spotted their airlock, cut roughly into the side of the *Amalfi*—they'd mated their ship and somehow avoided detection.

"Chellox, Olivet," Mud said, taking a moment to jab the Sweeper on the ground, convincing it to stay there a while longer, "get on their ship, see if you can figure anything out."

Mud set strands from his GravPack to the wall behind the fight and attracted himself to it quickly, coming in at speed and knocking over two Sweepers. Chellox and Olivet freed themselves from the melee and made for the airlock.

Mud worked his way into the scrum, still four Sweepers against only himself and Steelbox. Back to back with his teammate, Mud held his staff out, across his body.

"You know those other three are getting back up, right?" Steelbox muttered.

"Yup," Mud agreed, swinging his staff in an arc to keep the Sweepers in front of him back. "But I have a plan. Duck."

Steelbox hit the ground and Mud set his GravPack to attract. The Sweepers around them felt themselves being pulled over, forced on top of the two humans. Mud reversed the GravPack's setting and they went flying, finding walls and floors to stop their wild tumbling. Mud tapped his staff on the floor with a thunk and smiled. "Let's leave them and get on their ship."

They ran for it and found Chellox and Olivet standing over the controls. "You know we can't do anything here, right?" Olivet asked Mud.

Mud pulled his blaster and pointed it at the controls, waiting. "Not the idea. Just buying time."

The Sweepers came on board warily, stopping when they saw Mud and worked out his intent. He patted the air hastily then held up his hand, palm out, to them. "Stop," he told them softly.

"They can't understand us," Chellox pointed out.

"Oh, they get this," Mud assured him. "Bee," Mud said into his comm, "need your translator, engine room, on the Sweeper ship."

"On my way, just securing these three."

"Leave them," Mud said, "I think we can end this."

"Really?" Steelbox eyed the seven Sweepers in front of them. "This is your whole plan?"

"They have a ship. We've never seen one, any time we've been in their universe. So why now?"

"They need it to transfer a bunch of them at once," Olivet said. "So..."

"Exactly," Mud told him. He kept his hand raised toward the Sweepers, his gun pointed at the controls.

Bee entered the ship, three of the Sweepers turning to aim at her. "I'm with them," she said into her translator, "let me pass." They moved aside, very obviously against the idea but still giving in, and she walked over to Mud.

"Diplomacy, huh?" she asked him, shaking her head.

"We have not harmed your scientists. They are here of their own free will. We wish to help both sides," he said to her translator and waited.

One of the Sweepers took a half step forward, speaking as he did. "You will hand them to us," the translator said.

"We will discuss this with them, or you don't go home," Mud told them, waggling the gun a bit. "We do not want to fight you. Let us solve this with peace."

"They come with us," the Sweeper repeated.

"Talk to them first, with us. No weapons on either side," Mud said. "If they want to go with you, we will not stop you."

The Sweepers looked at each other and spoke in whispers so the translator couldn't hear them. Their arms waved in conversation. After a full minute, the Sweeper in charge said loudly, "Yes, leave our ship, we will leave weapons here. Bring them to us."

Mud nodded and holstered his Acadian blaster. "Dad, bring the group to the engine room, I guess. We can set up in a corner while they fix the relays, the damage is minimal. And bring the white boards, too, we'll have to work down here while we arrange some sort of peace."

"So it was the—"

"Yeah. I'll explain when you get here. No weapons."

CHAPTER 32

EVERYONE GATHERED in a corner of the engine room, trying to stay out of the way of the technicians fixing the *Amalfi*. The Sweepers had disabled the engine, but they didn't have a real understanding of human technology. As such, their work ended up highly creative, and ungainly to untangle.

They refused to help, insisting they weren't sure what they'd actually done to the engine. Mills grew ever more frustrated with them over this, but kept his calm as talks progressed. "Just *tell them* what you—" he started for the fourth time.

"Leave it," Mud said. "Look, they came here of their own will. We are *all* at risk," he told the new Sweepers—Traksit, Jomin, Wokha, and Pelith all agreeing with him. It changed nothing, though. The Sweepers, who Mud had started to think of as a reflection of his team, insisted only that they be allowed to return to their own universe, taking the scientists with them.

Jomin agued for staying, explaining the danger, but nothing seemed to sway the intruders. Steelbox and Olivet wandered away from the discussions for a breather, followed by Shae. "When you were in their universe, did they have many ships like this?" she gestured toward the rough edges of the airlock seal along the wall.

"We didn't see a single ship," Olivet said. "Wait, we didn't see any ships at all."

"Not that strange, is it?" Steelbox asked. "We saw less than a fraction of their...anything."

"But we've never recorded contact with them," Shae said, "until now. But here they are with devices to shuttle through to our universe, and now whole ships. Feel odd?"

"Our universe is *really* big, too. Bigger than theirs, even. So I don't know if it is."

"But you were on the ship," Shae said. "How did it look?"

"In what sense?" Steelbox asked.

"How new was it?" she asked.

"If I had to guess," Olivet said, "it'd been fairly decently worn. Not shiny new but well used."

Shae turned and left them, heading back to the larger group without another word. Olivet and Steelbox looked at each other, confused for a moment, and then followed. "Bee, ask them how long they've been coming to our universe and what they've been doing here," Shae said.

As the question translated, the Sweepers looked at each other and said they hadn't been to this side of the breaches before. Shae refused that and asked again. Another dismissal. She sighed and rubbed her temples. "So the breach device in your ship is new?"

That got only silence as a reply, to which Shae nodded. So she asked them again about their past transfers. This time one of the Sweepers nodded at her. "We have been to your side before," the translation came. "To explore, to find the problem."

"So you knew of the problem," Shae said. She looked at Mud. "How much of this has been a lie from the start?"

"I don't think it was in the way you're suggesting," he told her, turning to Wokha. "The different tribes, some knew, others did not. That's why you wanted to come help, isn't it?"

"Yes, we knew, others did not. Some were told and did not believe. We had to act."

"And this group, sent to bring you back?" he asked.

"We have heard of them, yes. They are not sent by our people, but another group."

"Why wouldn't you tell us this?" Bee asked, annoyed.

"When we go back, we do not want to cause trouble between the groups," Jomin said.

"If you don't work out a way to get them to back off, you won't stay without a lot of trouble, and then there won't be anywhere to go back to, will there?" Mud said, his voice rising as he spoke.

"You speak truth," Pelith said to him. Turning to the other Sweepers, he said, "These beings speak the truth. We will explain to yours when we get back. For now, we must stay."

"You must return now."

"We refuse. We invoke abstract," Jomin said.

Mud and Bee looked at each other. "What's—" he started to ask, even as she answered she had no idea. Slowly they worked around translations to figure out that the scientists officially sought a form of asylum, breaking with all tribes from their home.

They took a break from the talks, a short one, so everyone could eat. The Sweepers had brought enough food on their ship and were willing to share with the scientists, even though they were apparently no longer part of their own society. Mud didn't pretend to fully understand the status, much less why they had waited so long to invoke it with the fate of two universes hanging out there.

They tried to discuss it with Pelith, who seemed willing to explain, but the deeper they got into the subject the more confusing it seemed. There were so many cultural differences to be overcome that they could only accept what they were told and keep moving.

That in mind, they got back to negotiations and finding a way to solve the crisis. The *Amalfi* came back online, and Mills left to check on the ship. While he was gone, Mud called for the Brands and got them back to work on their catapult idea. The Sweepers weren't sure the concept would work, but with a reduction in long-range communications, they agreed a lure seemed a good idea.

Jonah kept reassuring everyone that he could convince the Council to drop the communications levels. Shae raised an eyebrow each time he said so, but let the matter slide. Their plans drawn up, they called Mills back.

"Here's the basics," Mud told him. "Dad will convince the Council, and Pelith and Traksit will stay on this side for now, to help. They'll also collaborate with the Brands to build a working catapult and test the theory. The Sweeper Task Force," Mud continued, gesturing at the ten Sweepers still standing in a group, looking unhappy, "will take Jomin and Wokha back, where hopefully whatever societal crap they need to cut through will happen. Then we can start working on this from both sides."

"But if they were coming here before, in secret, because of this—"

"We got that worked out, too," Bee said. "We think. Look, they didn't trust us, and have such a strange relationship with technology...they did a good thing bad."

"Not sure that's an explanation," Mills told her.

"They snuck over here to test substances to cut off communications from this side," Mills said, "before they built the sweep guns they use."

"Oh," Mills said, "so we just only missed a possible invasion."

"Mills," Jonah cut in, "don't make this worse than it is. We did the same."

"Kind of?" Mills said, tilting his head and thinking it through. "But not really at all."

"We leave it and move forward," Mud said firmly. "Look, we cut communications back and see if the barrier heals. If it does, we keep comms low usage but we can stop worrying. If the barrier doesn't heal, then we find a better long-term solution—but according to the math this buys us about a century."

"On your side," Pelith added.

"We're going to have to work out exact time translations, and new maps for guest breaching," Mud said. "This is going to be an ongoing thing."

Mills sighed and leaned against the wall. "So we don't even get to present a full, working plan when we tell the Council we need to fundamentally change the way the Gov works?"

"Think of it this way," Shae said, "they get to have input for a change."

"Oh, they'll love hearing that gracious tidbit."

Mud clapped Mills on the shoulder. "Let's walk and I'll explain the rest to you." He looked behind him at the assembled group as he led Mills away. "You guys start prepping things."

They walked along a corridor, grey and flat,

military issue with lights bright enough to reduce shadows and dim enough to not cause glare. Even the harshness of the illumination had been studied once and decided by committee, Mud knew.

This, too, would fall into the pattern. They would start the work, extend the shelf life of two universes, and then the majority of the long term would enter committee. Worse, it would spin like that across two universes, and the leadership of the other universe didn't even have a central head.

The only thing for any of it remained to start. Mud explained details to Mills, including his worry about committee spiral and the problems of finding ambassadors and diplomats for an entirely new-to-humanity universe.

Mills and Mud walked to Mills' quarters and sat there, having a drink and continuing to talk. At one point Mills smiled suddenly and Mud took a breath, preparing himself.

"Olivet needs to go back to Trasker Four," Mills said, "to explain the reality of the planet's situation to his people, right?"

"Yeah, we'll need to fill his slot on the team for a while, at least."

"Permanently, I think."

"Wait, why?" Mud asked, twirling his empty glass in hand.

"You said yourself we need an ambassador. He'd be good at it, and has experience in both universes, technically." Mills shrugged and poured himself half a drink, just staring at it.

"If he agrees, you can have him. I don't like it, but it makes the sort of stupid sense the Gov likes."

"Thanks. Now for the rest, huh?"

"Oh," Mud said, pouring himself another drink and sipping at it for a second. "My parents will be in charge of the long-term team."

"I don't know that you get to decide that," Mills said, knowing in his heart he'd already lost any possible fight about it.

"You can argue it with them, but you see how much they seem to want in already. It gives them something to do—less punching, more talking, but still saving the universe. Besides, the Council will hate it and worry about what they'll do next, even more than they'll worry about the Sweepers. Should ease some of the problems."

"I'm never going to hear the end of this, am I?"

"From either side," Mud agreed. "Maybe the Sweepers will be nice about it." They shared a laugh, the sort of gallows laugh you can trust a friend to commiserate with you on. Raising their glasses, they nodded at each other. "I'm considering this mission done, from my angle."

"Yeah, you're off the hook for it," Mills said. "You know, if you wanted to, they'd promote you. You could get your own ship. Give Bee the team, take it easy a while."

"You want to say something about my leg, say it."

Mills laughed again and drained his glass. "Not at all. I just thought maybe less getting shot at would be nice."

"And so I could host the team and you wouldn't have to deal with the problems we cause," Mud said, shaking his head.

"See, you're more than smart enough for a promotion."

"Pass."

"Well," Mills said, standing, "we should get back before your mother injures one of the Brands. I think I'll offer them some contract work in return for their turning their whole enterprise into something legal, working for us not against us."

"Good luck with that, but let's wait a bit more," Mud said, remaining seated.

"Why?"

"About now," Mud said, looking at his wrist display, "they're starting to think we're up to something. A few more minutes and they'll really start to bond about being annoyed with us. It'll work in our favor after a while."

"I want to argue with that. I really do," Mills said, sitting back down. "But I won't."

CHAPTER 33

DAYS LATER. The *Amalfi*'s night shift worked away the quiet hours. The bridge crew checked incoming reports, shuffling things around so the day shift could deal with anything that might wait. The shift commander scanned a readout and sighed, hitting a button.

The lights in Mud's quarters flashed on, and an alarm rang out angrily. He rolled out of bed, grabbing his staff as he did, to limp over to his leg brace. Getting dressed quickly and strapping on the brace, he called up to the bridge.

"S'Mud, what've you got?" he said, forcing himself fully awake. Even as he asked, he hit his wrist communicator and woke the rest of the Insertion Team. A slap on the doorplate and Mud walked toward the hangar while waiting for the details of their new mission.

He found himself smiling as he adjusted his goggles. Once more, he thought, to make the unknown known.

ALSO BY ADAM P. KNAVE

PROSE

Crazy Little Things

Stays Crunchy In Milk

Strange Angel

NYCWTF

I Slept With Your Imaginary Friend

This Starry Deep

COMICS

Amelia Cole

Never Ending

Artful Daggers

Laser Joan and The Rayguns

Sensation Comics Featuring Wonder Woman

The Once and Future Queen

ABOUT THE AUTHOR

Adam P. Knave has been telling stories since he was a small child. He never stopped, and hopes he never will. A New York native, he self-exiled to Portland, Oregon, not long before his fortieth birthday and now spends many evenings on his patio, whiskey in hand.

www.adampknave.com